'An excellent mystery featuring characters, in a well-imagined, precommended.'
Brian Price, author of the DC Mel (

'An accomplished addition to the Banyard and Mingle series. Suitable for teens and adults alike, I would recommend it for fans of murder mystery who enjoy a well-wrought whodunnit portrayed with captivating characters. First-rate!'
Jeff Parke, WiFi SciFi

'Ben Mears' books are rich with the sense of a world extending beyond the page, unexplored and full of promise.'
Anne Corlett, author of The Space Between the Stars

A
Banyard & Mingle
Mystery

Volume IV

SERAPH OF THE SALLOW GROVE

B J Mears

instant
apostle

First published in Great Britain in 2021

Instant Apostle
The Barn
1 Watford House Lane
Watford
Herts
WD17 1BJ

British Library Cataloguing-in-Publication Data

A catalogue record for this book is available from the British Library.

This book and all other Instant Apostle books are available from Instant Apostle:

Website: www.instantapostle.com

Email: info@instantapostle.com

ISBN 978-1-912726-51-6

Printed in Great Britain.

Thanks and Credits

Special thanks to my beta readers Keith Munro, Matt Cooper, Rev Dr Simon Woodman, Jeff Parke and Henna Mears.

My thanks to Edward Field, Alison Hull, Julian Roderick, Kate Coe, Dan Sefton, Simon Lupton, Dr Alistair Sims, Joy Mears, Céline Badaroux, Steve Fenton, Anne Corlett, Nicki Copeland, Nigel Freeman, Sheila Jacobs and Anne Rogers.

Special thanks to Brian Price for consultation and expert guidance on crime scene forensics.

Contents

Camdon City

Windstrome Bay

Grayton Mire

EASTERN SEA

Burrington Point Lighthouse

Hatch Head

The Northern Chase

Tynn

Highbridge

Lytche's Cove

Dockside

Eyes of Myrh

Deepning Sound

C A M D O N

Old Camdon

Tower End

Tower Bridge

Rook's Bridge

Southside

Dart's Cove

Crowlands

Holloway

Timlock's Farm

Womping Sound

Halser's Bay

Black Down Forest

Curlston Marsh

Drifter's Bay

Stonhaven

To the Borderlands & Mors Zonam

1 League

N

Camdon City & Surrounding Area

Old Camdon

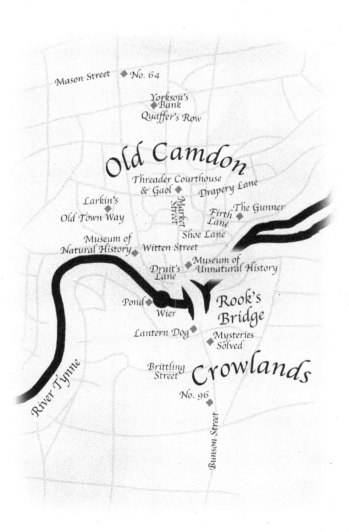

Mason Street ◆ No. 64

Yorkson's ◆ Bank
Quaffer's Row

Old Camdon

Threader Courthouse ◆
& Gaol   Drapery Lane

Larkin's ◆   The Gunner
Old Town Way   Firth ◆
Lane

Market Street

Museum of   Shoe Lane
Natural History ◆ Witten Street

Druit's ◆ Museum of
Lane   Unnatural History

Pond ◆   Rook's
Wier   Bridge

Lantern Dog ◆   Mysteries ◆
Solved

River Tynne

Brittling   Crowlands
Street

No. 96 ◆

Bunson Street

The Eleven Months of the Earthorian Year

1st: Tithemoon

2nd: Doblemoon

3rd: Trimoon

4th: Quartersmoon

5th: Thripplemoon

6th: Sixthmoon

7th: Fipplemoon

8th: Hexmoon

9th: Honourmoon

10th: Twinemoon

11th: Elventide

The threaders thread the silk.

The silkers wear the silk.

Prologue

1st Elventide, winter 1795 AD (after Doon)

A thick snow carpeted the field, though the fall had ceased some hours before. It now rested like a work complete. Like deep frosting on an endless cake, concealing all. Hiding who knew what beneath.

A boy threw a *stick*.

His wolfhound fetched it.

A tried and tested game. A scene familiar throughout ages.

And yet, there was something different here. Something wrong.

Over and again, he lobbed the missile to land it in the powdery drifts that marked the start of the Sallow Grove. The devoted hound snuffled in the icy bank, searched, sniffed out the thing, retrieved and returned it, tail wagging with delight. They played so long and hard that, in the end, great furrows of churned snow lay all about and the boy's feet were damp and numb, his nose rosy from the cold.

His breath fogged the air as he threw again.

'You there!' A voice startled him. The hound chased.

'Me, sir?' the boy said, although apart from the dog and the newcomer, he was alone. He watched the man approach: a farmhand from the nearby homestead.

'Yes, you. What's that you have there?'

It seemed a strange question to the boy. He shrugged. 'A stick.'

'I think not.' The farmhand trudged closer, leaving a trail of large boot prints. He reached the circle of play where his tracks became lost. The hound brought the *stick*. Dropped it as usual, at the lad's feet.

'What, this?' asked the boy.

'Here. Let me see.'

The boy stooped to collect the *stick* and handed it to the man.

'Lad, don't you know a bone when you see one? Where did this come from?'

'Don't know. The dog found it.' The boy realised then that on some level he had known all along it was not a stick, and yet, what did it matter? They were on farmland where the bones of livestock were no rarity, nor sinister, nor even mysterious. It was simply less disconcerting in his mind for him to be throwing a stick, and so a stick it had become.

Sensing the end of play, the hound set off once more and padded back through the drifts into the grove. The man looked again at the long bone in his hand before following. Intrigued, the boy tailed after, stepping in the man's prints as a game.

In the shadows of the great weeping trees, the excited hound dug – turfed up the whiteness of snow, first, and then the dark tones of frosted soil came spewing up behind him to scatter over the seamless blanket. The farmhand stood observing. There was a keenness in the hound, an urgency to unearth its treasure.

'Here! Fetch!' The farmhand threw the bone. The hound dug deeper. There was nothing else for it. The farmhand walked in to pull the hound away.

The boy covered his gaping mouth, staring at the dog's excavation. There, the partial remains of an arm protruded from the icy ground, its blackened hand curled in an eternal wave farewell.

1

The Sallow Grove

In which Banyard and Mingle visit an extraordinary crime scene

The icy pavement of Bunson Street is patterned with prints. Josiah Mingle, my hulking business partner, whose features might be described as *rugged* – if one were feeling particularly benevolent – adds the large tracks of his riding boots to the hotchpotch design as he walks at my side, marvelling at the frozen crust. The leather boots creak with each step. I glance down at them.

He shrugs. 'I need new ones. These leak.'

'That doesn't explain the squeaking.' I frown.

He shrugs again, removes his silken top hat to scratch his thick-boned head. 'Can I get some on expenses?'

'No. Use your pay. That's what it's for.'

He grunts as the winter wind tousles our lagging scarfs.

I fasten another button of my long coat. 'Anyway, we don't have cash to throw around now. Not since the last few threaders we helped. It costs a fortune, as well you know.'

Jemima Gunn, Willow Buxton, Annie Patch, Martha and Seth Landsdale, Mason Pyke: these are but a few of the unfortunates we've rescued from the dire circumstances of threader existence, not to mention *Old Squeaky Boots* himself:

Josiah, previously known as Silus Garroway. It's an expensive business and a stream of overheads – silk wardrobes including hats, boots and shoes, money for subsistence, forged documents and identification papers – has recently depleted our once bountiful funds. In short, a substantial windfall is needed before we might realistically think about resuming our clandestine (and thoroughly illegal) philanthropy. For the poor threaders – who are little more than slaves – are to be kept in their place, according to our government. Noble silkers, like me, are not allowed to set them up as equals.

Airships blot the sky overhead, a dark and ever-present reminder that war is pending. Camdon City is no exception: it's the same with every city across Londaland, the coasts too. Our country is in a rigid state of vigilance, never sleeping, always watching for the first signs of invasion from Urthia and we, like ants on the ground, are under constant scrutiny from above. Enemy spies are everywhere. Apparently.

The cobbled road at our side – where vehicles soon turned the snowfall to slush – is now icy and too slick for anything besides beasts of burden. A Clansly Haulage steam truck blocks the way, where it slipped and slid into the wall of a tailor's shop, this side of Rook's Bridge. A small crowd of spectators watch as troopers work to free it. A warning emblazoned across the side of the truck reads, 'CAUTION – ARMAMENTS ABOARD'.

Along with the whole of Amorphia, our government has imposed trade sanctions on the Urthian province of Morracib, to the east, and Urthia is, in turn, bristling for a fight. None of this would have happened if Morracib hadn't invaded Angula. Unrest that's been brewing for years is now intensifying into a palpable threat. For Londaland a war has yet to begin, but it seems inevitable.

'Do you think the war will change things?' Josiah asks, watching the men wrestle with the truck.

'Undoubtedly.'

'How?'

'For one thing, if war is declared, we'll be called up to fight. I fear it's only a matter of time, unless, of course, something remarkable happens.'

'Like what?'

'An unprecedented end of the nonsense. Unlikely, I'm afraid.'

'Are you... afraid?'

'My, you're full of questions today. I'm not afraid yet. But I will be. We all will.'

As we approach the Mysteries Solved office a tall figure in the black uniform of a Draker superior steps into our path: reinforced top hat; frock coat with a double breast of shining brass buttons; trousers like a pair of drainpipes. Lord Bretling Draker (the founder of Camdon City's noble establishment of watchmen, the Drakers) means business and seems keen to engage us before we reach the office.

'Young Banyard.' He tips his hat, his face drawn in a tight-lipped expression. His chin is broad and edged by thick sideburns. 'Mr Mingle.' For once his pipe is in his pocket and not his mouth. He must be busy.

'Good morning, sir,' I say while Josiah offers a simple nod. Our last encounter with Bretling was not entirely amicable, so I'm intrigued to know what he wants with us. 'May we be of assistance?'

'That remains to be seen,' he says, studying the two of us dourly. Deep shadows beneath his eyes suggest he's not slept for a while.

'Perhaps you'd like to step into our office.' I throw a hand towards the door of our private detective agency, over which stretches a large sign in faded golden paint:

BANYARD & MINGLE: MYSTERIES SOLVED

'I'd prefer not, if it's all the same. Do you still keep that lantern dog?'

The hairs on the back of my neck rise. 'Yes,' I say with a certain reticence. 'Why?'

Bretling's left eyebrow twitches, something I've not seen before. 'We've two shallow graves on Tinlock's Farm down in Holloway, and reason to believe there are more. They call the place the Sallow Grove. Out past Harrow's Copse. Meet me there within the hour. Bring the hound.'

He trudges away to climb aboard a Draker carriage that soon heads southwards at a brisk pace, drawn by a pair of stout black horses.

'Well, that was odd,' says Josiah as we watch it go.

'The mighty Lord Draker must be in a real pickle to have stooped so low.'

'Are we really going to help that malignant roach?' Joe's getting quite creative with his insults these days. His vocabulary's really coming on!

I dare say Bretling deserves the abuse after his appalling behaviour in that wretched Landsdale case. 'He's a powerful roach, so yes, we are.'

We find Bretling puffing on his pipe and pacing the snow to keep warm, looking like a rather frustrated and lanky crow. Behind him, the rime-frosted Sallow Grove provides an ominous backdrop to his staccato gait. The fall is heavier out here in Camdon City's most rural district of Holloway, a ragged patchwork of industry and farmsteads where the winds blow unfettered by the skyrakers of the inner city. From here southwards, the settlements only become sparser and the land less profitable as the soil grows poorer, until the Borderlands where cultivation is nigh impossible and, beyond that, the barren soil gives way to the poisoned deserts of Mors Zonam.

'Ah, there you are, Banyard.' Bretling juts his jaw at our snow-laboured approach.

I hug my winter long coat tighter about me. Josiah has Baker on a chain. The shaggy hound is huge and placid, although fiercely protective of us when threatened. And take it from me: you don't want to rile a lantern hound if you can help it (on account of their enormous stature and formidable teeth). Baker snuffles around, pauses to cock a leg, yellows the snow and continues his exploration of this uncharted field. Beyond him in the mid-distance, the low shapes of rundown farm buildings and a scatter of cottages darken the landscape and, nearby, a larger strand of trees, Harrow's Copse, spreads northwards. I don't know who *Harrow* is – or was – but he sounds like a grim fellow to me. To our south lies a large fishpond and, a mile on, the edge of Black Down Forest.

With a haunted expression, Bretling gestures for us to follow. 'This way.' Clamping the bit of his pipe between his teeth, he rubs his hands together and shoves them into his pockets before passing between a pair of Draker guards, and on into the grove.

The officer to our right salutes his acknowledgment. 'Lord Draker.'

An almost military respect follows this man around. 'Take a break, captain. I heard a rumour there's hot soup in the tent.' Bretling flicks his fingers to hurry them along. 'Your men, too.'

'Thank you, sir.' The Draker captain nods and waves for his officers as he heads off around the edge of the trees.

The ring of weeping sallows is roughly circular, their whispering branches drooping almost to the snow with a clearing at its centre, so that this space has the feeling of somewhere set apart. We ascend a slight ridge that surrounds the treeline and notice other Drakers guarding the perimeter beyond.

Bretling trudges on. 'Was a devil of a job to dig them out, on account of the frozen ground and these confounded roots. It's a poor choice for a place to dig a hole. Whoever this murderer is, he made his job all the harder. They found a third this morning while I was talking to you. A bleak prospect, I think you'll agree.'

We see them and come to a halt. Josiah makes the sacred sign, tracing a circle on his forehead before touching a point over his heart. I throw him a subtle scowl. Threaders tend to use the sacred sign; silkers more often the godly sign. It's one of

Josiah's old habits that could raise suspicion in those around us. Bretling doesn't appear to notice, though. He waves a gathering of Drakers away and they swiftly move out, leaving the three of us briefly alone in the grove. Needlessly, he points to the decomposing corpses that have been extracted from the icy ground and laid out on blankets at the sides of their open graves.

The three bodies form an arching line at one edge of the clearing. The remains are shades of yellow, brown, black and grey. The putrefying flesh, skin and fabrics are stained by the soil and in various states of decay. Next to them sits a small pile of red marker flags set on canes, and nearby, a collection of picks, spades and shovels leans against the trunk of a big old sallow. The open graves are indeed riddled with tree roots. In places the roots have been hacked apart when the graves were cut. Elsewhere, pale marks show where Draker spades have made fresh lacerations.

'Three silker gents, though there are more here beneath the sod,' says Bretling. 'I'd stake my name on it.'

I brush a lock of raven hair from my brow, adjust my old, battered tricorn and turn my collar against the cold. 'Because?'

'Six silkers have gone missing from Camdon City over these last months. Six silkers, not three, and each has disappeared on or around the 17th of the month. I fancy this is where their killer disposed of them.'

'Are you saying a man's vanished on that day each month for six months? That's extraordinary,' I say.

Bretling nods. 'On that day or close. A boy's dog turfed up the first of them and we brought in a Draker hound. He sniffed out the other two but there are more. I know it.'

'It's consistent with the state of the bodies.' I indicate the greenish-yellow corpse closest to me, which is dressed in what was once a smart ensemble, complete with leather shoes still in situ and a crumpled top hat, now perched at his side. 'This one looks considerably fresher than the others.' The body is a little bloated and stinks, despite the cold. 'Perhaps he was the last to be buried and has been kept mostly frozen.'

'Indeed.' Bretling regards the corpse as officers return to work. 'This is the Right Honourable Augusto Ritcott. As you can see, he's still recognisable, which can't be said for the others. Ritcott went missing on the 17th of Twinemoon, around two weeks ago. He's the latest to have disappeared – the one the lad's dog unearthed. We think other animals had already disturbed the grave. What was exposed has been de-fleshed.'

I study the grim sight at my feet. 'A member of parliament. A political grudge?'

Choosing not to speculate, Bretling takes a puff on his pipe before moving on to the next body, one with sunken cheeks and great patches of flesh withered and, in places, liquified to the bone. The remains have clearly been removed from the ground one piece at a time and reassembled. 'We think this one's the investor Uriah Mumford, on account of his estimated height. He was the first. Vanished on the 18th of Thripplemoon. Left his house for his city office that morning. As far as we know, he was never seen alive again.'

'And this one?' I ask, viewing the third body: swollen and blackened, still wearing a soiled brown silk suit and a gold wedding ring. I watch the attending officer take a wallet and a gold pocket watch from the clothes to bag them as evidence.

The officer opens the wallet to count the bank notes and informs Bretling. 'Fifty guineas, sir.'

Bretling nods. 'That's John Lancett, mine owner. He was found with a business contract and all his personal effects. It's the same with the others.'

'Not robbery, then.'

'My thoughts precisely.' Bretling hands me a waxed leather document case that has, to a degree, protected the vellum contract inside. I glance over the faded agreement details and see John Lancett's signature along with two others and a date of the 16th of Sixthmoon. Bretling continues. 'It's deteriorating but mostly legible, otherwise we'd be guessing. He vanished on the 17th or 18th of Sixthmoon. We can't be sure which as he was away from home at the time. None can verify the exact day, but...'

'Yes, I see. May we have a list of the missing men?' I ask.

'I made a copy.' He takes a folded page from the inner pocket of his coat and passes it to me. 'I'd hoped they would turn up alive, of course, but I think we can forget about that. Someone's killed all six. Someone with a grudge to settle.'

'I've seen nothing in the papers,' I say, unfolding the list to view the names and accompanying notes in Bretling's precise cursive script.

'I've had the press keep silent on the matter,' he says, 'but it'll come out one way or another now.'

I glance at the hanging branches that rattle in the cruel wind, and shudder. This place is forbidding. It's as though a phantasm has settled here. 'I suggest you keep them quiet for as long as possible. When this reaches the headlines, the killer will be forewarned we're hunting him.'

'Of course,' says Bretling, an edge of defensiveness creeping into his voice.

Josiah peers through the trees, out towards the water. Beyond stretches the dark line of Black Down Forest. 'Why bury them here? Why not just ditch them in the pond or use the cover of the woods?'

'A good question, Mr Mingle,' I say, wondering at the answer. 'Perhaps the grove has meaning.'

Josiah approaches Bretling. 'And why us? You could bring in dogs from a hundred other sources.'

I must admit, I've been wondering the same thing.

'Well, now,' says Bretling, 'it's not escaped my notice that you two have an affinity for threader clients. It sets you apart. You know threaders better than any of my lawmen. These silkers were murdered by a threader who resents his position, mark my words. Banyard here has something of his father's nose for a criminal. I've seen it. I want your help tracking this threader down – the pair of you – if that's acceptable. I need people with real insight into the backward ways of these folk.'

Josiah glares at Bretling. 'Threaders, you mean?'

Bretling ignores him. 'This is no run-of-the-mill villain we're dealing with. Your father was a fine detective, Banyard – I'd have signed him up like a shot if he was interested – but I trust a little of his nous has passed to you. I'm giving you and your team a chance to prove yourselves.' He becomes pensive and is quiet for some moments. 'I'll pay. Whatever your going rate. I admit I'm desperate. I've been on this case for more than five months and it's gone nowhere but down. These bodies confirm my fears. Today's the 1st of Elventide, so presumably we have just sixteen days before the killer strikes again. There's pressure from the government – from those who are in the know. I'm expected to sort this mess out and put a stop to it. A murderous threader taking down silkers unchecked? It's the wrong kind of message. Hapgood is deeply vexed.' Chivers Hapgood is our *esteemed* Prime Minister, a flatulent buffoon with the undeserving good fortune to be born rich – my opinion, for what it's worth. Bretling continues. 'When the story breaks, every silker in Londaland will fear for his life, and every threader will be encouraged to murder his master.'

Baker strains on his chain. Josiah drags him away from the remains and the hound begins digging in a slight hollow on the undisturbed side of the grove.

While Josiah handles the hound, Bretling steps closer to me and lowers his voice. 'I want this kept between us, Banyard. No blabbing to the papers. No loose talk. It's not the done thing, a Draker employing civilians like this. I'll need you to keep your hound on a short leash.' He glances across at Josiah. 'Do you understand?'

I suddenly see the reason for his reluctance to step into our office. 'Yes. Quite.'

Baker digs earnestly.

'Sir,' calls Josiah. 'I think he's on to something.'

Bretling moves in to view the spot. 'Take him on.' He stoops to take a flag from the pile and thrusts the marker's cane into the ground where Baker has dug.

Josiah leads Baker past the bodies but pauses midway,

heaving on the hound's lead. For several moments he stares at the nearest corpse. 'What's that?' His face wrinkles and he nods towards the body's grizzled head.

'Where?' Bretling leaves his newly placed marker to stand by Josiah.

'There, in his mouth. Something black.' Josiah points with his free hand while Baker threatens to unbalance him.

Bretling stoops for a closer look and plucks the black object from the decaying jaws of the dead man to study it. 'A piece of coal.'

I'm intrigued. 'Might it have fallen in from the surrounding soil? A mere natural aspect?'

'Perhaps,' says Bretling.

We watch as he checks the mouths of the other cadavers, using the end of a marker to push open their jaws and peering inside. Grimacing, he delves into the third open mouth before straightening to display a small find between a finger and thumb. 'Another fragment of coal. Strange.' He strides to the edge of the trees and shouts. 'Sergeant!'

Josiah frowns. 'Were they burned to death?'

'Unlikely,' I say, but that doesn't stop me from imagining the torture that may have been inflicted had burning coals truly been forced into the victims' mouths while they were alive.

Through drooping branches, we glimpse a grizzled sergeant who wears a long moustache and a sour expression on his craggy face. He hands a steaming copper cup to a fellow officer and hurries back into the grove. Bretling meets him as he arrives. 'Huntly, have your men check the graves for coal.'

'Sir?' Sergeant Huntly seems bemused.

'You heard me. Coal.' Bretling dismisses the sergeant with a *get on with it* gesture. 'And have them dig there.' He points to the newly marked location, his brow twitching away.

Baker leads Josiah on to trace a line around the inner edge of the grove around six feet from the tree trunks. Again, the dog alerts and paws at the snow. 'Here!' says Josiah.

Bretling plants another flag to mark the spot and, before

long, the hound indicates a third location. Bretling shoves yet another flag into the ground. 'Well, that's it. Looks like we may have all six. Will you wait until we've established the graves?'

'If you wish.' I watch Josiah and Baker as they continue to patrol the shadowed fringe. The dog sniffs at a spot and moves on, but then returns to thrust his nose back into the soft snow. He scrabbles at the icy ground beneath with his front claws.

Josiah glances from Baker to Bretling. 'Six, you say?'

Inside the soup tent we huddle around a large pot that sits upon a portable burner, collect hot black bean soup and stand warming our hands on the bright copper cups as they quickly cool. The wind beats against the hastily pitched canvas and moans beyond the entrance, where Josiah has left Baker tethered to a tree. The hound barks at the Drakers as they hack at the ground with picks and spades.

'I still think it's odd that the famous Lord Draker would bring us in on an investigation. I don't trust him,' says Josiah.

'Indeed.' I peer into the dark depths of my soup, which is possibly the worst I've ever tasted. 'Especially after that Landsdale business.' I refer to an injustice concerning an innocent boy, in which Bretling appeared complicit. I've yet to forgive him. In fact, I'm not sure I ever will. The tragic incident sparked the formation of an avenging secret society, a band of outraged threaders fighting the system from the shadows and calling themselves the Landsdale Rebels. 'If it were any other Draker I'd flatly refuse, but Bretling? He's a different sort. Complicated.' In truth, he's a better silker than most and his reform of the Camdon City watchmen has brought some definite improvements. For one thing there's less thuggery and corruption among the men – not that it's gone altogether, but it has diminished, and he does have a good history of policing, for which he's been handsomely rewarded by the state. The evidence is on proud display around his office walls. 'Do you think he wants to recruit us?'

Josiah looks doubtful. 'You, maybe. He wouldn't want me.'

'I don't know. The Drakers like a bit of muscle, don't they? Handy in a tight corner.'

He purses his lips, cocks his head. 'Maybe.'

If the Drakers were to learn of Josiah's true origins, we'd both be hanged in a trice. 'Listen, Joe. You'll need to be more careful if we're to be around these people for any length of time. You can't go making the sacred sign. It's a dead giveaway. Try to keep your head up, your back straight, and don't tread on any toes. It only draws attention.'

He glances at his boots and then at me. 'Are you saying I have big feet?'

'Metaphorically, yes.'

'Meta-what?'

Give me strength. He walks to the entrance of the tent to watch the Drakers dig. He's sick of my warnings and constant corrections but what else can I do? Poor fellow.

'Do you think there are seven?' he asks.

'We'll soon know for sure. I can't shake the feeling that there must be something special about the grove for it to have been chosen for the burials, though what *that* might be, I can only guess. Who would do such a thing?'

'Oh, you'd be surprised,' says Joe. 'They say everyone's capable of murder.'

'Yes, but seven? That's quite a commitment.'

'True. And there could be more. Someone must have been seriously vexed.'

'We'll examine the facts and see how each victim is connected. That's where my father would've begun.'

Josiah nods as a figure approaches, dark against the snowscape.

The officer pokes his head into the tent. 'Lord Bretling bids you come. We've found another.'

2

Coal

*In which further graves are confirmed
and Josiah questions the properties of snow*

We trudge the short way back to the grove and join Bretling towards the head of the latest find. The partially excavated corpse in the ground below us is blackened and appears frozen in a twisted pose: face turned to the left, legs bent at odd angles with one foot pointing to the right. The immediate impression is that of a once limp body, tossed unceremoniously into a pit that is at most two feet deep like the others. At its edges, truncated roots protrude, hacked apart by the original grave cut.

'Can you name him?' I ask.

Bretling shakes his head. 'It's too soon to say. As you can see, he's unrecognisable owing to decomposition. Hopefully, Dr Orkney will confirm how long each has been interred.'

I've a feeling we'll be seeing Dr Myrah Orkney, Camdon City's Coroner, very soon. Before Bretling can say more, one of the younger diggers from further on in the grove staggers out of his pit to double over and vomit at the side.

'Number five,' says Josiah, with a nod towards the newfound grave where a discoloured oval face peers heavenwards from the soil with sunken eyes.

'Here!' A digger knee deep in an excavation to our right signals another discovery.

'That makes six,' says Bretling.

'Seven!' calls yet another digger across the grove.

Bretling turns to a nearby Draker. 'Fetch Sergeant Goffings from the farmhouse.'

With a curt nod, the officer hurries away.

'Goffings?' whispers Josiah, leaning close. 'What in Lychling's name is *he* doing here?'

Sergeant Goffings is a hardened Draker posted at the Dockside station. At least, he *was*. We have an unfortunate history with the man, as he once falsely imprisoned us on the request of the Dockside harbour master. Goffings is a barrel-chested brute and a rogue (not in a dashing or handsome way — to the contrary, he's a rotter with a face like a potato) who'll kiss the boots of anyone he thinks will advance his somewhat limited realm of influence.

'Just behave yourself and we'll be all right,' I tell Josiah quietly.

'You mean I'm not allowed to punch him in the face?'

'Precisely.'

'I'll try,' whispers Joe.

'Do you mean you'll try to punch him in the face or you'll try not to?'

'The second, though I can't promise anything.'

We watch the excavations, glad we're not the ones handling the icy bodies. By the time the officer returns with Goffings in tow, another of the corpses has been lifted and arranged on a blanket by its grave.

'You sent for me, sir,' Goffings says to Bretling. He spots Josiah and me, stiffens and stifles a grimace. 'Gentlemen…' he manages to say, standing to attention, soldier-like.

'Ah, there you are, sergeant,' begins Bretling, stepping nearer. 'I want you to escort Dr Orkney. You'll find her in the morgue at the City Draker Headquarters. Bring her here. The sooner the better.'

'Yes, sir.' Goffings clicks his heels and hurries away.

I supress a smile at the thought of Bretling taking on Goffings as his latest lackey. I'm not at all sure it's a promotion from Goffings' point of view, and wonder what happened. In any case, I feel there's a certain poetic justice to the move. Goffings and Bretling: made for each other.

'I want the coroner to see the site, get a feel for it,' says Bretling, scraping ash from the bowl of his pipe with a pocketknife. 'There's something about this place…'

'You feel it, too,' I say with a shiver. 'Was Goffings questioning the farmer?'

'He was,' says Bretling. 'Men like him need to be kept busy or they…' He shrugs. 'Never mind.'

'His findings?'

'Don't matter. I've already questioned Farmer Tinlock and his family myself. They say they've nothing to do with the deaths and I, for one, believe them. They have no connection whatsoever with the victims and the grove is all but beyond view from the farmhouse. They can't be held responsible if some maniac trespasses on their land in the small hours.'

'Hardly the work of a maniac,' I say. 'Our killer has struck down seven prominent silkers, successfully disposed of all evidence and done so without alerting a single individual. It would take an organised mind to do that.'

Bretling points at me with the stem of his pipe. 'Perhaps, Banyard, though we *have* been alerted, have we not?'

An officer interrupts. 'Sir, more coal – here in the mouth.' Stooping, he prises open the jaw of the seventh body to reveal a slick, black lump cushioned on a bloated tongue.

'Interesting,' says Bretling. He thumbs a fresh pinch of Old Beauty into his pipe. 'Not a happenstance of nature, then, this coal…'

'It seems not,' I say. 'But why would the killer place coal in his victims' mouths?'

Bretling strikes a Sulphur and tries to light his pipe as a northerly promptly blows out the match. 'I don't know.' He strikes a second – which also fails – and fixes upon the horizon, a slab of slate grey that bodes further snowstorms. 'Well, gentlemen, would you care to join me in the tent while we await the good doctor? I should like to step out of this confounded wind.'

Back in the tent I make a cursory study of the notes from Bretling, while he serves himself black bean soup. The list runs down the left side and is, I note, in chronological order.

> *Uriah Mumford (financier – investor) – missing 18th*
> *Thripplemoon...*
> *John Lancett (mine owner) – missing 18th Sixthmoon...*
> *Davey Brindle (industrialist and mining consultant) – missing*
> *17th Fipplemoon...*
> *Wulfric Hemings (the honourable) – missing 17th*
> *Hexmoon...*
> *Abraham Ketting (investor) – missing 18th Honourmoon...*
> *Augusto Ritcott (the honourable) – missing 17th*
> *Twinemoon...*

'This is quite a gathering,' I say, thinking that perhaps Bretling is correct about the motive for the murders. After all, these were all silkers of considerable power and influence. I read the information on the first known victim aloud for Josiah while Bretling listens in and finally manages to light his pipe. 'Uriah Mumford, financier and investor, reported missing on the 18th Thripplemoon by wife, Victoria Mumford. Uriah left home in Highbridge as usual on the morning of the 17th to attend his office in Old Camdon, never to return. Sons Jethro and Samuel–'

'Ah, yes,' says Bretling. 'I've already questioned the family extensively. I'd be obliged if you'd leave them be. It's all been a bit much and there's no chance they're involved. They all have alibis cast in iron.'

'And of course, they're silkers,' mutters Josiah at my side.

'Very well.' I continue reading. 'Business associates Ranalf

Harmon, Otis Jacks.' There's a space on the page before two further names. 'Larkin. Kenwigs.' I'm left slightly confused, my head already swimming with names. 'Sir, who are these two at the end? Other business associates?'

Bretling sips his soup while dredging his mind. 'Larkin… Larkin…' He brightens. 'Ah, yes. Stanley Larkin – a fascinating man. A talented toymaker. Runs a shop down Old Town Way. The other is a Madam Kenwigs, the crone who runs The Gunner.'

'The Gunner – also in Old Camdon,' I note.

'On Firth Lane, I believe,' confirms Bretling. 'Both Larkin and Madam Kenwigs were expecting visits from Mumford on the day he went missing. I questioned them. Mumford failed to make the appointments, suggesting his murderer found him before both meetings. The first was set for eleven o'clock that morning, so he was probably dead by then. Dead or otherwise detained by his murderer. When we're done here, I suggest you start by revisiting those whom the deceased were supposed to meet.'

'Very well.' I take a pencil from my coat's inside pocket and add the details to the page. Bretling responds to my further questions and I scribble information about meetings missed by the other silker victims and the names of the corresponding participants. There are three more to add, none of whom I know, and each unconnected in any other way as far as I can see: Simon Forbes, an excavations consultant who should have met with mine owner John Lancett on the 18th of Sixthmoon; Master of the Dockside Forges Markus Hinton, who should have met with industrialist and mining consultant Davey Brindle on the 17th of Fipplemoon; and head tailor of Thackory's (a Highbridge gentlemen's outfitter) Zachariah Sterling who, on the 17th of Hexmoon, should have met with MP Wulfric Hemings. Again, I lose hope of remembering all these names, which as yet mean little to me. We shall learn more about them in due course.

I view the list again. 'John Lancett, mine owner. Not a coal mine, by any chance?'

'Some coal, some iron ore. He owns several mines south of here,' says Bretling.

There's a pause in our conversation.

'You should set a watch on the grove,' says Josiah. 'The killer could return at any time.'

'Thank you, Mr Mingle,' replies Bretling with forbearance. 'That has been arranged.'

I gaze back at the graves through the entrance as the wind tears at the tent. 'Someone has given this consideration. A grove of weeping trees – weeping for whom? Coals set in the mouths of the dead... Someone has thought about this a great deal. In fact, I'd say every detail has meaning for the killer. All those tree roots: who would choose such a laborious place to dig graves?' I wish my cousin Mardon were here. His insights would be most welcome. Alas, I'm stuck with Joe, though I mean to recount all of this to the rest of the Mysteries Solved team at the first opportunity. I suppose I shouldn't be too hard on Joe. He did notice the coal, after all.

He joins me near the entrance to look pensively out at the snow and the icy pond beyond the grove. 'There's so much of it.'

'Of what?' I ask.

'Snow and ice. Where does it all come from?'

'The atmosphere.'

'Mr Banyard, you told me snow and ice and steam are all water, but surely they're different.' He turns to look down at me with an almost apologetic expression.

'Yes, Joe.' I lower my voice so Bretling can't hear. 'They are the same and they're also different. I thought I'd explained...'

'I know. I just don't understand how one thing can be a solid, a liquid and a gas all at the same time.'

'Not at the same time, Joe. At different times. It's the temperature that makes the difference. When it's very hot, it's steam. When it's very cold, it's ice. Anything in between is just water.'

He nods, but judging by his wrinkled brow he still doesn't get it. Oh well. That's Joe for you: one minute he's the only one who's noticed there's coal in a dead man's mouth, the next he's lost all grip on the basics. I can't say he's the most reliable of assistants. To be honest, most of the time I wonder why I endure him.

Bretling's smoke fills the tent between erratic gusts of wind that breach the entrance. From our shelter we contemplate the graves in silence – at least, I do (who can say what Josiah's thinking?) – until a Draker enters to shake us from our stupors. 'Sir, the coroner is here.'

'Good.' Bretling pockets his pipe and strides back to the grove. We follow.

Dr Myrah Orkney, accompanied by a Draker imographer who has already set to work, stands at the centre of the ring of graves, seemingly unsure of where to begin. Her hair, as usual, is tied up neatly at the back. Behind her round-lensed spectacles, which seem overly large for her face and give her an owl-like appearance, her eyes are a little bloodshot from the drink. 'When your man said seven I thought he must have been mistaken.'

Bretling greets her with a modest tip of his hat. 'No mistake, doctor. I'd like a full report on site and a more detailed analysis once we have the remains back at the morgue.'

'Yes, of course.' Myrah seems stunned by the scene before her, unusually disturbed. She removes her spectacles to polish them with one end of her scarf. 'So, your six are here?'

'I believe so, but I'd like you to confirm it if possible.'

'And the seventh man?' she asks.

Bretling shrugs. 'Someone who's not been missed, I suppose.'

'Then we'd better start with...' Myrah consults her notebook, '... Uriah Mumford. He was the first, according to your information.'

'This way.' Bretling ushers Myrah towards the decayed remains that lie in pieces, yet reassembled. The body's fragmented, soil-stained silks have been arranged to one side. Following behind, the imographer sets a tripod on the ground near the remnants and makes some fine adjustments to his Yately Boxer. He strikes a Sulphur and lights a charge of flash powder in the camera's flash pan. The sudden white glare is blinding against the snow. A small cloud of smoke rises into the air.

'Mid Thripplemoon. Yes. Late spring. Five and a half months in the ground would do this.' Myrah makes a few corrections to the positioning of the remains, measures the approximate height, studies the blackened fingers, and wipes her hands on a handkerchief before jotting notes in her pocketbook with a pencil. 'Six feet and eight inches. Manicured nails. That was a nice suit, once. It all tallies.' She points to the lump of coal that's been placed by the rancid skull. 'What's this?'

'It was found in his mouth,' says Bretling. 'Most of the others are the same.' He calls to the sergeant. 'Huntly, what of the coal?'

Huntly hurries over to report. 'There's one in each grave, sir. Five bodies had a coal in their mouths and two appear to have fallen loose since they were interred. Those found without coal in their mouths have the signs – small fragments and coal dust on their tongues and thereabout.'

'Thank you, sergeant. As you were.'

The sergeant returns to his place, overseeing the excavation of the seventh body.

'That's new,' says Myrah.

'Yes,' Bretling concurs.

'Do you think their killer forced them to eat coal?' asks Myrah.

Bretling draws on his pipe and exhales a plume of fragrant smoke. 'I don't know what to think.'

'The autopsies will tell us.' Myrah appears to notice Josiah and me for the first time since her arrival. She knows us well enough from previous exploits and inclines her head cordially. 'Gentlemen.'

Bretling clears his throat. 'I've asked these gents for some assistance. A fact that is to remain between us.'

'Understood.' Returning her attention to the remains, Myrah asks, 'Why coal?'

No one can answer, though the question triggers a memory, and during a protracted silence I probe my mind for more details. I've read something about coal and lips in the same passage of text yet cannot place the source, though perhaps it is only a tentative and irrelevant link after all. Without rereading it, it's hard to say.

Myrah works her way around each of the bodies in turn, checking with Bretling that she has the facts right, taking care to visit them in the order upon which they were reported missing. At each blanket she stoops to examine its cadaver and make notes, pausing to inform us all that the remains of a man believed to be Davey Brindle have also been disturbed by animals, some small bones being absent.

'Sergeant,' says Bretling. 'Have that grave checked again for small bones.'

The sergeant calls his men to work and they start combing the grave again.

Myrah says little else during her examinations but confirms with Bretling that the degrees of decay are indeed consistent with the timeframe of his list. The imographer shadows her, capturing each body on film beneath the blackout hood of his Yately.

And so, it seems there can be no conclusion other than Bretling has indeed found his six missing silkers.

I ask him, 'Sir, my cousin is an experienced surgeon and part of my team. I wonder if he might be allowed to assist the good doctor here with the autopsies for the case. He's reliable, trustworthy.'

Bretling considers this briefly and nods approvingly. 'I don't see why not, if Dr Orkney agrees with the idea.'

Myrah ends her circuit of the grove at the grave of the unnamed man. I've seen more than my fair share of corpses and

I'm no expert – not like the coroner – but even I can see that this body is in the worst condition of all.

'I should have begun here,' she says. 'This was the first to be put in the ground. Another male. Sir, I'd advise making enquiries into any silker who has not been seen since the 17th of Quartersmoon.'

An excerpt taken from the gawper file,
as written by Reginald Francis Banyard.

I shall endeavour to record here collated my examination of the enigmatic beings popularly known as gawpers, thereby furthering our knowledge, to understand them, and thus to reveal their many mysteries in an academic study acceptable to men of modern science. The beings in question are, to my knowledge, known by different names in other countries: in Amorphia they are called the Witchety Nava; in Urthia, the Gankatan; and in the eastern lands of Icta, the Barrow-morty.

I shall begin by explaining what I so far have gleaned on the subject, although this is limited, before moving on to accounts of those who claim to have encountered these strange beings. While endeavouring to remain impartial, be that in argument for or against belief in their existence, I shall also, however, record encounters of my own and leave the reader to draw his or her conclusions.

Gawpers, to the general populous, are beings of myth and legend, like ghosts, if you will.

3

Mysteries Solved

*In which Banyard communicates with a gawper
and the team studies the case*

We leave Myrah and the others loading bodies into Draker carts
by lanternlight as the winter darkness closes in. There's nothing
more we can do at the Sallow Grove today, though my mind is
a whir of thoughts and names.

The lamplighter has already made his rounds by the time
Josiah and I call at The Dog for a long-needed drink, shocked
by the events of the last few hours. We're quick to order at the
bar and find stools around a barrel table in a nook where we can
talk.

'I wonder who this seventh man is,' says Joe, cradling a
tankard of Ruby's Finest Ale.

'Bretling's enquiries will likely tell us.' I allow the names we
know to consume me. I read and reread the notes, forced to
admit that I know very little about any of these dead silkers.
Seeking a link between them, I try to summarise the group. 'An
industrialist who's been in the papers once or twice in recent
years, one mine owner – whose name I have never before heard
– two rather zealous MPs...' I know of them '...and two
investors. Investors in what? They are strangers to me.' But

there's no point in asking Josiah about any of this. He doesn't even read the papers. 'There's certainly a lot of money here. Perhaps that's what lies behind the killings. It occurs to me that they're all either wealthy or in control of wealth. In the cases of the two politicians, probably both.' This line of deliberation leads me to a possible motive that might involve some business deal turned bad. 'Are these men swindlers, fallen foul of a shared victim who is exacting revenge?'

Josiah nods and sips his ale. 'Perhaps Bretling is right and this *is* about a grudge, though a *threader*?'

'If it concerns money dealings, unlikely.'

Later, Mr Jinkers, our reclusive and neurotic neighbour, catches us on our way into 96 Bunson Street.

'Good evening, Micky, Josiah.' He's eager to talk but we're both tired and hungry. Jinkers doesn't work, doesn't know what it's like. He lives a leisurely lifestyle by means of the considerable inheritance his parents left behind. You'd think he'd be happy but he's far from it. 'Busy day?' he enquires as a smoky black-and-grey striped cat winds a figure of eight around his ankles.

'You could say that. And you?'

'Indeed. Mr Kaylock and I have been very busy.' There's a loneliness in his rheumy eyes that he's incapable of concealing. Mr Kaylock fixes upon me, arches his back and hisses: his usual response to my presence.

'Doing what?' asks Josiah, pointedly.

'Oh, you know. This and that.' I suspect he's been down at the weir catching frogs, or perhaps out searching for gawpers. These are his two favourite obsessions. 'What have you been up to?' Expectantly, he looks at us in turn, his face an ashen blue in the glow of a nearby watch-lamp.

'We have a new case,' I say. 'Though we can't talk about it, as you well know.'

'Yes, I see. There was a lot of fuss in the city earlier this evening. Drakers coming and going. A host of lanterns flooding the streets. Was that something to do with it?'

Josiah and I exchange glances. 'Perhaps. What exactly did

you see?'

'Nothing, really. Just an unusual number of Drakers accompanying a couple of covered carts, a rum smell following in their wake. They crossed Rook's Bridge into Old Camdon and headed out towards Tower Bridge. I suppose they were taking something to the Draker Headquarters in Tower End.'

'Yes, I suppose they were,' I say, stamping snow from my riding boots and making a move for my front door.

He leans closer and lowers his voice. 'Micky, you would let me know if there's anything I might help with, wouldn't you?'

'Help... with what?'

'With the case. There's something big happening. I can tell.'

'It's against company policy for employees to share confidential information.' I weary of repeating this. 'I'm not sure how you could help–'

'I could spy!' he whispers. 'Find things out for you. Nobody notices me.' Again that melancholy... 'I swear, no one even sees me walk by, even in broad daylight. I sometimes think I'm invisible!'

Josiah smirks. I flash him a warning look. 'You're not invisible, Mr Jinkers, but perhaps we will bear your offer in mind. I bid you goodnight.'

'Before you go, I was wondering...' His eyes roam wildly. 'Have you seen any gawpers lately?'

'Not in person,' I say, and we leave Jinkers to enter the house.

'I do hope Jinkers doesn't start any rumours.' I hang my hat and slip off my long coat.

'I wouldn't worry,' says Josiah, following suit. 'Even if he did know something, who would he tell?'

I spend most of the evening at home in the green room, slumped in a Grand Wexford, pondering the case while warming myself before the fire with a glass of fine port in my hand. Baker sprawls out at my feet in the glow of the dancing flames, while Josiah busies himself drafting yet another letter to his sweetheart in Rochington. I've a surprise in store for him. Next Tuesday, on the 9th of Elventide, his threader sweetheart will be secretly transported to friends in Camdon City, under the guise of a well-to-do silker lady. She already has her fake documentation, her wardrobe of silks and accessories. I'm looking forward to seeing Joe's face when Willow Buxton arrives.

I consider the impending impact of war. Londaland's troops are already on the move and more set forth each day from Dockside aboard ironclads and galleons that have been drafted into the auxiliary navy. Our streets are busy with redcoats coming and going, our iron foundries pounding out armaments at full speed. And all this leads me to another possible reason why someone might secretly kill seven silkers from Old Camdon and hide their bodies in shallow graves out on the fringe of the city: could this be the work of a Morracibian spy?

A boy limps into the smoky room, a glass of milk in hand. He peers around with his one functioning eye. The other, as pale and featureless as the milk, was damaged by a wound that stole his sight and healed with an occlusion. 'Goodnight, Mr Banyard, Mr Mingle.'

Josiah nods. 'Goodnight, Shoe Shine.'

'Goodnight,' I say. Ebadiah Joseph – or Shoe Shine as he's often called – was a street boy before we took him in. Now he makes himself useful spying for Mysteries Solved when Mother's not schooling him. 'Oh, Ebadiah, would you join us at the office first thing? We're briefing the team with a new case and we'll need your help.'

'I will.' He nods and leaves as Mother appears briefly in the doorway to usher him upstairs to bed.

Across the room from me, my cousin Mardon reclines, smoking his pipe and perusing the *Camdon Herald*. A surgeon with a practice in Loncaster, he's lately spent more time here helping with Mysteries Solved cases. I give him a cursory account of our visit to the Sallow Grove, promising full details at the coming meeting, and he appears too weary and distracted to pass comment. Huffing, he refreshes his pipe with a pinch of Royal Gold and continues to smoke, burying himself in his newspaper.

'I see the Landsdale Rebels claimed responsibility for the bombing of Regent House,' he says.

'Indeed. Three dead and fifteen hospitalised. Terrible.'

'I'm surprised at you, Micky. I thought you of all people would have more sympathy for their cause.' Mardon exhales a vast plume of smoke.

'I don't see that anyone will listen to their arguments if all they do is kill and maim. There must be a better way.'

'Quite.' Mardon turns the page.

Widow Blewett (the old lady who also lives with us) retired an hour before, so once Josiah and Mardon have made for their beds I find myself alone and, tiring of my spinning thoughts, soon follow them up the stairs. In my room, I slide a hat box out from under the bed and remove the lid. Wrapped in an oil cloth inside rests the yellowed skull of a gawper. It looks like a man's skull but is a little larger and elongated, its cheekbones high and broad. Its teeth also appear longer than a man's. The skull was given to me by a gawper named Magwitch, in a cavern deep beneath the poisonous desert of Mors Zonam.

I lift the skull and hold its brow against mine, prepare for the disconcerting pressure in my head that accompanies these meetings of the mind, and open my *mind gate* (a term of my own invention).

Magwitch! I think his name, call him to me. There's a rush of notions and feelings, most of which I don't recognise as my own. It's an odd sensation, as though my psyche were brushing past a crush of others and absorbing a little of each along the way, and when the noise and confusion dissipates, his response is as clear as my own thoughts.

Michael Banyard has seen death this day, he thinks, already sensing my mood. I picture him as I saw him in the cave: looming over me, tall and grim, his hooded outline ragged in the lamplight, his robes woven from shreds of the black weed that grows in the streams running through their caverns, his lower face obscured by a mask formed from the same rubbery material.

I have, I reply in kind without speaking a word. *Seven dead silkers buried in shallow graves, south of the city.* I tell him all about the gruesome discoveries at the Sallow Grove before asking, *Were you aware of these deaths? Did you sense them on the fourth plane when they happened?*

I hear him laugh: a sound like gravel sluicing in a barrel or pan. I've heard it before but this time it's a mirthless response to my naivety. *Dagomites cannot sense every death that occurs in an entire city of humankind. Too many, are they.*

Of course, he's right. For one thing, the bodies of threaders who have been killed by their silker masters or who have drowned themselves are frequently pulled from the dark waters of the looping Tynne, and there are others who end their lives in a variety of other ways, then to be discovered in back alleys or dismal corners of the city. There are natural deaths as well, but plenty of threader executions. A regular turnover, in fact.

The Drakers have set a watch on the Sallow Grove in case the killer returns, but they are often useless. Will you watch over the grove?

Michael Banyard must wait. I feel Magwitch leave me, his mind gate closing. A few moments later he returns, reaching back out to reconnect. *A ring of weeping trees near a pond, farm buildings over a ridge and there, hiding, a watcher in black.*

That sounds like the place. The man in black must be the Draker who's watching the grove.

I have it. Magwitch will watch. This one (a quirk of the gawper dialect – he means me) *must call Magwitch again. Magwitch cannot always find this one in a moment.*

I marvel at his odd turn of phrase. *I shall call. Goodnight, Magwitch.*

Farewell for now, Michael Banyard.

Our minds separate and I wrap and place the skull back into its box as a trickle of blood runs from my temple.

Tuesday, 2nd Elventide

Outside, the snow has partially melted, reducing the road of ice to a more traversable surface, only perilous in part. It means traffic can flow again, albeit at a tentative pace. The noise and clatter of it also return. There's an envelope from Bretling waiting on the doormat when Josiah and I reach the Mysteries Solved office. It's marked for my attention and has the word 'SENSITIVE' stamped cross the front in bold red capitals. I take a letter opener from Lizzy's desk and slide it across the seal before taking out a collection of grim imographs taken at the Sallow Grove.

As army steam trucks pass on the road outside, rattling our windows, Josiah peers over my shoulder at the black-and-white images. 'Lord Draker seems serious about involving us. Though I don't see why *we* should help.'

'Believe me, I share your sentiments. But for the meantime we must humour him. It's that or have him turn utterly against us, and we don't want the mighty Lord Draker as an enemy.'

We're the first to arrive at the office but it's not long before the others begin to gather for the briefing in the case room, around nine o'clock in the morning. Lizzy, striking and sharply dressed, sits primly, her curvaceous legs crossed, a ledger perched on her knee and a sharpened pencil at the ready. Her blonde hair is today pinned in a high bun atop her head and she wears an expression of alert anticipation, a reflection of the mordantly sharp mind behind the glamour.

While she studies her notes, I lean in and whisper to Josiah, 'Is it my imagination or is Lizzy making more of an effort these days?'

He shrugs. 'The make-up, you mean? I thought the same. Not that she needs to…'

'Indeed.'

'She must have her eye on someone.'

Cousin Mardon sits reading a journal on the latest developments in surgical procedures, his leather surgeon's bag sagging on the floor at his feet.

Josiah chews at his nails, looking bored.

Ebadiah takes a seat and watches me with his good eye as an auburn silker lady in a green dress enters the room to take her place. That's Penney. We're courting but our last outing was nothing short of a disaster, though I can't fathom why. It's as if we're missing something. She throws me an apologetic smile.

'Good,' I begin, brushing the memory aside. 'Now that we're all here, I have much to divulge. Yesterday, no fewer than seven shallow graves were discovered in the south end of Holloway.' I go on to tell them all there is to know about the circumstances of the Sallow Grove and pin the seven imographs of the silkers' remains to the large corkboard in descending chronological order. There is also an image of the business contract discovered in John Lancett's pocket, unfolded, from which we may extract further details. The board is on the wall opposite the frosted glass windows that protect our case room's secrets from the prying eyes of passers-by on the pavement outside. Seeing the imographs, Ebadiah makes the sacred sign and clutches his cap to his chest, mouth agog. When I explain about the discovery of coal in the bodies' mouths, my team exchange unsettled glances.

Squinting at the imographs, Penney breaks the stunned silence. 'That's rather odd, isn't it?'

'I'd say so,' agrees Lizzy, jotting down the details in her ledger.

'Any thoughts, cousin?' I ask Mardon.

'Yes, well,' he says, reaching for a set of optical lenses from his bag. 'It means something, of course, but what?'

'Thank goodness *you're* here,' says Josiah.

Mardon throws him a glare. 'I suppose *you* have all the answers.'

'Not at all.'

I intervene. 'It's possible their killer was force-feeding the victims coal.'

'Some sort of punishment,' adds Josiah.

'There'll be post-mortems, I presume.' Mardon crosses the

room to scrutinise each imograph in turn, having selected a large magnifying lens.

'Indeed.' I explain all about Bretling's warning to keep the case and our involvement quiet. 'We may utter a word of this to no one. The consequences of such a blunder would be unthinkable.'

'Understood,' says Mardon.

Penney frowns. 'I'm sorry, Michael, but it sounds like you're saying we're to work with Lord Draker on this.'

'That's precisely what I'm saying.'

'Do you think that's wise after that Landsdale business?' asks Lizzy, looking disturbed by the idea. She's not the only one. They all glare at me as though I've made a pact with a devil.

'I'm not entirely sure we have a choice,' I say. 'And this case is already huge. For these reasons I must ask you all to set aside any ill feelings you may have towards Bretling Draker. And think of the publicity if we were to solve it. A killer of seven men. This will be the biggest story to ever hit the papers.'

A cynical half-smile spreads across Josiah's face.

'What?' I ask him, my irritation growing.

'I'm beginning to like this fellow, whoever he is. He's different: a killer loose in the city who only targets silkers.' His expression becomes serious. 'It could be any one of you next—'

This is a foolish blunder, even for Joe. 'It could be *you*!' I hear the anger in my voice. Josiah will always view himself as a threader but my team see him only as a silker – although Mardon knows the truth. 'What makes you think the killer hasn't already marked you out? That he wasn't watching us out there as we studied his handiwork at the Sallow Grove? Our man is cunning, careful and devious. He may already know we're on to his trail. Each one of us must be on guard.'

'Yes. Of course,' says Josiah. At least his slip-up was not in front of the Drakers.

'In any case, it seems to me that he's only interested in killing men,' says Penney. 'So I don't think Lizzy and I should worry unduly.'

'Good point,' says Josiah.

I feel no such assurance. 'Nonetheless, you must take every precaution. You are each to carry a pistol, concealed or otherwise.'

'Your concern is touching, Michael.' Penney smiles, but it's a flat gesture. I fear our romance is dwindling into something more akin to friendship and can only conclude she's feeling what I'm feeling: that we've become more like siblings than suitors. The upshot is we're left in an awkward *no man's land*, too genial to retreat and yet too uncertain to advance.

'Ladies, do you have your pistols?' I ask.

'Yes,' says Penney tapping her clutch bag.

'Always,' says Lizzy, who carries a snub-nosed pistol beneath her skirts, strapped to the inside of her thigh.

Josiah takes his gun belt from the deep drawer of his desk and buckles it around his waist, a pistol on each hip. Mine are at home in a chest at the foot on my bed. I'll fetch them later.

Ebadiah interrupts my contemplations. 'So, what's the plan?'

'I'm not sure I have one,' I confess. 'We might glean more information from the post-mortems, as Mardon suggests, but I doubt we'll learn much. How are your other investigations? Can anyone spare some time?'

'The Cross Keys case is closed,' says Mardon. This was an investigation into the disappearance of a cook from a silker mansion house out at Cross Keys to the west of Camdon City. Mardon traced the missing man to a patch of woodland nearby and there discovered the body. It appears the cook, who had an unfortunate drinking habit, was taking an evening stroll and, under the influence, tripped on a tree root and tumbled into a gully, striking his head mortally on a rock on his way down. No sign of foul play.

'Penney, Lizzy?'

'The Langdons have some family issues to deal with,' explains Penney. The Langdons are a silker couple from Highbridge who are convinced their banker is conning them. 'We met yesterday. They've called off the investigation until

51

further notice.'

'Just as well,' I conclude. 'We must throw everything we can at this. Put any new jobs on hold. I want everyone on the Sallow Grove. Lord Draker has requested our assistance, and our assistance he shall have.' I pin notes alongside each of the imographs, detailing the missed meetings that concern the dead silkers.

Mardon is quick to examine the facts. 'All disappeared, presumably murdered, on the 17th of the month.'

'We can't be sure of that,' I say. 'The mine owner John Lancett was only noted to be missing on the 18th when he failed to attend a meeting with excavations consultant Simon Forbes.'

'Well, I doubt Forbes is your man,' says Mardon. 'Lancett was killed on the 17th like the rest of them. It's the only logical conclusion.'

'Time will tell,' I shrug. 'Girls, I'd like you to research the grove and its surrounding area. I want to know who lives there, what goes on at Tinlock's Farm, all the gossip. Bretling's already questioned Farmer Tinlock and his family, so if you approach them, it may be best to use a guise. Also, the Sallow Grove itself – I think you'll agree – is an unlikely choice for a burial site, what with all the roots. As Josiah has astutely noted, why not dump the bodies in the nearby pond? A few stones in their pockets and in they go. Job done. Or why not use the forest? It's nearby and would have provided much better cover. The victims were all from the heart of the city. Why risk discovery by transporting them all the way out to the edge of Holloway at all? Whoever did this must have reasons for their actions. See what you can learn about sallows and any history of the grove.'

Lizzy and Penney nod.

'And me?' asks Mardon.

'I thought you might like to assist Dr Orkney with the post-mortems. It's already cleared with Lord Draker. I'm sure the coroner would appreciate help with seven bodies on her hands, and I'd like a man on the inside of the Draker HQ.'

'Very well,' says Mardon as a page of notes escapes Lizzy's

grasp to flutter to the floor. Both Lizzy and I stoop to retrieve it, meeting brow to brow over the paper.

'Oh!' she says as we almost collide.

'Allow me.' I collect the page, surprised to find that we both linger close a little longer than necessary. In the moment, the reason why evades me, though I own it feels rather marvellous to be near her. She gives a subtle smile as though she feels the same.

'Looks like I'm keeping shop, then,' says Ebadiah, with an air of disappointment.

Straightening, I hand the page back to Lizzy. 'For now, but don't get too comfortable, Shoe Shine. I've an idea in mind for you.'

'Right you are,' say Ebadiah as Penney throws me a scrutinising look and, like an idiot, I just smile vacantly back.

When Ebadiah has resignedly installed himself at Lizzy's desk in reception and the others have left, I fetch my coat and tricorn from the corner stand.

'Where are we going?' Josiah collects his topper and long coat.

'To the Museum of Unnatural History. There's something I need to check.'

4

The Seraph

*In which Banyard and Mingle
search for the right words*

There are two grand museums in Old Camdon – the oldest and most central district of Camdon City – and they are both situated on the northern banks of the Tynne, overlooking a broad curve of the river. As the name suggests, the Museum of Natural History exhibits all things considered natural: flora and fauna, geology, that kind of thing. But it's the other one that interests me today: the museum that deals with humankind, with the Old People and with anything else considered set apart from the natural world. There is, of course, a section on gawpers, which some consider nothing more than a joke, there purely for novelty's sake. For me it's a favourite, although I can't spare time to visit it today.

We climb the impressive outer steps of golden stone and pass beneath a gothic arch to view the antechamber where signs dictate, 'Do not touch the exhibits'. There are a few ancient amphora and broken marble statues on display here, but it's a small collection, merely a taster to decorate the room that leads on to the museum proper.

The first two floors are given over to relics of the Old People

– those who lived before the cataclysm thousands of years before our time. We pass glass cases holding bottles and other objects of moulded ware: a substance that is not rubber and not glass, but like something in-between. We do not know how to recreate it, though scientists have melted examples to prove the material can be reformed by heat, and so reused. Some specimens are transparent, others opaque and coloured.

To one side is a row of plinths bearing rusted and broken parts of what look like engines and bits of what we believe were various types of powered carriages. Whatever advancement this was, it was lost to us long ago. Of course, there are engineers working on it, trying to figure out and remake what once was, though as yet the closest we've come to these engine-driven vehicles are the clockwork car and the noisy, smoke-belching steam truck. We have several Londaland manufacturers of each but neither has quite produced anything to match the forementioned artefacts.

A long glass display case shows a range of other finds, each one a tablet-shaped object of glass, or metal or moulded wear, and each of a size that might fit well in the palm of your hand. They are various thicknesses, and none has survived fully intact. Their inner workings appear minute and complex, though of course rusted and decayed. Again, our science is sadly lacking in the interpretation and understanding of these things.

Further in are exhibited large pieces of a huge white vehicle: propellers; strange, curving, windowed panels; rubber wheels more than two feet in diameter, cushioned seats, cables and bits of wings and bodywork formed from a metal we call alumin. The text printed on the display cards informs visitors these are parts of a colossal and ancient flying machine, capable of transporting crowds of people through the sky.

All this we pass with little interest and, turning onto a broad marble staircase at the end of the room, ascend to the second floor – the reason we've come. I think that perhaps somewhere here are the words I've been trying to recall, old verses on fragile pages that have survived from an ancient sacred book.

'What's this?' asks Josiah, frowning at a glass case where some page fragments are displayed.

'They're from a tome thought to be already thousands of years old at the time of the Old People.'

'Is this what we've come for?' He seems disappointed and looks down the lengthy aisles of display cases filling the room.

I nod. 'We're looking for anything that mentions coal.'

'That could take all day!'

'Or longer, so the sooner we set to, the sooner we'll be done.'

He shakes his head miserably. 'If we must.'

Separating, we work along row after row of fragments – clay tablets imprinted with lines of strange archaic hieroglyphs, papyrus covered in pictograms, and parchments and papers scribed in languages both known and unknown. After half an hour of searching, Josiah calls me over to see a fragment of printed paper he's found. It's a yellowed section of a single torn page, frayed thin at the edges. I read the faded words aloud:

> *Then said I, Woe is me! for I am undone; because I am a man of unclean lips, and I dwell in the midst of a people of unclean lips: for mine eyes have seen the King, the* LORD *of hosts.*
>
> *Then flew one of the seraphims unto me, having a live coal in his hand, which he had taken with the tongs from off the altar:*
>
> *And he laid it upon my mouth, and said, Lo, this hath touched thy lips; and thine iniquity is taken away, and thy sin purged.*

We exchange a triumphant glance as a charge traverses my spine.

'That's it,' I say. 'You've found it!'

'Do you think it has something to do with the case?'

'*"Thine iniquity is taken away, and thy sin purged",*' I say. 'Do you not think the killer is trying to tell us something with the coals?'

'His victims were all sinners? And they have paid the price…'

'Indeed.'

'Maybe. But then again, perhaps he's just a madman, like Bretling says. Can we go now?'

I ponder the meaning of the scripture as we ride our horses from the museum. Mine is a sleek black gelding named Blink, Josiah's a muscular dappled grey mare named Willie. We turn down Druit's Lane to head across town. If anything, the verses have dampened my notion about a connection between the coal and the dead mine owner, John Lancett. Perhaps there is no correlation there at all. Again, I feel the sheer number of victims and potential suspects overwhelming, and we've barely begun to investigate. In fact, I don't think I've worked such a case before; nor, to my knowledge, did my father before me.

We follow the road around a sweeping bend of the Tynne, making our way to the western edge of Old Camdon, and soon rein in the horses outside a toy shop. This is also the residence of Stanley Larkin, who was expecting victim Uriah Mumford to visit on the day he disappeared.

The bay window displays a broad range of toys: puppets dangling on strings; automatons; spinning tops; kaleidoscopes; dolls and their houses; bottled ships; rocking horses and more. At centre stage, an automated woodcutter chops endlessly at a log with his hatchet. Above all this a large sign painted in gaudy shades of red, green and yellow reads, 'Larkin's'. We dismount and tether the horses to iron rings set into the wall nearby.

Taking off his hat and stooping beneath the lintel, Josiah enters the shop. The opening door triggers a peal of chimes from a cleverly rigged system of levers, springs and silver bells fixed overhead. We both pause, craning our necks to take it in as the chimes play out their melody.

Seeing a man behind the shop counter, I remove my tricorn and ask, 'Is that a creation of yours?'

'It is. How may I help you, gentlemen?' he asks, looking every bit a hardy silker gent with an open, oval face that's edged by a thick beard and shaved around the mouth. His silvered spectacles glint. His hair is as brown as his beard and his full lips form an amicable smile amid otherwise rugged features.

'My name is Michael Banyard. This is my associate, Josiah Mingle. We're here about Uriah Mumford, the missing man,' I say, wishing to impart the importance and sobriety of our visit.

His smile wanes as he offers a sombre nod of acceptance.

'Ah, yes. Mr Mumford commissioned a rather intricate automaton but has yet to collect it. Tell me, have you heard something from him?'

'Nothing I'm at liberty to share,' I say. 'You are Stanley Larkin, I presume?'

'I am.'

'You mentioned a commission...'

'Yes, the piece is in the workshop out back. You're welcome to see it, if it would be of interest.'

Josiah wanders the shop, lost in wonder – his boots squeaking. He gazes at the multitude of toys arranged around the edges of the floor, filling shelves and hanging from the ceiling. It's an impressive selection. He finds a zoetrope and gives it a spin to animate a leaping aurochs. 'Do you make all these yourself?' he asks, a childlike expression on his face.

'Indeed, I do,' says Larkin amicably. 'I'm rather proud of my creations. Do you like them?'

Josiah nods. 'They're rather good.' I don't suppose he had any real toys as a child. He finds a kaleidoscope and peers in through its lens, turning a brass ring at the end of its length. 'This is amazing. The colours and patterns move!'

'I'd like to see the commission,' I say.

Josiah replaces the kaleidoscope.

'Please, step this way.' With a welcoming smile, Larkin gestures towards an open doorway and leads us down a hall and into his workshop where benches are scattered with half-finished toys. Across the rear wall, an array of wood and metal-working tools hangs from pegs. To one side sits a half-barrel full of rough-hewn wood, ready to use, and another half full of sawdust and waste. He stops near a corner of the room where an intricately made automaton sits upon a shelf near a pair of rear doors.

'It's the engine from the wheal house at Mine Head Berta. A scale replica.' He gives a small brass key several turns and stands back to watch it work. At once the model engine springs to life, its wheels revolving on drive belts with a ticking sound, its little cage on delicate chains first lowering and then rising over the shelf's edge.

'It's a wonder,' I say, marvelling at the complex system of cogs, pistons and crankshafts. 'A triumph of minuscule engineering.'

Larkin beams. 'Well, I'm glad you think so. Tell me, gentlemen, would you like black bean soup? Or there's tea. I'm rather partial to it, though I take either. I can find chairs and we can talk more comfortably.'

'That could work,' says Josiah.

'Very well,' I add. 'We'll take black soup. Thank you.'

Larkin fusses around, fetching chairs and clearing space for them in his cluttered workspace.

'What about the shop?' asks Josiah.

Larkin smiles. 'Don't worry. The chimes will alert me to any visitors.'

'Of course,' says Josiah, while Larkin sets an iron kettle over the workshop stove and a distinct *thump* reaches our ears from somewhere upstairs.

'What was that?' asks Josiah, peering at the ceiling.

'Oh, just Mrs Figgins, my housekeeper.' Larkin adjusts the height of the flames on his stove.

'Why the wheal house engine?' I ask, taking a seat and watching him pour ground black beans into a little pan and adding water that's already steaming. Josiah walks around studying the tools, and I wonder if he's hunting for traces of blood. He delves into the half-barrel of sawdust yet appears to find nothing.

'Oh, it was to be a birthday gift for one of Mr Mumford's sons. When he commissioned it, we set a date upon which he would collect the piece. As I say, he has as yet failed to do so.'

'You think him still likely to collect?' asks Josiah.

'I have no reason to believe otherwise,' says Larkin, stirring the brew with a long spoon. He takes three copper cups from a cupboard and, with precision, sets them in a line on his workbench. 'May I ask what's prompted your visit? You don't look like Drakers.'

'We're private investigators,' I explain. 'We're not at liberty to divulge anything about our clients or the case.'

'I see. Well, I aim to be as helpful as I can be. What may I tell you?'

'We'd like to know more about the meeting you arranged with Mumford. Was there an agreed time?'

'He was supposed to arrive at eleven o'clock on the morning of the 17th of Thripplemoon. I had the automaton ready and waiting but I've not heard anything more from the man.'

'But why a wheal house?' I ask. 'Is his son particularly keen on mining?'

'Yes, at least, so he said. Mr Mumford also has an interest in Wheal Berta, I believe. He said he had personally invested in the mine, among others.'

'So Wheal Berta is an actual working mine?' I ask.

'Indeed, it is. A coal mine south of the city, owned by one John Lancett.'

I stare at him before pulling Bretling's notes from the inside pocket of my long coat. I unfold the page and scan it to confirm that John Lancett was, according to the state of the bodies and the date of his disappearance, the third silker gentleman to be murdered and buried in the Sallow Grove, and Uriah Mumford was the second. Judging by the look Josiah throws me, he's also made the connection.

Larkin pours three cups of hot black bean soup and passes one each to Josiah and me. We sit and drink. I watch Larkin with suspicion.

'A scale model... What did you work from?' I ask. The soup is good and strong, much better than the Draker brew we sampled out at the grove.

'Mumford procured detailed drawings of the wheal house

and its engine. I worked directly from the plans. In fact, I have them right here.' He gestures towards a long roll of papers tucked behind the model on the shelf.

'I see. And he didn't return at any time to see how your work was progressing?'

'No.' Larkin sips his soup, his expression intensifying. 'Listen, I'm not stupid. Something must have happened for you to come calling. Is Mr Mumford dead?' We remain silent. He continues. 'If he is, you should say so. I have my accounts to consider and the piece has not been paid for.'

Josiah leans forwards in his chair, resting his broad forearms on his knees. 'Your accounts? A man may have been murdered!'

'I have other reasons,' says Mumford defensively.

'Like what?'

'I might be of help to you. I've not considered him dead. Not thought about that at all. Is he dead? I will need time to revisit every word that passed between us. I may recall something of use.'

'Then do so,' I say. 'Do it, believing he may be dead, but give no mention of this to any other or there'll be consequences.'

'Sir, are you threatening me?' He sounds shocked by the idea. 'I'm only trying to help.'

I hand him my business card. 'It's not a threat, Mr Larkin, but you should understand my client is a ruthless and powerful man. If any word of this escapes, you will have to deal with him.'

He pales. 'Very well. Not a word. You must give me a few days before you return.'

'We *shall* return. I promise.' Leaving our cups half full, we go.

Outside, we untether the horses and mount up, though I'm left feeling a little sorry for Larkin. Perhaps we were too rough on him.

'He seems all right,' says Josiah. 'I quite like him. You don't think he had anything to do with it, do you?'

'I wouldn't if it wasn't for Wheal Berta. A connection we can't ignore.' Unsure of Larkin, I say no more on the subject.

On one hand he seems agreeable and harmless; on the other, he appears to know about two of the victims. And with Wheal Berta connecting the three men, I'm back to pondering the presence of coal in the dead men's mouths.

Josiah grunts. 'If he were guilty of anything, why insist we return to question him further? He's clearly a silker and Bretling says the killer is a threader.'

'Bretling could be wrong.'

'I suppose.'

Our next stop is The Gunner, a dowdy tavern on the east side of town where we hope to meet the owner, who was also supposed to meet with Uriah Mumford around the time he disappeared. We cross Old Camdon and, passing the threader courthouse and gaol, find the tavern in Firth Lane, dismount and tether the horses.

Inside, we're welcomed by a roaring log fire and a smoky, stale atmosphere. The place is quiet with a few lone customers scattered at its edges. I approach the central bar to address a drably dressed serving girl with ratty hair and a waxy complexion. 'Good day, miss. Please fetch Mistress Kenwigs. We have important business with her.'

'Begging your pardon, sirs, but she's out and won't be back for nigh on an hour.' The girl watches us, seeming unsure of how she might help. 'Who are you, sirs, if you don't mind?'

'Banyard and Mingle, private investigators. And you are?'

'Patty Primshaw, sirs. You may wait, of course. Have you eaten? The stew's good.'

A glance at my pocket watch tells me it's past one o'clock.

'We should eat,' says Josiah. 'I'm famished.'

'You're always famished,' I say, but looking around at the grime-coated bar and walls, I mutter to him, 'Are you sure it's safe to eat here?'

The girl aims a withering look at me. 'It's perfectly safe. The food is good. I cook it myself.'

That seals it. We *have* to order now. It's the only decent thing to do. 'In that case, bread and stew for two, if you please.' Thanking the girl, I pay for the meal and she quickly disappears into a back room.

While we await our luncheon, we take in the drab, patterned carpet that must have once been red and gold, the dusty chandeliers and wall lamps that were the pinnacle of fashion and taste ten years ago, and the worn bar in dire need of refurbishment. At length, Patty returns with a steaming bucket of water and begins scrubbing down the bar. We feel her judgemental eyes upon us. When she's finished glaring, she works hard, never pausing to rest. Halfway through the job, she drops the scrubbing brush into her pail and leaves again to attend to the kitchen. Minutes later, she's back to finish the bar. She towels it dry before fetching several trays of tankards and setting them down, ready to serve. She hefts a new keg of ale into place behind the bar, straining under its weight, and hammers a tap through the corked hole. She vanishes into the back rooms again and, moments later, brings out our food on a single large tray, placing it down upon our table and setting everything in place. We take up our spoons and eat.

Josiah slurps his stew, dips bread and chomps it hungrily down. 'A pint would go well with this.'

'It's too early. We need clear heads. There's a lot of thinking to be done.'

He nods grudgingly. 'This is good!' He sounds surprised.

'It *is* good. *Very* good.' The stew is flavoursome and thick, full of meat, onion and chunks of potato and carrot. There's something else: stout, I think.

While we eat, the girl labours on and I start to feel exhausted just watching. She finishes the bar, collects dirty plates and tankards from the various alcoves and corners, dusts the tapestries and paintings that surround us on the walls, mops the tiled entrance hall and polishes the brass candle holders that sit in wall niches. She seems to have been left completely alone to run the entire establishment and I regret my former comment. That said, for all her labouring, the tavern retains a grimy feel and I think she could clean and polish away for a year and that wouldn't change.

Josiah seems to notice as well, his eyes following her every move. 'My word, she's a worker.'

'Indeed.'

Our thoughts are interrupted by the arrival of a silker lady – I use the term loosely, for the woman in question is most unladylike, being stocky, hook-nosed and with a grimy patina about her that well matches her premises. She walks in pompously and instantly begins berating her maid. I'm reminded of Bretling's comment that she's a crone, which I felt at the time was harsh and perhaps undeserved, yet now understand.

'Have you swept the stairs? Scrubbed the front steps? Look at these dishes! This glassware's filthy! Clean yourself up, girl! You're nothing but a sweat stain! What you goggling at? Get back to work!'

Pretending to be unaffected by the tirade, we mop the last excellent morsels of stew from our bowls with the bread, which is wholesome and freshly baked with a good, crisp crust.

A few minutes later, when Kenwigs has ascended the stairs, Patty visits us to clear our table. 'I'm sorry, masters. I shall bring Mistress Kenwigs to you shortly when she's more settled,' she says, hurriedly loading our empty bowls, plates and spoons onto her tray and turning away. We glimpse raw-looking scars from a lash across her shoulders, partially hidden beneath the straps of her dress.

Josiah calls her back. 'Hey, girl, the food was fine. Are you alone here or do others serve with you?'

She pauses to face us. 'I'm alone, sir, apart from Mistress Kenwigs.'

'You mean you run this entire tavern? Does she help at all?'

'Not so much, sir.'

'And what does that woman feed you?' he asks.

Patty throws a nervous glance across the room. The crone is still upstairs. 'If I'm caught tasting the food before it's served, I am lashed.'

'What? Even though you're the cook?'

'Yes, sir.' She pauses, seeming suddenly unsure of our motives, concerned that we might land her in trouble. 'I've no complaints, sirs. My mistress is kind. I am allowed to eat the scraps that others leave behind.'

I imagine dining this way, taking half-chewed bread from someone else's finished plate, with someone else's saliva still adhering to the crust. The notion disgusts me.

Josiah nods and eyes the bowls we've mopped clean with bread. There's not a crumb left. 'Have you eaten today?'

'No, sir.'

'In that case, I'd like to order another bowl of your fine stew with plenty of that marvellous fresh bread and butter. Be sure to use a clean bowl and plate. Thank you.' He takes his wallet from his long coat pocket. 'How much is that?'

She takes payment and leaves us to fetch the stew. When she returns to deliver the order, Joe pushes the plate and bowl back to her across the table, untouched. 'I'm sorry, Miss Primshaw. I've rather lost my appetite.'

'Thank you, sir.' Patty makes a brief curtsy, collects the food and heads for the kitchen.

'That was a kindness,' I tell him.

'Yeah, well...'

Josiah knows all too well what it means to live a threader's life. He has similar scars across the muscles of his back, though they are old now, healed and pale.

Madam Kenwigs enters the room from the stairway and, seeing no serving girl, makes a beeline for the kitchen.

An excerpt taken from the gawper file,
as written by Michael Banyard.

Having experienced them at first hand, I can tell you that at least one tribe of gawpers dwells in the subterranean caverns of Mors Zonam, a toxic desert that begins some fifty miles or so to the south of Camdon City. This wasteland is considered deadly and is used as a place of mortal punishment, where convicted threaders are often banished, should hanging be deemed too lenient a penalty. The gawpers there call themselves Dagomites, which brings me to the Dagomite named Magwitch, whom I encountered when I undertook a perilous expedition to locate a missing girl.

Magwitch has become something of an ally, one I have met with on several occasions.

5

Manner of Death

*In which Banyard and Mingle
attend a party at the morgue*

I hate to think what would happen if Kenwigs were to find Patty eating from a full bowl, something I'm not about to let happen. I rise and hurry to intercept her, with Josiah close on my heel.

'Banyard and Mingle, private detectives.' I offer my hand, which she regards with disdain through eyes that are toad-like, puffy and heavy-lidded. 'Madam Kenwigs, may we have a word?'

'Will it take long? I'm rather busy.' Her accent is unusually ignoble for a silker, one that I imagine comes from spending much time in the company of rogues. With deepening dislike, I decide not to trust a word she says. She sweeps a stray lock of hair from her capacious wig of blonde curls. Her make-up is overdone, the rouge on her cheeks a vivid shade of plum over a stark white foundation.

'Not long at all. Might we sit?' I gesture towards the nearest table, where we settle.

She dumps an oversized carpet bag on the bench next to her and glares at us. 'Well, then, what is it?'

'We've come about a missing man, an industrialist named

Uriah Mumford. He was due to meet with–'

'Not this again!' She glares. 'I thought I was done with the whole business.'

'I'm sorry to disappoint but we're looking into the disappearance.'

'For whom?'

'Our client wishes to remain anonymous.'

'Is that so?'

'Apparently, you were scheduled to meet with Mr Mumford on the day he vanished. Is this correct?'

'It is,' she admits resignedly. 'We were to meet for luncheon but he stood me up.'

'Why was your meeting arranged?'

'I rather think Mr Mumford had taken a shine to me.'

'You mean…' I'm surprised and it probably shows. 'He was courting you?' I sound a little incredulous.

'Yes, that's exactly what I mean.' She looks offended. Her eyes narrow. 'Is that so unthinkable?'

'Not at all,' I lie. Moving on. 'Was there perhaps a secondary reason he might have had in wishing to meet?'

'None of which I'm aware. Sir, I find your tone offensive.'

'I do apologise. I can assure you no offence was meant.'

'Be that as it may, I must ask you to leave.' She takes a handkerchief from her bag and dabs at sweat that is beading on her brow. She feigns tears – or so I believe – and mops at the corners of her eyes. 'Really, this entire affair has been most upsetting.'

'Then we shall leave you be, madam, but may I ask, had you met with Mr Mumford before?'

'Oh, yes. Several times. Not that it's any business of yours. Now, if you don't mind, I'd like to be alone.'

We rise, bow a polite farewell and leave.

We're descending the stone steps outside when the serving girl, Patty, hurries out of the doors after us, looking furtive. She calls in a hushed voice. 'Sirs, a word.' We pause and turn at the bottom of the steps as she approaches, laden with a mop and a pail of soapy water. 'I'm sorry, sirs, but I couldn't help overhearing. Are you seeking Uriah Mumford?'

Josiah and I exchange a glance. 'We are,' I say.

'I was here that day, the day he was meant to call.' She glances over her shoulder back at the tavern entrance. 'I wouldn't trust a word my mistress says. Did she tell you Mr Mumford had a thing for her?'

'She implied it,' I confirm.

'Pah!' Patty snorts derisively. 'Not a chance. I don't know why they were supposed to meet but it weren't that. More likely he was arranging lodgings or something of that nature.'

'Thank you.' I tip my hat.

'No, sirs,' she says, fixing upon Josiah. 'Thank *you*.'

There are thirteen of us gathered and I've never seen the mortuary so full: Sergeant Huntly, Myrah, Bretling, Mardon, Josiah, the dead men and me. Myrah has them arranged flat on their backs upon gurneys across one end of the room. The stench of decay is heavy, more so than out in the cold of the grove. There is nothing else that smells quite the same as putrefying human flesh. It's a scent I've come to loathe. The place is a mess: blood and other bodily fluids on the floor, some of it spread around the boards where it has adhered to shoes or boots. Myrah looks exhausted, haggard and pale in her lab coat and apron, stained and smeared with dark substances. Mardon wears the same. 'Poor blighters,' he mutters absently, standing over the dead men.

'Any news on the unnamed man?' I ask.

'Nothing yet,' says Bretling, who also appears gaunt and grim. 'My officers are looking into it, but let me know immediately if you learn anything.'

'Of course, sir,' I say.

At Myrah's lead, we encircle the first gurney, which holds the remains of the unknown silker. His toe badge reads *Tobias 42960*, the name synonymous with the unidentified dead. We stare at liquifying flesh that's still clinging to grizzled bones. A dark cavern in the centre of the torso shows where Myrah extracted the rotting stomach. What's left of the organ itself sits in a steel bowl to one side of the disarticulated corpse.

'From the advanced state of decomposition, we can be fairly sure this was the first of the burials.' She consults a clipboard with notes on the post-mortem examination. 'No coal in the mouth, but then, there was very little flesh of the mouth left that would have contained it. This was found in the spoil heap.' With a hand she indicates a lump of coal that sits near the bowl. 'Further examination has confirmed my previous estimated date of death, that being sometime in the spring of this year. My best guess, with all things considered, is Quartersmoon, which means he may have been buried a month or so before Uriah Mumford here.' She gestures towards the remains on the adjacent gurney.

'You studied his stomach contents, as requested?' asks Bretling, peering at the bowl.

'I did. No coal, nor coal dust present as far as we can tell, although – as with the mouth – the tissues are decomposed to a problematic degree. That said, our findings are the same for all of them.'

'After close examination it's safe to say none of the recovered coal was ever fired,' Mardon explains.

'So, the killer didn't make them eat coal,' I say.

'Correct,' confirms Mardon. 'As far as we can tell.'

'What difference does it make?' asks Josiah.

'It means it's more likely the coal was placed in their mouths after they were dead and was therefore ritualistic.' I pass a copy of the verses from the museum to Bretling. 'I recalled something I'd read from an old scripture. We tracked it down in the Museum of Unnatural History.'

Bretling reads aloud.

> *Then said I, Woe is me! for I am undone; because I am a man of unclean lips, and I dwell in the midst of a people of unclean lips: for mine eyes have seen the King, the LORD of hosts.*

> *Then flew one of the seraphims unto me, having a live coal in his hand, which he had taken with the tongs from off the altar:*
>
> *And he laid it upon my mouth, and said, Lo, this hath touched thy lips; and thine iniquity is taken away, and thy sin purged.*

He fixes upon me. 'That's interesting. You think our man is some kind of religious fanatic?'

'Perhaps. It suggests to me that he is educated, that he can read and either owns a copy of the scripture in some form or has at least read it somewhere. Perhaps he too visited the museum.'

His face creases with concern. 'Educated? But that would...'

'... make him a silker.' Josiah completes the thought.

'Unlikely,' says Bretling. 'This is a threader's doing. I'd put money on it.'

Josiah moves to speak but closes his mouth when he sees my subtle shake of the head. We can't risk the fallout that could transpire over a wager.

'It could be either,' reasons Mardon.

Bretling makes a blustering, huffing kind of sound. 'Anything else of note with this one, coroner?'

Myrah gives Mardon a nod.

'We found this, Lord Draker,' says Mardon, presenting Bretling with a dissection board bearing several fragmented and decayed scraps of what appears to be newspaper pinned in place. 'From a pocket of his jacket. If I can match them with a back copy of Camdon's papers it may confirm the date of his disappearance, though I can't promise anything. They're rather small and disintegrating.'

'Very good,' says Bretling. 'It's worth a shot.'

'Can you tell us how they died?' asks Josiah.

Mardon corrects him. 'You mean *how they were killed*.'

Josiah flashes him an agitated look. 'I think you'll find it was a perfectly good question.'

'I was merely pointing out that they were clearly killed and did not simply die,' says Mardon.

Josiah attempts a comeback. 'You're just being per... per...'

'Pedantic,' I whisper at his ear.

'... pedantic!' says Joe.

Mardon scowls at us both. 'I was being accurate. There's a difference.'

Josiah's clenched knuckles whiten as he leans in, narrowing his eyes. 'I'll show you a difference,' he growls.

I clear my throat. 'Perhaps we might move on?'

'I believe we can now confidently say that each was killed by a single stab wound entering through the eye and into the brain case,' says Myrah, looking irritated. 'Every victim has an orbit pierced by a narrow blade. It was impossible to see through all the decay at the scene, but when we cleaned them up, it became quite clear.'

Bretling leans on the gurney for support. 'A dagger wound? Are you sure?'

'I'm certain. A dagger or something similar. The blade that caused these wounds was around half an inch across. Mostly it's the right eye but sometimes the left.' Myrah uses a wooden pointer to indicate the shattered bone at the back of the cadaver's eye socket.

'That's odd,' says Josiah.

'Why would someone choose to stab through the eye?' Bretling ponders, but no one can answer.

We take a cursory tour of the other bodily remains but there is little Myrah can add, and despondently, Bretling mutters something about another appointment and leaves.

'Mardon, a word.' I lead my cousin out into the corridor, although his gaze remains on the gathering we've left behind. He continues to peer through the gap in the door, which makes me wonder exactly what or who he's looking at. 'Listen, you're going to have to take it easy on him.'

'On Josiah? *Why?*' Mardon looks at me briefly before gazing back into the room. '*Why* on Earthoria did you partner with him in the first place? He's a dullard. I've never understood it.'

'Granted, I may have rushed into it, but he's making progress. He's trying hard and needs all the help he can get.'

'You know you could have had me as your business partner.' I think I see now where this is coming from. He continues, 'You only had to ask.'

'You were busy in Loncaster, mending bones and stitching wounds. You weren't interested. Not back then. Not when I saved him from the noose.'

'When *we* saved him from the noose. Remember? I was right there with you!' Now he's affronted.

'Yes, I recall half-dragging you there. You were quite reluctant. Detached, I would say.'

'Well...' His words run dry. 'I admit it wasn't until later...'

'It's done now. I'll not end the arrangement. Not as long as he wants the position.'

'Very well. I'll finish this case and return to Loncaster. But you've built your tower, Micky. Don't cry to me when it crumbles into the sea.'

I hold his glare, my face like granite. 'I promise, I won't. Why does he aggravate you so? You've barely taken your eyes from him this whole time.'

He shakes his head before turning away. 'I wasn't looking at the dullard, man! I was admiring the beauty.'

For a moment I'm baffled until, by a process of elimination, understanding dawns. 'The coroner?'

Around seven o'clock, I ready myself for romance and take a carriage to Highbridge through Camdon's lamplit streets to collect Penney. Little do I know that, like a galleon following a doom light, I am bound for rocks.

The evening begins well enough. She looks stunning in a purple dress and black bodice that accentuates her curves. Her hair is dressed high in a sophisticated coif. When we greet with a kiss, I smell sweet mint and a floral scent, and we talk amicably of trivialities, nestled arm in arm while sharing a cosy bench in the cabin. Though once installed in a nook at The High

Commander, an expensive inn located at the heart of Highbridge, our conversation soon takes a more pragmatic turn. Penney launches into a series of questions about our investigation – referring to it as the *Seraph case* – and what's worse is I'm happy to oblige: anything to avoid discussing us and the apathy that's slipped between us.

'What about all these bodies? So many. Can it truly be the work of just one man? Are you sure we should be working with Lord Draker? I've a terrible feeling we're making a mistake. What if something goes wrong? We really don't want that man as an enemy…'

The questions roll on and on. I answer them as best I can. Those that have no answers we discuss at length and, before long, our food arrives, and very fine it is too. We eat. We sip wine and continue the debate long after the serving girl collects our empty platters. I walk Penney home and bid her goodnight. Unfortunately, our final exchange returns to the subject of us working alongside the Drakers and is a weighty contention. There is no kiss when we part, no loving touch or gesture. Just a *goodnight* and a disappointed, empty feeling.

I flag down a coach and ride miserably home.

Wednesday, 3rd Elventide

Simon Forbes is next on the list. My notes remind me he's an excavations consultant working down on the east coast, beyond Drifter's Bay, on an edge of land known as Stonhaven. Josiah sits on the cabin bench opposite me as our carriage trundles along the open track that skirts the eastern fringe of Curlston Marsh. The wheels splash through meltwater and slip on patches of ice and snow that cling stubbornly to the verges.

'Listen, Joe. What's this business between you and Mardon? It simply can't continue.'

'Tell that to your abnoxious cousin.'

'You mean obnoxious. With an "o".'

'That too.'

'Well?'

'I can't help it, Mr Banyard. He picks on me. Argues against everything I say. I can't work with him.'

'You must. He's on the team.'

'Only because you say so. You could kick him out any time it suits.'

'It doesn't suit. Not at all. We need a man of science like him.'

He stares out of the carriage window, nonplussed. 'He can't be the only scientist around.'

'Promise me you'll try.'

He takes a penny dreadful from his coat pocket and flicks it open. 'I will, but he'd better mind his step.'

For the remainder of the journey he loses himself in *Jack Marlsdon, the Butcher of Rat Tail Alley*, while I'm forced to accept the situation. I read and reread my notes until a bump in the road prompts me to glance up as we near our destination. Beyond the window, the land ends in an abrupt line: cliff edges revealing an expanse of sea that's a shimmering inky black in the afternoon's shallow winter light. There's a westerly howling in to raise huge choppy waves and I'm glad to be on dry land, even if I am jostled by the road and trapped in a coach with Joe. Ahead, the cliffs drop steeply to a cove on a rugged coast of surf-battered rock, and over the next rise, the tall chimney tower and high roof of Wheal Berta slide into view. By all accounts, this is where we should find our man.

From a little digging I've learned that, since the disappearance of the owner John Lancett, Wheal Berta has remained in the family as a working coal mine managed by Lancett's widow. Of the other two signatories on the contract found in Lancett's pocket, only one name is legible, Avory Steverus. My plan is therefore to find and question not only Simon Forbes but also this Steverus fellow, hoping to uncover the third individual involved in what may well have been the last business deal Lancett ever made.

Our driver – a rough-looking retired soldier named Fletcher, wearing a coachman's hat, a patched scarf and long coat, and sporting a blunderbuss at his hip – calls the horses to halt and the carriage stills around a hundred yards from the mine. From here a gravel path too narrow for vehicles winds down a gentle slope between hillocks of gorse and heather. The track is busy with barrowmen steering carts heaped with rough-hewn gains from the mine, while others wheel the empties back. There's a never-ending cycle of collection and transportation as the loads are drawn up Wheal Berta's deep mineshaft on the steam-powered winch. From the crown of the stack, smoke spews into the glowering sky, and further down the path several wagons collect the coal to carry it north.

A cold wind hits us as we descend the carriage steps and I pay Fletcher. We leave him with the promise of recompense for his wait while we investigate, our first stop the mine itself. The workers we pass on our approach are all wiry thin and seem broken in spirit, never lifting their soot-blackened faces from the path nor acknowledging our presence. They simply trudge, manoeuvring their barrows, their ropey muscles showing here and there through tears in their ragged clothes. They are threaders trapped in a joyless existence, born and bred for the purpose of labour, or so our silker society would have us believe.

Outside the entrance, I pause to address a barrowman, accompanied by the repeating *clinks* of a distant hammer.

'Is your foreman about?'

The weary-looking man nods to a knoll beyond the mine that overlooks the sea. 'He's yonder, masters.'

Peering up, we see a lone figure silhouetted against the sky at the peak of land and set forth to climb the hill. Beyond it to the south lie a scatter of hovels, a blacksmith's workshop and other stone buildings that form a small village where presumably the workers dwell.

I'm panting by the time we reach the figure, who is crisply dressed in a tartan brocade beneath a dapper fur-trimmed coat. He watches our approach through astute grey-blue eyes and tips his top hat of shimmering black silk in greeting as we near. He is tall and slender, though handsome – I suppose – and very smartly turned out with a narrow face. His coat tails flutter in the breeze along with a mop of pale blond hair that protrudes beneath the brim of his topper.

'Good day. Are you the foreman of the mine?' I ask, tipping my tricorn in return and glancing at the expansive sea vista.

'I am, sir. May I assist you in some way?' His accent is that of a high-born silker.

'Perhaps,' I reply. 'We're investigating the disappearance of John Lancett. May we ask you some questions?'

'By Lychling! How terribly exciting! Yes, of course you may. Tell me, are you employed by Mercy Lancett?'

'I'm afraid we're not at liberty to divulge such information.'

'Who's Mercy Lancett?' asks Josiah. I scowl.

'Why, John's wife, of course. Oh my, we should really find somewhere to sit and take shelter. It seems you have much to learn.' He offers a half-smile, enjoying the encounter a little too much for my liking.

'By all means,' I say with a nod. 'Lead the way.' We follow as the foreman takes us back down the knoll, along a gravel lane and into what appears to be a ramshackle tavern that's been strewn with a few old benches and barrels, though the place has no sign to name it.

'It's not palatial, but we'll be out of this confounded wind,' the foreman says, rubbing his chilled hands together and ducking to enter through a low doorway. 'Take a seat. I'll fetch us a warmer. Rum? It's that or ale, I'm afraid.'

Josiah's quick to nod. 'Rum, thanks.'

'I confess, that sounds good. Does this place have board and lodgings?'

'There are several modest rooms above,' the foreman explains.

For a few moments we're left alone to find a suitable bench and peer at our humble surroundings. The foreman orders drinks from a spindly serving woman at the bar: a trestle table, behind which are arranged a half-dozen kegs. In a corner by the fireplace, a solitary lame man sits smoking a clay pipe, watching us with his bandaged leg outstretched. A pair of crutches lean against the wall by the injured man.

The foreman soon returns steadying three pewter cups in his hands and sets them down carefully on an old, upturned barrel.

'That's an interesting hat you have there.' He directs this at me.

'I'm quite aware it's unfashionable, but it was my father's and I'm rather fond of it.'

He nods. 'Now, gentlemen, tell me what you would like to know,' he says in his oily manner, sipping his rum and smiling assuredly.

'We're looking for two men who may or may not be connected to the disappearance of John Lancett. The first is Simon Forbes, an excavations consultant at the mine. He was supposed to meet Lancett on the 18th of Sixthmoon but Lancett never showed. The second is a fellow by the name of Avory Steverus.'

'Well, I can certainly help you there. Simon Forbes still works at Wheal Berta. In fact, he's down the shaft this very minute, examining a seam for purity.'

Josiah and I exchange a glance. 'And the second man?' I ask.

'Oh, that's easy.' He grins knowingly.

'Why so?' asks Josiah.

The foreman shrugs and takes another sip. 'Because you're speaking to him.'

6

Stonhaven Hall

In which the questioners become the questioned

Mingle narrows his eyes at the foreman. 'You're Avory Steverus?'

'I am. And you may ask me whatever you like. I've nothing to hide.'

'Do you know anything about the disappearance of John Lancett?' Thinking twice about the rum in my hand, I set it down. Josiah knocks his back in one swig and glances disappointedly into the bottom of his cup.

'No, although I can give you some detail of John's situation as it was before he vanished. Might that be of use? I say, he's not dead, is he?'

'Missing for more than four months,' grunts Josiah. 'Doesn't look good, does it?'

'Do tell us what you know,' I prompt.

'John's disappearance came as a shock to everyone. You see, for many a year he was discontented, a harsh man, some would no doubt say, but the last year or two were kinder to him. His mines were doing well, yielding rich ore and coal, earning a respectable name on the market. Prices were high and he was reaping a good profit. He was planning to expand his business, to purchase other mines, though he vanished before he could. His family were happy, as far as I could tell. Mercy, his wife, believes John to be dead and so remains in mourning. There are rumours, of course. People can be cruel. A story circulated that he had fallen for a common country lass and eloped. But it's nonsense. For one thing, why would he do that when it would mean abandoning his business, his life's work? Mercy will confirm to you nothing of his has been taken. Not a single guinea was drawn from his account, not a stocking missing from his wardrobe. She's convinced he's dead. I'd rather hoped it wasn't the case.'

'I see. We shall seek her out.' I pause, constructing my next words with care. I must not give too much away. 'Mr Steverus, your name is reported to have been upon a business contract alongside John Lancett's. Can you explain your involvement with him? There was another name also...' I watch him closely to evaluate his reaction, which is neutral and unreadable.

'Ah, yes, a signed agreement between shareholders to take our coal to a new market in Loncaster. I have a copy somewhere. We were selling to Rochington before that, until word reached us of better prices elsewhere.'

'You're a shareholder in the mine?' asks Josiah, shoving a thumb over his shoulder towards Wheal Berta. 'As well as the foreman?'

'A shareholder, yes, although I was not the foreman until a few months before John's disappearance. I've been a shareholder for much longer. I stepped in to assist when the previous foreman abandoned his post and left John in the lurch. John approached me for help and I was happy to oblige. I've been the foreman here ever since.'

'So, the three of you met to sign the agreement on the 16th of Sixthmoon,' I prompt.

'Indeed. We gathered at The Gunner that evening, John, Simon Forbes and I. That was the last time I saw John.'

'And yet Simon Forbes had a second meeting set for the 18th. Why?'

'I'm afraid I don't know. You'll have to ask him.'

'Did the three of you get on well?' asks Josiah.

'Absolutely. We were–'

Steverus is interrupted by a coal-dusted worker in shirt sleeves, who throws the door open to rush in. 'Master Steverus, hurry, sir! The shaft is emptying on account of an issue from the lower jenkin. They're saying it's either firedamp or whitedamp. Master Forbes has ordered work to cease until we know more.'

Downing the last of his rum, Steverus rises. 'If you'll excuse me, gentlemen, it seems I'm needed.' He pauses before adding, 'Better still, why not accompany me? How might you feel about a lesson in mining?' He follows the messenger outside and back down the pathway towards Wheal Berta. Josiah helps himself to my rum and we hasten to catch up.

'What's firedamp? Whitedamp?' probes Josiah.

'Gas, deep in the mine. Neither are good news,' explains Steverus. 'Whitedamp's toxic. Firedamp's explosive.'

'So, what will you do?' I ask, striding briskly alongside Steverus.

'Empty the mine of workers, increase ventilation, hope it's a small pocket of fumes that clears. We'll pump air for an hour before testing the jenkin with a fire drop and then take a flame down the level, just to be sure.'

'What idiot's going to go down there with a naked flame?' scoffs Joe.

Steverus gives a half-smile. 'Well, I'm the foreman, so...'

'You?' asks Josiah, astounded.

Steverus nods. 'It'll be all right. I've done it before. You fellows can go on if you'd rather observe from a safe distance. Mercy Lancett lives up on the hill.' He gestures to a mansion, partially screened by trees around a quarter of a mile away on a high ridge overlooking the mine and the sea. 'May I suggest you talk to her while I deal with this?'

'We must speak with Simon Forbes also,' I say.

'Forbes and I shall be busy here for a while. We're not going anywhere. I'll find you at the Lancett place when we're done.'

Steverus tips his hat and heads down the gravelled offshoot of the coastal path that leads to the mine. We watch him go before turning for the manor house.

'What do you make of him?' I ask Josiah.

'He's a dandy,' says Josiah, meaning it in a derogatory sense. 'Though I suppose he has guts.'

'Yes,' I agree. Returned to the mercy of the elements, I feel the bite of the cold and am glad of the warming hike up the hill and the promise of shelter in the Lancett mansion. Before we get far, a fine sea fret gusts inland and we turn to see the mine head still emptying of workers, all huddling, cold in the shadowed dampness of the tall stack. Among the men are barrow boys and women.

We leave the scene behind and are dampened by the time we reach the hilltop where a sweeping gravel drive terminates at a grand entrance to the main building. A coach house sits solidly to our right and, beyond that, the stables edge the side of an open yard that surrounds an old well. The stonework is a chalky golden brown, not the local sandstone but material that's been carted in specially to impress visitors. The house glows in the dramatic landscape like a gilded jewel, even in this watery half-light. Over the entrance a black iron sign announces in white letters, *Stonhaven Hall*. We climb a half-dozen steps to the door and I rap thrice with a brass ram's head knocker (complete with horns) and stand back to await a response. A blond-haired threader boy in serviceable yet modest attire answers to look up at us. He cowers visibly at the sight of Josiah. For a moment I think, in his fear, he might close the door in our faces.

'Good day, masters. May I help?' he forces the words out as though they were stones in his throat.

'Good day to you. We've come to see Mrs Mercy Lancett. Is she here?' I ask.

'Who should I say is calling?'

'Banyard and Mingle, private detectives.' I give him my card.

He disappears into the house but returns quickly to bid us enter and follow him through to a drawing room where Mercy

Lancett – of middle age and wearing a black mourning dress of silk and lace – rises to greet us with a slow curtsy. 'Do come in, gentlemen. I am Mercy Lancett. Will you take tea?'

We leave the doorway and find seats of cushioned red velvet with gold trim. The building's interior is fine, if a little old-fashioned, though clean and well kept. Mercy Lancett seems amiable with a gentle nature. There's something about the lines of her careworn face that reminds me of my mother.

I begin by introducing ourselves, although she already holds my card in her hand. 'We're investigating your husband's disappearance, among others. Will you tell us what happened around the time you last saw Mr Lancett?'

She peers at us one after the other. 'As I understand it, the matter is in Lord Draker's hands.'

'The Draker investigation is still underway, you can be assured. Unfortunately, we're not at liberty to discuss the case or our employer.'

'Very well, though it seems most odd. My husband left for Camdon on the morning of the 16th on business. Usually, he takes a room at The Gunner when he needs to stay overnight.' Josiah raises an eyebrow and we exchange a glance. Mercy continues. 'He must have done so on this occasion too because his bags and belongings were found there after I reported him missing. A few days later, I had to send a man to collect everything and deliver it back to me here.'

I nod. 'What time did your husband set out from here for The Gunner?'

'It must have been late morning, around half past eleven. I recall he visited the mine first to check all was well before returning to the house for his things.'

'And that was the last time you saw or heard from him?' asks Josiah.

'That's correct. I know for a fact that he met with the other shareholders that evening. You can ask them yourselves. Beyond that, what happened to him is a mystery to me.'

'You wear mourning dress,' I say.

'Because he is dead. He would have returned to me if it were not so. We were inseparable.'

'Very well, Mrs Lancett. May we know who else lives here with you? Do you have children?'

'No children of our own. It's just myself, my cook, a gardener, the boy and the maids. We've had to let some staff go since John's disappearance.'

'However do you manage?' says Joe, his sarcasm lost on her. Mother runs our house without a finger of help from anyone, but then, we are poor compared to most silkers because we channel the majority of profits into our secret and illicit hobby: resituating threaders.

'Needs must,' says Mercy. 'We manage well enough. Master Steverus looks in from time to time to see how I fare.'

'That's good of him,' I say, frowning at Josiah. 'Do you find him a reasonable man?'

'He's flamboyant but kind.'

'And Simon Forbes?' asks Josiah.

'He's surly though not wholly unpleasant. Has a sharp mind. Sharper than Mr Steverus, I'd say.'

I jot a few notes in my pocketbook. 'Perhaps we might see John's study before we leave, if he has such a room. It may tell us something.'

'By all means. I've left everything as it was.' Mrs Lancett rises to lead us out into the hallway and across a floor tiled in tones of russet and cream to a door, which she unlocks and opens for us. The study has the feel of a modest-sized library, comfortably furnished with a walnut desk and a green glass lamp, three Grand Wexford chairs, darkly panelled walls, and shelves of leatherbound books. A freestanding set of shelves at one end of the desk holds various documents and scrolls. I withdraw a few, studying them briefly to confirm they are all business contracts, mining rosters, records and accounts.

A distant knocking informs us someone else has arrived at the house.

'Mrs Lancett, it is my understanding that you now own and

manage the mine and yet you say you've left all here untouched. Have you not had cause to use the study for business purposes since your husband's disappearance?'

'Once or twice, I suppose. In general, I prefer the light of the drawing room for such tasks.'

'I see.' I consider again the coals found in the victims' mouths and in the graves as their decomposing faces flash in my mind. 'Would you object to us having a look around, madam?'

'Not at all.'

Without really knowing what to look for, Josiah and I begin a search of the room.

Mercy watches us work. 'You must let me know immediately if there is anything I can help you with. I would have John home if I thought there was the faintest chance he may yet still live. You would tell me if there was something I should know?'

It seems word of the shallow graves has yet to reach Stonhaven. 'I'm afraid we can offer no news and little hope. I fear your inclination to wear black is entirely appropriate.' I'm about to ask a final question about Wheal Berta when the threader boy enters the room carrying a sealed letter to Mercy. She opens and scans it, steadying herself with a hand on the desk before quickly dropping into one of the leather chairs as though faint.

'Are you all right, Mrs Lancett?' I ask, stepping closer in concern.

'It's from Lord Draker,' she says, turning her paling face towards me. 'They've found John.'

I look to the boy. 'Do you have brandy in the house? Your mistress may need a tot.'

The lad nods and departs.

'I'm sorry,' I mutter with a pang of guilt and at a loss as to what I could say that might help.

She stares blankly at a panelled wall of the room, her expression bleak. 'It is nothing more than confirmation of what I already believed.'

'All the same…' I peer at my boots.

'Lord Draker has asked me to tell no one. I shouldn't have told you.'

'It doesn't matter, madam. I can assure you Lord Draker would not mind us knowing. We are under strict instructions from our employer to share nothing of our investigation with any other.'

The boy returns with a crystal decanter and glasses on a tray. Josiah is quick to pour a drink for Mercy, handing her a heavy glass, which she accepts with a subtle nod. She sips brandy, letting the news seep insidiously in. When her gaze returns to us, it holds something of a suspicion that leaves me wondering at her thoughts.

There are times in life when one's mere presence creates an atmosphere, and this is one of them. Rather than wait awkwardly at Stonhaven Hall, Josiah and I make swift farewells and descend the hill. We plan to find Steverus and Forbes at the mine, but instead meet them along the way as they climb the trackway towards the house.

'Here,' says Steverus with a confident sweep of a hand. 'I've brought Forbes to you.'

Forbes reaches out to shake our hands in turn, though his face remains poised in a stoical expression, greeting us with a single nod. 'Gentlemen, Mr Steverus tells me you have questions.'

'Indeed.' Not wishing to linger in the icy wind that continues to pound up the hill from the clifftops, I ask, 'Perhaps we might take shelter.'

Steverus grins. 'Well, our little drama at the mine seems to be under control. Shall we return to the tavern?'

'I wonder, might we instead see the mine?' I ask. 'I have a natural curiosity for such things. Perhaps there's somewhere within we might talk.'

'My, you're brave,' jokes Steverus, 'though I'm sure it's quite safe now. We'll take you there.'

We head back down the hill towards the mine, hugging our

long coats tightly about us, and I've an inkling the temperature is falling. 'Tell me, is that a storm coming in?' We peer at a barrelling dark-grey band of cloud that appears to be approaching over the sea.

'I rather think it is,' says Steverus in his flamboyant way. The thought seems to amuse him and I wonder if it's because Josiah and I may become caught out here in the inclement weather.

'Doesn't the mine flood, being so close to the sea?' Josiah asks.

'Not often,' says Steverus, enigmatically.

Josiah aims a question at Forbes as we trudge. 'Any theories about Lancett?'

'Oh, not really. I try to steer clear of such speculation. Though one thing's for sure, he didn't run away with a lover as some have suggested. I can vouch for that. He was true to his wife.'

Was? I say. 'Do you believe him dead, as Mercy does?'

'I can see no other explanation.' Forbes says no more on the subject and we walk the rest of the way to the mine in its craggy setting, greeting workers as we pass. Steverus leads us into the wheal house and opens a door to the foreman's office. The walls are covered in excavation charts, pinned in place, and a rudimentary desk and chairs occupy one end of the room where we settle, Steverus himself taking his place behind the desk. From a rough-glassed window arch, he watches the storm roll in.

Forbes declines the offer of a seat, preferring to stand before us. 'So, gentlemen, with what may I assist you?'

I continue my line of questions. 'We know that you, Avory and John met at The Gunner on the evening of the 16th of Sixthmoon, and we know why. What we don't know is why you and John had a second meeting set for the 18th.'

Forbes considers this briefly. 'I'm afraid I can't tell you. John requested the meeting and I simply agreed. The reason for it remains a mystery to me.'

We follow several other lines of enquiry but learn little from

Forbes. 'No, Wheal Berta was in no peril shortly before John's disappearance... Yes, I got on well with John Lancett. He was a good friend. John, Avory and I enjoyed each other's company, in the traditional sense, if you take my meaning... No, I don't have a clue as to his whereabouts or what may have befallen him... Yes, I was happy with our financial dealings... No, to my knowledge there is no way Mrs Lancett might have had anything to do with his absence... No, I don't know of any who may have held a grudge against him. He was a fine businessman, well respected in these parts and in the city.'

I pause, plumbing the depths of my mind for any pertinent areas we may have missed.

'And now, sirs, a question for you, if I may be so bold.' Forbes clears his throat for effect. 'How is it that Lord Draker has employed two civilian would-be detectives to investigate the disappearance of a lowly mine owner?'

An excerpt taken from the gawper file,
as written by Reginald Francis Banyard.

Gawper physiology is perhaps the largest of the mysteries surrounding their existence. My experience has taught me they are not the same as our kind, appearing somehow removed from the Earthorian realm and yet at the same time moving through it without any construct of discernible propulsion. Do they have legs upon which to walk in some way? I cannot say. Nor can any of those who have so far rendered accounts to me. How, then, do they move? They seem to glide or float through thin air, their lower extremities either hidden, gaseous or indiscernible. For now, it seems, this must remain an unanswered question.

As to their less curious features, it can be gleaned from existing reports that they are always tall and usually steeped in shadow, their outlines undefined. Although of all their peculiarities, it is their eyes that are the most striking, being consistently described as points of ethereal white fire or light.

7

The Absent Suspect

*In which Banyard and Mingle find a man missing,
and Jinkers speaks of rumours*

Josiah grimaces, forcing words through his teeth. 'I should watch your tone if I were you.' His right hand moves to the butt of a pistol on his belt.

I catch his arm. 'Wait.'

Forbes shrugs, unarmed and unperturbed. 'It's an honest question. It doesn't make sense.'

I intervene. 'And what do you know of Lord Draker's methods? He's at liberty to operate in whatever way he sees fit.'

'I'm sure he is,' says Forbes. 'Never mind. I did not mean to rile you.'

I'm intensely irritated because Forbes now believes Bretling has commissioned us, which he has. What's more, I feel every bit as affronted as Josiah clearly does.

'Apology accepted,' says Josiah pointedly, somehow managing to make the words sound like a threat.

Forbes frowns. 'Oh, but I didn't apologise.'

I wince, unsure I'll be able to hold Josiah back if he's drawn into a fight. 'Mr Mingle, we'd best be going before the storm hits.' Leading him by the arm, I steer him out of the room and say grudgingly, 'Gentlemen, you have our gratitude.'

'I'm sure you'd be welcome to stay and ride out the storm here,' says Forbes in a menacing tone.

I swallow my annoyance. 'Thank you for your hospitality, gentlemen, but we must go. We have much to do.'

Once outside and safely beyond earshot, I mutter to Josiah. 'I don't think much of Mr Forbes.'

'Are you going to let him get away with that slur?'

'I'm sorry, but for now we must.'

'*Would-be* detectives? How dare he!'

'Let it go, Joe. Perhaps he'll prove to be the killer and we might bring him in.' I smile at the thought.

'I sincerely hope you're right. What a despicable cad.'

'Don't let him get to you. Some people have no pleasure except to irk their fellow man,' I say, although I'm failing to heed my own advice. With that one little snipe, Forbes has enraged me. On some level, I fear his comment might hold some morsel of truth and that Josiah and I are in some way pretenders. I try vehemently to shake off the notion.

Leaving the mine behind, we hurry to wake Fletcher, who we find sleeping in the carriage's cabin, and climb aboard as a lashing sleet sets in. Fletcher takes one look at the coming storm clouds and clambers up onto the driver's bench, flicking the reins to quicken the horses and turn us about.

Shielded behind the glass of the carriage windows, we watch the maelstrom sweep across the coast towards us. I have an eerie feeling that we're being chased away by some insidious, unseen force and, peering back, glimpse Forbes poised in the entrance, his dispassionate face staring as we're borne home. I'm haunted by the gaunt figures of workers ever trudging from the mouth of Wheal Berta, through a shroud of grey sleet.

It's evening and fully dark by the time we arrive to alight wearily from the coach, Josiah complaining about his damp feet and leaking boots. The streets are puddled with water. I pay Fletcher and, with a tip of his hat and a flick of the reins, he drives his horses on. Josiah and I make for the front door as one of our neighbour's lower windows flies open and, there, Jinkers' pale face appears in the glow of a tallow candle, which he brandishes as he beckons.

'Another day detecting?' he asks. 'How's progress?'

We pause on the cobbled pavement. 'Well enough,' I mutter vaguely.

'I've heard rumours,' he continues. 'Wondered if you might care to confirm or deny their truth...' Jinkers licks his flabby lips in anticipation and his bulbous eyes, which at the best of times have a habit of roving about for no apparent reason, roll uncontrollably before settling upon me.

I should probably brush him aside but I don't have the energy, and anyway, I'm interested to hear what he thinks he knows. 'What rumours?'

'Of bodies...'

Surprised, I peer intently at him.

Pre-emptively, he makes the godly sign. '...bodies found in shallow graves at the edge of the city. Is that what you're investigating? I wondered if that's what the Drakers were bringing in on their carts.'

'Mr Jinkers, we can't discuss the matter, at least not here and now. Promise you will say nothing of this to anyone. I shall call upon you at a more civilised hour.'

'Tomorrow, then?' His eyes gleam.

'Tomorrow. I bid you goodnight.'

Thursday, 4th Elventide

Standing at the iron-studded door, I check my notes. Markus Hinton lives here but that is all we know of the man, other than the fact that on the 17th of Fipplemoon he was supposed to meet with victim number four, who was an industrialist and mining consultant named Davey Brindle. That is Hinton's only mention in Bretling's notes. I show Josiah the page.

He raises an eyebrow. 'Mining again...'

The imposing house is stark in the shallow morning light. I snap my pocketbook shut, slip it back into my coat and rap the iron knocker thrice. I glance at our surroundings as we wait. The Old Camdon property is a tall townhouse built of pale stone. The modest grounds are defended by wrought-iron railings that are topped with spikes and look like rows of black spears. We can't be far from The Gunner, I muse, taking in an excellent view of Crowlands across the sluggish Tynne to the south and of Dockside to the east.

An old threader servant in a gilded waistcoat opens the door to peer out at us. 'Yes?'

'Masters Banyard and Mingle to see Mr Hinton,' I say, passing my card.

The man bows and promptly disappears into the house, closing the door behind him.

I glance at Josiah. 'What do you think this Hinton fellow does?'

He shrugs with a hang-dog expression that says it all: *This case is awful; too many victims; numerous suspects when we've barely begun; it all adds up to a lot of work.* At least, I assume that's what he's thinking, although there's a good chance he's simply pining for his sweetheart.

Roll on Tuesday!

The servant returns. 'If you'll follow me, masters. Mr Hinton will see you now.'

We enter and walk a broad hallway that leads to a study. The threader stands to one side of the entrance and announces our arrival. 'Masters Banyard and Mingle, sir.'

We hear a jovial voice from within. 'Come in, come in. Banyard and Mingle... I feel I've heard your names before but – forgive me, gentlemen – quite where, I can't recall.'

I stride into the room and offer a brief bow of the head. 'Perhaps you've seen our premises near Rook's Bridge or read about us in the papers.'

'Ah, yes, of course! Aren't you the fellows who recovered the bones of Great King Doon?'

'The very same,' I say. 'Michael Banyard. My associate here is Mr Mingle.'

A bespectacled, round-faced silker in his middle years with a jolly countenance, Hinton thrusts out his hand enthusiastically. 'Marvellous, quite marvellous.' He shakes my hand and quickly moves on to shake Josiah's. 'Delighted to meet you. Please, do sit down and make yourselves comfortable. Will you take some refreshment?'

'A cup of black bean soup, if you have it,' says Josiah, dropping into the nearest Grand Wexford.

I nod. 'The same. Thank you.'

Hinton sends his threader off to prepare the drinks before turning back to us. 'And why have the famous private detectives sought me out, I wonder?' His expression sobers. 'Is it about that business with Davey Brindle?'

'How very astute you are,' I say. 'You and Mr Brindle were supposed to meet, were you not, around the time of his disappearance? And he was never to arrive.'

'Correct. We used to meet often, as friends do. It was most unlike him to miss the meeting. I don't know why and have neither seen him nor heard from him since. It's my belief that something terrible befell the poor chap.'

I check the date of the meeting and ask about the venue.

'Why, it must have been The Gunner, of course.' He says this as though thinking aloud. 'Davey and I always met at The Gunner by habit.'

I make a concerted effort to avoid Josiah's gaze. 'And what is it you do, Mr Hinton?'

'I'm Master of the Dockside Forges. You're lucky to find me at home. I'm usually down on site. I was just preparing some papers for a meeting in town.' He gestures to a scatter of business documents and technical drawings on his desk.

'At The Gunner?' asks Josiah.

'No,' says Hinton with a smile. 'Not this time. It's at the office of Ricardo and Manson, the architects. They're working on the new bridge in Loncaster – need some arches casting and have enlisted my help.'

'Very good,' I say as the threader returns to pour steaming

black bean soup into three shellware cups. I receive one with thanks. 'This meeting – the one that Davey Brindle missed – you are sure it was in no way business?'

'I am, indeed, though I can see why one might wonder. An industrialist in mining, meeting with the Master of the Forges. Coal, iron ore... It could make sense. But no. I assure you we had no business together. The apparent theme is purely coincidental.'

'Did Brindle ever work at the coal mine, Wheal Berta, as far as you know?'

Hinton's eyes widen. 'Why, yes! I do believe he did, though it was a long time ago now.'

'How long?' asks Josiah.

'Twenty years or more. I think he said it was his first commission.'

'I see. Was he well when you last saw him? Was he worried or concerned about anything?'

'He was quite well, as I recall. In good cheer, in fact. He had just received a raise in pay and so we made merry.' Hinton smiles as though reminiscing. 'I'm afraid we may have rather overindulged in our celebratory libations!'

Josiah frowns.

'Where were you on the 17th of Quartersmoon?' I ask.

'I was likely here or at the foundry. Wait there. I'll check.' He fetches a diary from his desk and flips through it, stopping to examine a page. 'Yes, I was at the foundry. Why?'

'I'm afraid I'm not at liberty to say. What about the 17th of Thripplemoon?'

He turns pages and reads his entries. 'I was at home all day, unwell. Had to cancel several meetings.'

'What about the 17th of Sixthmoon, of Hexmoon, Honourmoon and Twinemoon?'

He gawps at me, astonished, but patiently searches for each of the dates in turn. 'At the foundry. The foundry again. And then I took a trip to Amorphia on business for two months. That was Honourmoon and Twinemoon.'

'You were away for the 17th of both months?'

'I was. Only returned last week, in fact.' Hinton takes a gold watch from his waistcoat pocket and glances at the dial. 'Well, gentlemen.' He sips his black bean soup. 'I must apologise but I'm due at Ricardo and Manson's in fifteen minutes. Do stay and finish your refreshments. Smedley will let you out when you're quite ready.' He gathers his papers into a document case, tucks this under one arm and bows politely. 'With your leave. Do call again if there's anything else I can help with. You fellows are welcome here any time.'

'Thank you. We may well do so,' I say.

Josiah stands, stepping towards Hinton as though he intends to stop him. I give a subtle shake of the head and stand also, but only to bow to Hinton. 'You're most kind.'

Heading off to his meeting, he leaves.

'Well, he cut that short,' complains Joe.

'Yes. Though I'm sure he has nothing to hide. Why else would he trust us, alone in his study? We should go.'

'You're not even going to have a look around? He could be bluffing.'

'We have another missed appointment to investigate and a briefing with Lord Draker at midday. We don't have time to search the place. Not properly, anyway. But don't let me stop you.'

Josiah glares at me and briefly scans the room. 'No. I'll leave it, thanks.'

Our final call investigating the missed meetings is to the residence of one Zachariah Sterling, head tailor at Thackory's, a gentlemen's outfitters in Highbridge, though it's not far from the fringes of Old Camdon. We ride there in less than ten minutes and stand once more before the door of a grand townhouse, awaiting a response. A few moments later a threader answers and looks quite baffled when I ask for Mr Sterling – who was supposed to meet with a member of parliament, Wulfric Hemings. My notes remind me that

Hemings was due at Thackory's, presumably for a fitting, on the 17th of Hexmoon but instead became victim number five.

'Mr Sterling?' questions the thin-faced threader, his brow furrowing.

'Mr Zachariah Sterling.' I check my notebook and peer up at the house number emblazoned in golden glass, leaded over the door. 'This *is* 64 Mason Street...'

'It is, sir,' he says. 'But there's no Mr Sterling residing here. No Sterlings of any kind. Perhaps you have the wrong address.'

I take out Bretling's original page of notes and check that, too. 'The address is correct. May I please speak with your master or mistress?'

'Of course, sir. Who should I say is calling?'

'Masters Banyard and Mingle. We're private detectives.'

He accepts my card with a nod and disappears into the house. A few moments pass before he returns to lead us through to a sitting room where a finely dressed older woman rises from her chair. We remove our hats.

'Lady Dunston, Masters Banyard and Mingle.' The servant promptly bows before leaving.

'Private detectives? Whatever do you want with me?' she asks.

'We have this address down as the residence of a Zachariah Sterling, but your man tells us he doesn't live here.'

'And he's correct. I think you should check your facts.'

'Then I'm sorry to have disturbed you.'

The woman frowns. 'Wait. I do believe there was a man of that name here before us. We purchased the house from his master, a Mr Jennings.'

Jennings clearly valued and trusted Sterling highly to have set him up with his own house, but then, he was Jennings' head tailor.

'When was this?' I ask.

'We moved in on the 3rd of Honourmoon.'

'Did Mr Sterling leave a forwarding address?'

'No, but I can give you Mr Jennings' address, if that helps.'

'Very well.' I take down the address, thank her for her time and we leave.

Outside, we collect the horses.

'What do you make of that?' I ask Josiah.

'Very suspicious,' he mutters, climbing into his saddle.

'I quite agree. Perhaps this fellow Sterling realised his appointment with Hemings might make him a suspect. That alone may have caused him to flee.'

'Who told Bretling about the appointment, I wonder?' He turns his dappled grey mare.

I mount Blink and we set off at a trot, back towards Rook's Bridge. 'We must ask Lord Draker when we see him. There's a little time before we're due at the Draker Headquarters. Let's give Mr Jinkers that call.'

Josiah rolls his eyes. 'If we must.'

'Good day, Mr Jinkers.' I doff my tricorn.

'Micky!' Standing in his doorway, Jinkers fights for a grip on his wretched cat, who seems determined to escape. 'All right, Mr Kaylock. There, there… Off you go.' With a squeal, Mr Kaylock darts away. 'Oh dear. Mr Kaylock is rather out of sorts today. I'm sure it's all these strange happenings in the town.' By which, I presume he means the crowd of Drakers and the carts that he saw, but perhaps he's also unsettled by the general talk of war across the city. 'Won't you come in?' Jinkers gestures towards his hallway.

I suppose it's this or the tavern, I think. I'd rather we met at The Dog, but that would take longer and Josiah would demand ale, which I'm trying to discourage this early in the day. With mixed feelings, I nod and enter the dim and joyless interior of Jinkers' family home.

I find myself wondering what his parents were like and try to recall, but back then, when they were alive and we were boys, I had little to do with them. I can only suppose they were every bit as eccentric as Jinkers himself. Instead of a recollection involving his parents, my mind carries me back to a childhood memory to revisit an event in which Jinkers was cruelly bullied – one of many unfortunate incidents. It all began when the Jinkers family moved into the house next door to ours. The Jinkers were different from Camdon dwellers. They spoke 'funny', carried customs and superstitions that locals had never heard of before. They even looked strange. They hadn't moved from across town, or even across the country, but far across the sea from Eyrlanda and that, so it seemed for most people around here, was an unforgivable offence, although I cannot for the life of me reason why. In any case, *that* was the beginning of Jinkers' downfall.

The boy shoving him hard to the ground was a classmate of his, although the scene was a narrow alley somewhere near Rook's Bridge, and not in school.

'Weirdy, weirdy, weirdo,' his assailant chanted, following up with a good kick to the ribs.

Jinkers moaned. The other boys gathered around and picked up the mantra, lining up to take their turn to 'boot the weirdo'.

I watched with horror, a few years younger than any of them and feeling powerless to help. Yet, summoning courage, I stepped out into the entrance of the alley to plant my feet on the cobbles. 'Leave him be, you cowards!' My message delivered, I turned and fled, soon losing the boys in backstreets I knew better than they, and so doubled back to help the sorely wounded Jinkers to his feet, and then on to his home. *This* home, into which we now enter.

Keeping step, Josiah sniffs at the stale air, which carries an odd, dank odour. Jinkers leads us into a grimy sitting room and throws back the drapes, releasing a thousand billowing motes of dust. The sudden light reveals a threadbare carpet and several dreary, ancient-looking armchairs. The walls are covered with a patterned paper that may have been fashionable fifty years ago and is hung with several dark portraits, presumably of family members long departed. I single out a pair of tall, shady characters with grim features, suspecting they are his mother and father, but soon look away when I realise I'm staring.

'Come, sit,' says Jinkers, keenly. His eyes widen with sudden inspiration. 'Tea! I'll fetch tea! No, black bean soup! Cake! This calls for cake! Wait right there.' Our protests go unheeded as he scurries away into the malodorous depths of the house. Josiah and I occupy seats and study the room.

He brushes a layer of dust from an arm of his chair. 'What on Earthoria *is* that? It smells like a dozen mummified rats.'

'Long lost Aunty Myrtle, perhaps? Your guess is as good as mine.' I take out my pocket watch and glance at the time as precious minutes trickle by.

When Jinkers eventually returns, he's laden with a silver tray bearing cups, milk, cake, black bean soup, sugar and a steaming teapot, cosied with what looks like a tramp's woollen hat. 'Here.' He sets the tray upon a table. 'Shall I pour?' Without waiting for an answer, he begins pouring tea. 'Oh, dear me. I quite forgot to ask which you would prefer!'

'Nothing for me,' says Josiah, eyeing the cake dubiously. I resist the urge to ask if it's been baked *with* or *without* frogs.

Josiah's refusal births an obligation for me to accept something. 'Tea. Thank you.'

Appearing relieved, Jinkers tips more tea into the cup. 'Milk?'

'A little. Mr Jinkers, about the investigation – I really must insist that you refrain from spreading hearsay or personal conclusions about things you may or may not have witnessed. May we confide in you, trusting this will go no further?'

He fixes his eyes upon mine as he thrusts the platter of cake at me. 'Yes, of course. What is it you wish to confide?' He quickly adds, 'Cake?'

I shake my head. He returns the platter to the tray and sits in a chair, rearranging the objects on the table as though preparing a still life. He's desperate for this to be the perfect social call, but it's nothing of the kind.

'We'll share confidentialities with you on the understanding that you'll keep them to yourself,' I say. 'You must give a solemn promise. The consequences of this information leaking would be undesirable in the extreme.'

'I swear on my mother's grave.' He glances at the painting. 'I will speak to none.'

'Very well, but before we go further you must tell us of these rumours and their origins.'

'The rumours. Yes. Of course.' He takes tea for himself and sips as though to calm his nerves. 'Well, it's like this. I was taking a stroll down Quaffer's Row when I came to the corner near Yorkson's. There I overheard two Drakers talking and, I confess, I lingered somewhat in the shadows of the wall. I was interested in what they were saying, you see.'

'And what *were* they saying?' I ask.

'They were talking about bodies, bones and such.' Here he pauses to make the godly sign. 'Human remains found south of the city, all in the same patch. I thought they were talking about an old graveyard that had been rediscovered, but no, they were unlawful burials in shallow graves. With that and the fuss they made with those carts – well, it all seemed to add up...'

I sip tea. 'A number of graves *have* recently been discovered. I can't say for certain they were in the carts you witnessed, but it's likely. Lord Draker has requested our assistance in the ongoing investigation – but no one is to know of our involvement, no one at all. Not even you. If Lord Draker were to learn of this conversation, he would probably throw us in gaol for betraying his confidence. Mr Jinkers, we are entrusting you with our careers by telling you this. Am I making myself clear?'

'Perfectly. Let me assure you – nobody listens to me even when I do speak with them, which is rarely. I shall certainly tell no one, in any case. Is there anything else you can tell me? My offer to spy was serious. I could help, but it would be better if I was informed.'

I shake my head. 'It's out of my hands, really. Company policy. You understand.' I invent some official-sounding drivel. 'No person or persons may act as an agent within or regarding any case, thereby, who is not an employee of the company. Rule number forty-three.'

'That's it! Employ me!' he says, shuffling to the edge of his seat with eyes wide.

'It's not that simple. We can't afford–'

'I don't need money. I'll work for free. Mr Kaylock, too!' He laughs nervously.

'If we're not paying you, you're not an employee.' *How did I get here?* From the corner of an eye, I glimpse Josiah massaging his temples.

Jinkers also notices. 'Ah. Oh. I see. Never mind.' Now he's deeply disappointed. 'Yes. Yes, of course. How stupid of me...'

'Now, don't be disheartened,' I say. 'Perhaps there is a role for you in all this, after all, though it could not be an official one.'

He brightens again and I'm regretting the entire visit.

'Listen,' I conclude. 'Leave it with me. I'll see what I can do.'

Josiah throws me an astounded look. I rise, set my cup down and we leave.

On the pavement outside and safely beyond earshot, Josiah chastises me. 'You've really lost it.'

'Believe me, there's nothing you can say that I'm not already thinking. Why didn't you stop me in there?'

'Hey, this is your show. You've made your bed. Now you have to sleep in it.'

'The expression is *lie in it*.'

'Whatever.'

8

Briefings

In which Banyard reports to Lord Draker and Mingle stuffs his face

We ride to Tower End, arriving at the Draker Headquarters precisely two minutes late for the meeting. Bretling looks worse than ever: stressed and weary. This case is seriously getting to him. Wearing a tight expression, he paces restlessly back and forth at the head of the assembly room, a cavernous chamber panelled in age-darkened oak and lit by a series of frosted-glass windows at one side that cast stark shadows from our gathering. On the board behind him is pinned a set of the same morbid imographs that grace our case room wall, and to one side stands a chalkboard with notes written in Bretling's distinguished hand. The scripture about the seraph has also been copied out there.

'Ah. Welcome, gentlemen.' He beckons us in and we find seats at the near end of the group. Goffings sits nearby, looking smug, his bulky form nestled among his peers. Watching Josiah and me, he offers a sly smile. Bretling makes no mention of our arrival, who we are or why we are there, so presumably he's already explained our involvement to his men and cautioned them to silence.

'Now then, what have we learned since the discoveries at the

Sallow Grove? You are my key investigators, and the onerous task of capturing this killer of silkers lies as heavily upon your shoulders as it does mine. Have any of you made progress?' I begin to feel the weight personally. 'Well, gentlemen, who would like to begin?' Bretling fixes upon us each in turn. 'Huntly, why don't you start? How goes the search for our as yet unnamed victim?'

'Not well, sir. There's little to go on. We're making enquiries around the city to see if anyone's missing a man, but his approximate height is all we have to work with.'

'Right,' says Bretling, quickly turning to another sergeant. 'Smeaton, how's the list of threader suspects coming on?'

A thin sergeant with oil-slicked hair stands to answer. 'It's a long list, sir, a very long list. I have officers working to narrow the field but it's going to take time. Thirty or so discounted so far. Another four hundred to go.'

'All males?' asks Bretling.

'No, sir. Fifty or so women are on the list. I thought the victims may have been drugged or otherwise inebriated before being stabbed. Or perhaps poisoned, sir.'

'And poison is a woman's modus operandi.'

'That is my belief, sir,' says Smeaton.

Bretling nods. 'Quite right, too.'

Josiah raises a hand as though to disagree but I quickly grab his arm and give a subtle shake of my head. We must choose our battles wisely where Lord Draker is concerned.

Bretling continues. 'Are there any other advancements? I don't need to remind you that the 17th of Elventide is but thirteen days away.'

'Sir, might we warn each of the prominent silkers in the city? They would then know to guard themselves against attack on the 17th.' The hapless sergeant, a brawny fellow with a balding pate, seems to realise he's miscalculated even before Bretling opens his mouth.

'And have the entire city in a state of panic? No, we might not.'

I lift a tentative finger. 'On that point, sir, if I may interject...'

'Yes, Banyard.'

'I should like to remind all concerned to keep a tight lip where details of the case are concerned. It only takes one careless comment to spark a rumour.'

'Good point.' Bretling turns to his sergeants. 'Now, I'm honour-bound to inform the widows and close family of the six victims we've identified, but that's as far as it goes. All will be cautioned to keep quiet on account of the ongoing investigation, and each will only be informed of the death of their respective loved one. I'm taking care of that personally. But remind your men to watch their tongues. They're on the streets to gather information, not hand it out.' He follows this with a question directed at me, one I've been dreading. 'And what do *you* bring to this table?'

I glance nervously at the glaring sergeants and stand to approach the displayed imographs, pausing before Bretling. 'If I may...'

'Be my guest,' he says, stepping aside. I take his place before the men.

'Mr Mingle and I have revisited all of the individuals who were supposed to meet with the victims – those meetings that never took place.' I wonder exactly how much information I should share, as part of me baulks at the thought of working with these Drakers. 'There are a number of common threads. The coal mine Wheal Berta links several of the victims, namely the mine owner John Lancett, Uriah Mumford and Davey Brindle.' I point to the images of the victims' remains, one after the other.

'Yes, we're well aware of Wheal Berta,' says Goffings. Several other sergeants snort.

I ignore them. 'The name of a certain tavern in Old Camdon also keeps cropping up.'

'You mean The Gunner,' says Bretling knowingly.

'Indeed.' I refer to my notes and indicate each of the imographs on the board as it becomes relevant. 'John Lancett –

the third victim – was lodging there when he disappeared, and it was the location of a meeting the day before, between him and two shareholders in the mine, Simon Forbes and Avory Steverus. The owner of The Gunner, Madam Kenwigs, had an appointment with victim number two, Uriah Mumford, at the tavern shortly before he disappeared. The meeting between Davey Brindle – victim number four – and Markus Hinton, Master of the Dockside Forges, was also supposed to take place at The Gunner. Of course, the presence of coal in the victims' mouths is obviously another possible connection with the mine. We plan to investigate both Wheal Berta and The Gunner more thoroughly.'

I feel the sergeants' resentful looks bore into me: a reminder that we are only here on invitation by Bretling. His men, who mostly loathe us, would much rather we were excluded.

'Good work, Banyard. You do that and report any findings directly to me. Understand?'

'Yes, Lord Draker.' I retake my seat.

'Though I should forget about Kenwigs as a suspect. And any other silker, for that matter. Do you have anything of value to add, Mr Mingle?' asks Bretling. Goffings smirks derisively.

Josiah stands, a determined look on his face. 'Only that Simon Forbes – he's an excavations consultant down at Wheal Berta – was supposed to meet again with John Lancett around the time of his disappearance. This was arranged to be just the two of them. Forbes maintains that John Lancett requested the meeting and that he does not know why the meeting was called, but I think it suspicious.'

I nod in agreement, surprised by Josiah's sudden turn of eloquence. 'Well said.'

'Duly noted, Mr Mingle,' says Bretling. 'But is Forbes a silker or a threader?'

'He's a silker, sir,' says Josiah.

Bretling strikes a chalk line through Forbes' name on the board.

'Oh, and another thing,' I add. 'We couldn't question

Zachariah Sterling because he's moved away and left no forwarding address. Again, this seems suspicious. We plan to question his master, Mr Jennings, to hear the full story.' One glance at the vacuous sergeants tells me they're struggling to keep up. I sympathise. This case involves far too many people.

'That's more like it. This Sterling fellow's a good fit for the crime,' says Bretling.

I add, 'He is a threader, sir, one surely valued and trusted by his master. Though without questioning him...'

Bretling underlines Sterling's name on the chalkboard, where his notes remind all that Sterling was a head tailor at the time of Heming's murder. It's the kind of position that might be held by a working silker or otherwise a threader who's doing exceptionally well. 'Sterling was all set to measure up the fifth victim, the politician Wulfric Hemings, but claims Hemings never arrived. I interviewed him myself at Thackory's soon after Heming's disappearance. His personal secretary informed me of the appointment.'

'So, Sterling didn't volunteer the information,' says Sergeant Huntly.

'He did not,' confirms Bretling, taking out his pipe and priming it with tobacco.

I check the notes I made at Sterling's old home. 'Well, at some time after your visit and before the 3rd of Honourmoon, he packed his bags and vanished, and his master sold the property.'

'Then perhaps Sterling killed Hemings and, thinking himself beyond suspicion, was then startled by your visit,' says Josiah.

'Perhaps.' Pensively, Bretling strikes a Sulphur and lights his pipe. 'It's a lead. A good one. Huntly, I want you to follow up on Sterling's present location. Find him and bring him in.'

Descending the headquarters' front steps, I confide, 'That wasn't too bad, I suppose.'

'It went quite well, I thought,' says Josiah, with more than a hint of pride.

'Just promise me you'll not run off to become a Draker. It

would be your ruin.'

'Scared you'll lose me?'

I throw him a sideways look. 'Perhaps I am.'

Halfway down the steps a hand grabs my shoulder from behind, bringing me to a halt. Turning, I'm faced with Goffings.

'Just so's you know, I'm watching the pair of you,' he says. 'Don't forget it.'

'And we're watching you, sir,' I shake loose from his grasp. 'And I'll thank you to keep your sausage-fingered paws off me.'

'I'm warning you, *Barnyard*. One toe out of place and I'll be down on you faster than a raging bull.'

'Well, you certainly have the build for it. It's Ban-yard, by the way, with one R not two.'

'I know!'

'Good day to you, sergeant.' I tip my hat and we leave.

He calls after us. 'I'll see you behind bars, *Barnyard*. Just give me an excuse.'

Our next briefing is comparatively relaxed and begins with black bean soup and lemon cake in the Mysteries Solved case room. Josiah stuffs an aurochs sandwich into his face, followed by several colossal slices of the tart, sugary cake, while I spend an hour or so bringing Penney, Lizzy, Mardon and Ebadiah up to speed with developments. There's a sadness in Penney's gaze whenever she turns my way.

Attempting to make the information more digestible, I pin the names of those involved to the board alongside the victim imographs, which are already labelled – excepting the first, who remains unknown – and add notes on the six whose identities we think we know. By the time we're through, there's a bewildering mass of information clustered around the images. I add to that a map of Camdon City that also covers a portion of the east coast, before pointing out Wheal Berta's situation and its proximity to the Sallow Grove.

'I can't help feeling we're terribly late to the party,' says Mardon, viewing the wall with an uncharacteristically bemused look.

'We are,' I say, taking a secret pleasure in his bafflement. This is perhaps a new experience for him. *Welcome to my world...* 'Bretling's been investigating the disappearances for months without any sign of a body.'

'It's a shame we weren't in on it from the start,' says Mardon. 'Who knows what we might have learned by now?'

'I'm sure he's told us everything he can,' I say.

'Hmm.'

'Have you anything to add from the morgue?'

'Nothing new,' says Mardon. 'Though I'm studying the coal that was found in the graves. Not all coal is the same, so we may learn something from it.'

'What about you, Lizzy, Penney?'

Lizzy takes out a notebook and opens it. 'We visited the Sallow Grove, took in the general area and, posing as two lost wanderers, spoke with the Tinlocks. The place has quite a history and the sallows are said to have grown there for hundreds of years.'

'According to whom?' asks Mardon.

'Farmer Tinlock told us, but the locals confirmed it. We took luncheon at a tavern nearby and made enquiries. The landlord was most helpful.'

'I'm sure,' I say.

'The grove is flanked to the south by Black Down Forest and otherwise surrounded by farmland and industry,' explains Penney. 'There's a tile factory within half a mile to the north and to the east lie the workers' cottages, some miners' among them.'

Lizzy continues. 'The trees themselves are significant. They naturally thrive near water and so have been linked with places considered mysterious or spiritual, meaning that the ancients used to believe that bodies of water were sacred places, entrances into the otherworld.'

'No doubt some fools still do,' says Mardon.

'Indeed, they do,' says Penney. 'Fools like the landlord of The Pike and Musket. Sallows traditionally symbolise sorrow because of their weeping branches and, as such, appear in numerous folklore beliefs. The combination of these elements makes the sallows meaningful.'

'In conclusion,' says Lizzy, 'we believe this symbolism may have influenced the killer's choice of site for the burials.'

'How's that?' grunts Josiah.

Lizzy gives him a disparaging look. 'By choosing the Sallow Grove, the killer is expressing sadness over the deaths of his victims.'

'Remorse?' asks Mardon.

'No,' says Penney. 'I wouldn't go that far. He has murdered them, after all.'

'It would make sense of an otherwise troublesome location.' I pause to jot notes in my pocketbook, which is filling by the minute.

'This case is huge,' says Mardon. 'Our greatest challenge to date.'

'Indeed.' I stand back to take in the board and make a sweeping gesture towards the display. 'Although it is my hope that this process will aid us in forming a more discernible list of suspects.'

'All threaders, of course,' says Josiah, mocking Bretling's prejudice.

'Actually, they're mostly silkers.' I pin strands of red string between the names of those who are connected in some way and things seem to simplify. Our chart now exhibits the following notations:

Victim number 1. Unknown: no leads

Victim number 2. Investor in Wheal Berta, Uriah
Mumford:
Stanley Larkin (toymaker); Miss Kenwiggs (owner of
The Gunner); Victoria Mumford: sons Jethro and
Samuel; business associates Ranalf Harmon and Otis
Jacks

Victim number 3. Owner of several mines (including Wheal Berta), John Lancett:
Simon Forbes (excavations consultant at Wheal Berta); Avory Steverus (foreman at Wheal Berta); Mercy Lancett (widow and inheritor of the Lancett estate and mines)

Victim number 4. Mining consultant, Davey Brindle:
Markus Hinton (Master of the Dockside Forges)

Victim number 5. MP, Wulfric Hemings:
Zachariah Sterling (head tailor at Thackory's), Sterling's master, Mr Jennings

Victim number 6. Investor, Abraham Ketting: no leads

Victim number 7. MP, Augusto Ritcott: no leads

'Shouldn't we write up silker or threader accordingly alongside the names?' asks Mardon.

'What for? They're either the killer or they're not. Now, I wish to hammer out theories for each likely suspect. Of course, we may need to add further names to the list later, but it's a place to start.'

'Madam Kenwigs, she's definitely one for the list,' says Josiah.

I'm reminded of the poor threader who runs The Gunner beneath cruel Kenwigs as I underline her name on the board. 'Your theory?'

Josiah's face wrinkles as he cogitates. 'Kenwigs said Mumford had a thing for her and that's why they were supposed to meet, but Patty, her threader girl, told us that was a lie and that Kenwigs couldn't be trusted. Why lie about the meeting unless she has something to hide?'

'Good. And then there's the fact that at least three of the victims were supposed to meet at The Gunner, where Madam

Kenwigs had opportunity...' adds Lizzy.

'Yes,' says Penney. 'Perhaps these other victims also visited The Gunner and were never seen alive again. We should search the entire premises. She must have many rooms where she could hide evidence – bodies, even.'

I make a note. 'Good. Other suspects? Josiah and I took a dislike to Simon Forbes at the mine and he acted a little oddly, I thought.'

'Did you see the way he stared at us as we left?' asks Josiah.

'I did. He was also supposed to meet with John Lancett on the 18th but can't or won't tell us why. I appreciate Lancett was probably killed on the 17th but I'm adding Forbes as a likely suspect anyway.' I underline Forbes' name.

'What about these others?' asks Mardon. 'Avory Steverus, Markus Hinton, Zachariah Sterling and Stanley Larkin?'

'We spoke with Steverus and Forbes together,' explains Josiah. 'Steverus is the foreman of Wheal Berta and it seems he, Forbes and Lancett were on good terms. Steverus seemed all right.'

'We'll leave him for the time being,' I say. 'Though I suppose he and Forbes could be in cahoots. Markus Hinton has a solid alibi for the last two murders as he was out of the country when they happened.' I draw a line through Hinton's name. 'Which leaves Sterling and Larkin.'

Josiah rubs at his jaw. 'Sterling has disappeared since Lord Draker called upon him. He's a wanted man.'

'You think he's made a run for it?' asks Mardon.

'That or he's lying in a shallow grave somewhere,' says Lizzy.

'Are we sure there are no more bodies at the Sallow Grove?' asks Penney.

'The chances are slim, but there could be older graves the dogs failed to detect. Without digging up the entire place, we may never know. There's a Draker watching the grove from a hidden location, so we should hear if anyone attempts to make another deposit.' I think of Magwitch, also spying from his subterranean cavern in Mors Zonam, and I'm glad we've a more reliable watchman.

'So, what about Larkin?' asks Mardon. 'Have you questioned him?'

'Oh, yes,' says Josiah. 'The man's a genius. Makes the most amazing toys. Seemed helpful. You should visit his shop.'

'Pah,' says Mardon.

'I'm leaving Larkin off the list for now, but only because we plan to question him again anyway. He said he may remember things that could help, given some time.'

At the end of all our musings we have narrowed down the suspects: Kenwigs, Forbes and Sterling. 'In conclusion, we think it could be one of these three,' I say.

Josiah shrugs. 'Or none of them.'

I consider our next steps. 'Ebadiah, we need someone on the inside of Wheal Berta.'

'You mean down the mine?' he asks.

'Let's hope it doesn't come to that, but perhaps. For now, I'd like you to go to Stonhaven and find somewhere to stay — there's an inn, of sorts, though I'd advise you take an extra blanket for your bed. Get to know the locals and see what you can dig up, metaphorically speaking.'

'Will do,' says Ebadiah with a nod.

'Penney, you take the MP Augusto Ritcott. Find out precisely what he was doing in parliament, what he was pushing for.'

'I shall,' says Penney.

'Then that leaves me with Wulfric Hemings,' says Lizzy.

'Tread lightly. These were respected men with powerful connections and families. People won't appreciate it if they think you're poking around in the affairs of their dead. We'll leave Sterling to the Drakers for now.' I glance at the gathering, at the wall full of gathered information, and feel a wave of pride in our little outfit. 'Right, let's get to work.'

An excerpt taken from the gawper file,
as written by Michael Banyard.

The Dagomites — I cannot speak for the other gawpers — hold the art of writing in such high regard that it extends to almost sacred significance. They even name themselves, by tradition, after characters from books or manuscripts in their possession (mostly written in antiquity by the Old People) that survived the ancient cataclysm. Magwitch, Deadlock, Robespierre, Falstaff and Tacitus: these are the names I have so far learned. They are peculiar to my ears. There is one other I should mention: a large and menacing Dagomite who rules over the rest. His name is Skallagrim.

There is still much to learn about the gawpers, I am sure, and perhaps Magwitch will divulge more soon. I recall part of a conversation that played out in a joining of minds.

Magwitch: Dagomites sense the killing thoughts on the fourth plane. They are like ripples on the surface of cool waters. Robespierre sensed such thoughts and conjured the mire to investigate.

Me: The fourth plane?

Magwitch: Humankind feel the deepest of emotions on the fourth plane. The third plane carries other thoughts and feelings.

Me: We know nothing of these planes.

Magwitch: You use them but are unaware of them. Only Dagomites can wander the planes.

9

The Hunched Man

*In which Jinkers becomes a problem that can
no longer be ignored*

Despite my intentions, progress is slow over the following few days. We make sure Ebadiah is well provided for, have him promise to return with any news twice weekly, and see him onto a coach bound for Stonhaven. Appearing as a homeless boy from the streets of Camdon, he will beg for work at the mine. I worry some harm may come to him while beyond reach, but he's a tough sort, rough and ready, and as canny as a street boy could be. He's also doing well in his studies. As a threader, he's not allowed in school, but Mother is teaching him from home when he's not spying for us. He seems pleased to have an active role in the case at last and grins as we wave him off.

Mardon studies his coal in true scientific fashion and vanishes for hours at a time, doing who knows what or where.

We visit Mr Jennings, Zachariah Sterling's master, to question him, but learn little.

'Sterling didn't show up for work one day and I haven't seen him since,' says Jennings. 'The Drakers are searching, of course, but what else can I do?'

'Do you think he's run away?' asks Josiah.

'I can only guess as to the reason he's missing. He had a good life here, you know, better than most threaders. I see no reason why he would run. I'm worried something terrible has befallen him.'

Josiah and I revisit The Gunner, this time with Patty Primshaw in mind. Secluded in a corner of the tavern, we observe her until she spies us and makes her way over, wiping her hands on her apron. 'If you've come to see Mistress Kenwigs, you're out o' luck.'

I smile at her. 'We're here for the ale, Miss Primshaw. Two pints of Ruby's, if you please.'

'That's tuppence.' She holds out her hand to receive the coins before fetching our drinks, which we gladly receive.

'How would you feel about a different life elsewhere, Patty?' Josiah asks. 'Somewhere away from here – away from your mistress?'

'I'm sure I'd feel fine, sir, but that'll never 'appen. Ain't no 'arm in dreamin', though, I suppose.'

'No harm at all,' I say, taking a sip of ale. 'Have you heard anything more about Mr Mumford, the missing man?'

At the mention of the dead man, Josiah makes the sacred sign without thinking and the girl notices.

She shakes her head but then narrows her eyes. 'He's dead then, this toff Mumford?'

'Quite possibly,' I say, scowling at Joe.

'You know what? There ain't a single silker I know who makes the sacred sign.' Her attention settles briefly onto me before flicking back to Josiah. 'You wears the 'at, but you ain't no silker. I thought you was an odd one the moment I laid eyes on you.'

I feel my scowl deepening.

Josiah reddens. 'I am a silker, how dare you say otherwise?'

'All right, all right. Ain't no concern o' mine. But you don't need to fret. I wouldn't tell no one.' She leaves to serve other customers.

I warn Joe, hissing through my teeth. 'You're going to get us hanged if you carry on like that!'

'Sorry,' says Josiah.

A few minutes later, when my anger has cooled, I ask, 'What do you think? Should she be next on our list?'

'Let's see if she can hold her tongue first.'

We drink our ale.

Penney and Lizzy report in on the 6th but only to say they need more time. That afternoon, feeling somewhat thwarted by the case, Josiah and I revisit Stanley Larkin at his toy shop on Old Town Way. It seems a desperate move but we said we'd return, so return we do.

Wearing a crimson silk cravat and a charcoal grey suit, Larkin greets us genially, summoned by his ingenious entrance chimes. 'Ah, Masters Banyard and Mingle. Do come in, gentlemen. You are *most* welcome.' He appears brighter than the last time we visited and I wonder why. We enter and he's quick to invite us through to the back of his shop where he brushes wood shavings from chairs with a sleeve. 'Black bean soup?' He slips his soup pan onto the workshop stove and stokes the fire beneath the hot plate.

We accept the offer. 'Mr Larkin, have you thought any more about your encounter with Uriah Mumford?' I ask, taking a seat.

'Of course, poor old Uriah. I read his obituary in the papers.' Larkin makes the sacred sign. 'I've gone over his visit as I recall it. Yes. I've thought a great deal about it all and I have remembered a detail. It *may* be of interest to you. I don't know...' For a moment he looks doubtful.

'Tell us, then,' grunts Josiah, looking bored and frustrated.

Larkin pulls an apologetic expression. 'Of course. Let me take you through that day as it happened. I think that will give you the fullest picture of what took place.'

Josiah appears to physically deflate, giving a long sigh and letting his arms hang either side of his chair.

'Very well.' I glance out of the rear windows where a pair of double doors lead out onto a cobbled yard and a dismal, crooked backstreet.

We hear footsteps descending stairs beyond view and, before Larkin can begin, another voice cuts in. 'Master Larkin, do I hear guests? Would you like refreshments brought through?' A grey-haired threader woman, in neat cotton clothes and a white apron, appears in the doorway to the rear hall. Her eyes seem large in her thin face as she sees us.

'Gentlemen, this is Mrs Figgins.' To the housekeeper, he says, 'No, thank you, Mary. I have everything in hand.' He turns back to us. 'Now, where was I? Ah, yes, the day of Mr Mumford's disappearance. I live over the shop.' Larkin points at the ceiling. 'And it's my habit to come down to open up each morning at nine. It was so on the 8th of Quartersmoon when Mr Mumford first visited and I worked on a carrousel for some time, painting its merry horses.'

'How do you know that was the date of his calling?' I ask.

'I have it here in my order book. He signed for the commission. See for yourself.' Larkin takes a ledger from a shelf that's otherwise crammed with wooden toys in various states of completion, opens the book and presents it for inspection. Sure enough, there is Uriah Mumford's signature, along with the details and agreed price of his wheal house automaton order.

'Yes, I see.' I hand the ledger back to him and he replaces it on the shelf.

'I made tea and worked until the shop bell disturbed me. He was my first visitor that day, arriving precisely at eleven. I remember *that* because I recall thinking it fitting that he should arrange to collect the finished work at eleven also on another day.'

'The 17th of Thripplemoon…'

'Indeed.' The water boils. Larkin adds the ground black beans.

'What happened next?' I ask.

'Mr Mumford enquired about the automaton, asking if I was able to make a working model of the engine and winch from Wheal Bertha. It's a complicated business and I hadn't made one like that before, so I asked to see the plans before committing to anything. He carried them with him, you see. When I saw that I would be able to manage the work, I agreed, and we settled upon a price.' He takes the simmering black soup from the stove and pours it into three copper cups. 'Here, gentlemen. Drink up.'

'Was he in a good mood when he came to you, or was he distracted, worried about anything?'

'He seemed perfectly happy.' Larkin shrugs. 'We went on to decide upon a date for the collection.'

'And how long would you say he stayed?'

'Around half an hour. No more. But – and here's the thing – another customer came in around then, a strange fellow.' Larkin takes a sip from his cup.

'Oh?' I say.

'Looked at us both most oddly. That is to say, it seemed to me that he was pretending to browse but all the while I had the distinct impression that he was watching us. When I bade Mr Mumford farewell, the odd fellow took a sudden interest in the shop window and soon left as well. Never spoke a word to me, even when I wished him good morning.'

'And this is the detail you recalled?' asks Josiah, shifting to the edge of his seat and looking more interested.

'It is,' says Larkin.

'The Drakers do not know of this?' Josiah presses.

'They do not. When they questioned me, I had no idea of the seriousness of it all. I'd forgotten about the stranger and, in all honesty, the Drakers were rather rude. I didn't much like them.'

'Can you describe the man?' I ask, taking out my pocketbook and pencil to make notes.

'He was a scruffy sort, hunched over. His hair was dark, black or brown, I can't quite remember. He walked with a stick but also seemed well built, strong, you know... I remember thinking I wouldn't like to get in a tussle with him, never mind his hunch and his walking stick.'

'Did he limp, then?' asks Josiah.

Larkin closes his eyes briefly as though picturing the encounter. 'Do you know, I couldn't say. I think that, if he did have a limp, it was not pronounced.'

'Age?' I ask.

'Around forty.'

'You say *scruffy*. Was he a threader?' I ask.

'Either that or a silker who'd fallen on exceptionally hard times. He had a look about him as though he'd been sleeping rough. And there was something strange about his eyes and the way he peered at me before he went. Something... threatening. I did wonder if the fellow was quite sane.'

'Which way did Mr Mumford go? Did the odd man follow him?'

'I'm sorry. I really couldn't say. I went back to work.'

Retrieving our horses on the street outside Larkin's, we speculate beneath a darkly foreboding sky that suggests snow is on the way again.

'A new suspect. We should report this to Bretling immediately.'

'I suppose we should,' says Josiah. 'What do you make of it all?'

'It's the best lead so far. A madman following one of the victims? This could be it, Joe. This could be our man. We'll have his description circulated as soon as possible.'

'But we'll tell the team first, right?' Josiah heaves himself up into his saddle, the oiled leather creaking under the strain.

'Agreed.' I mount and we trot from Old Camdon's claustrophobic streets to clatter our way across Rook's Bridge, wind tearing at our coat tails, before slowing to a stop outside Mysteries Solved, where we tether Blink and Willie to the well-worn wall rings. Hurrying in, we find Lizzy at her desk in reception, working her way through a tall stack of back copies of the *Camdon Herald*, searching for information on Wulfric Hemings, presumably.

'Lizzy, gather the team,' I say as she glowers at my lack of manners. 'Where's Mardon? Does anyone know?'

She taps a half-dozen papers on the desk to align them. 'He's at the Museum of Natural History, I believe, consulting an expert. Really, Mr Banyard. Is it too much to expect a "Good afternoon"?' She seems disproportionately affronted.

'I'm sorry, Lizzy. I've a lot on my mind. Penney?'

'Visiting an MP she's been working on, digging for more on Augusto Ritcott.'

'Right.' A meeting will have to wait. I decide instead to write out the hunched man's description on a scrap of paper for the case room display. 'Here. Pin this to the wall with everything else. We have a new suspect. Tell the others to keep a sharp eye out for the man. I want to know the minute he's spotted.' I turn for the door.

'Wait. Where are you going?' asks Lizzy.

'To inform Lord Draker.'

Bretling is slumped in his chair, smoking his pipe, when he bids us enter. His voice is listless. We open the door to his office and view him through a tobacco haze: a ghost of his former self. 'What is it, young Banyard? In the name of Lychling, I do hope it's good news. I swear I can't take much more of this.'

'It *is* good news, sir.' I tell of our visit to Larkin's and of the strange fellow who may have followed Mumford from the shop, giving him a full description, at which he brightens a little. He straightens in his chair and copies down the description, asking me to repeat everything. When sure he has it correctly noted, he hurries to the door and calls into the corridor for an officer.

'At last we're getting somewhere. I knew I'd not regret bringing you fellows in.'

'We're glad to be of assistance, sir,' I say.

The officer arrives, his face drawn with concern. 'Yes, sir?'

'Take these notes to the steam press. I want copies in the hands of every sergeant within the hour. Understand?'

'Yes, sir.' The officer takes the paper from Bretling's

outstretched hand, turns on his heel and leaves.

'Yes. Good. Right.' Bretling slides open a drawer from his desk, takes out a bottle of Scolanda Glen Mordoon and pours three glasses. 'Here, we'll drink to the foreseeable capture of this hunched man, and an end to this wretched business.'

We stand, raise glasses and slug the fine whisky.

'I'll have a sergeant run over to Larkin's to check the details. Make it official, but well done, gentlemen. Well done. We'll soon have posters up on every street corner in Camdon. This rogue will be caught and I'll see that he hangs.'

'Will you have a sketch made?' asks Josiah.

'Yes, by Lychling, I shall, Mr Mingle.'

As he pours another round, I worry about the state of Bretling's mind. He's bounced from the darkest depression to a state of ecstasy in two minutes flat. 'Sir, may I suggest caution in our optimism? The fellow is as yet far from capture.'

'You know, Banyard, that's just the sort of thing your father would have said.' Bretling gives a half-smile and wags a finger at me. At least he's cheered, which isn't such a bad thing. 'A wise man, your father was.'

This evening Josiah and I find ourselves settling in the green room before the fire with a glass of port, as our habit dictates. Outside, the night air is filled with a thousand pale flakes of falling snow. I watch it for a time, mesmerised, before throwing another log onto the fire. We're alone because it's late. I sit to read the *Camdon Herald* for a while, planning to climb the stairs for my bed at any moment, when from a rear window there comes a faint tap-tapping sound. Rising and turning towards it, we're startled by a pale face pressed up against the pane.

'Jinkers!' I say.

'What does *he* want?' complains Joe. 'Why can't he use the door like everyone else?'

'Never mind. We'd better let him in.' I cross to the window, release the catch and heave up the lower sash. A gust of cold air chills the room. Snowflakes invade to settle and melt on the floor.

Jinkers swings a leg over the sill and clambers awkwardly in, shedding snow from his shoulders and shoes. 'G-good evening,' he stammers, apparently unsettled by the daring nature of this act.

'What on Earthoria are you doing?' I ask, though not unkindly. I draw the window closed.

His face breaks into a nervous smile. 'I need to speak with you and, well, thought it best to be discreet. You know, now that I'm spying for you and all...'

Josiah places his hands on his hips, towering over Jinkers. 'You're not spying for us.'

'Ah, yes!' he points at Josiah conspiratorially before tapping his nose. 'Very good! That's precisely the reason I thought I should visit.'

Joe looks baffled. 'What?'

I begin to speak. 'Mr Jinkers—'

'You see, I wanted you to know that I understand. You can't employ me, but I got the message.'

'Message?' says Josiah, screwing up his face so that it looks like a giant prune. 'What message?'

Jinkers lowers his voice. 'The message that you need me to spy for you but you can't tell anyone. Not even me!'

I attempt to set him straight. 'Mr Jinkers, we can't employ you because—'

'Now, Micky, don't say another word.' His eyes flit around the room as he gabbles. 'Message received loud and clear. I've read the papers. Seen the obituaries. Thought there was something odd about it all, so I executed a little research. Did you know that six of those obituaries announced over the last two days were for silker gents who were reported missing months ago? It's all very strange.' He pauses, his gaze flitting between us. 'I'm right, aren't I? This is the case you're investigating. And those men went missing but have turned up dead, south of the city.' He makes the godly sign.

Josiah and I exchange a glance. Joe shrugs and shakes his

head in resignation. 'Might as well tell him everything if he knows that much. Let's face it. He's going to spy for us whether we like it or not.'

I invite Jinkers to sit and I find another glass. This is going to take a while.

Later, when Jinkers has left for home, beaming at his newly found purpose, I make my way to my bedroom, close the door and take the gawper skull from its box beneath the bed. Magwitch is quick to respond to my presence. For a moment, a mess of thoughts and half-formed ideas swirl chaotically through my mind and then his presence stills all.

Michael Banyard, Magwitch is here.

Magwitch, are you still watching the Sallow Grove?

Magwitch has been watching. Deadlock is now watching.

I picture Deadlock — a severe, towering gawper who unsettles me — peering into Holloway from the caverns of Mors Zonam with flaming white eyes, and am glad I'm not in either place. A shiver travels the length of my spine.

Has anyone tried to visit the grove at night?

No. All has been quiet. Drakers have visited in daylight.

You will let me know if someone comes in darkness?

Magwitch will find this one. Fear not.

Very well.

The watchman sleeps.

You mean the Draker guard is asleep right now?

This very minute.

He's supposed to be watching.

This is truth.

I'll see to it. Keep watching, Magwitch. I'm relying on you.

10

The Interment of John Lancett

In which Ebadiah reports and Banyard chases shadows

Tuesday, 9th Elventide

Josiah is late to the breakfast table. He's still buttoning his shirt as he takes a seat opposite me. Mother fusses around him, fetching milk and honey, slicing bread and doling a thick creamy porridge into bowls. He dollops honey on top of his and is about to shove an enormous spoonful into his mouth when I take a large box from under the table and place it before him.

The spoon hovers three inches from his chin. 'What's this?' he asks, shovelling the porridge into his mouth and swallowing.

'Open it and see,' I say.

He lays down his spoon to shake the box, as though guessing. He tears the brown wrapping paper open and lifts the lid. 'New riding boots!' He grins.

'Size twelve. Oiled leather,' I say, feeling gratified.

'Caramel brown. Perfect.' He kicks off his old, leaky squeakers and pulls on the new boots. 'Oh yes! But why? You said I should spend my wages on them.'

'Today is a special day, Joe, and we can't have you squelching around in ruined boots.'

He peers at me suspiciously. 'What's so special about today?'

'Ah! You'll have to wait and see.' I take a mouthful of porridge.

That's confused him. He doesn't know whether to be pleased or concerned. 'Are we going somewhere?'

'Well, we'll start at the office.'

'Tell me!'

I smile. 'You'll find out, soon enough.'

We ready ourselves and ride out, passing a gaggle of urchins who skip and circle in the street while singing an old plague song.

> *Ring a bell for Rosey,*
> *A-sleepin' with a nosebleed,*
> *Call for a doc-tor,*
> *We all fall down!*

At Mysteries Solved we greet Lizzy, already working at her desk in reception.

'Lizzy, do you have any news?'

'I have a report ready. Would you and Josiah like black bean soup first?' She sounds pleased with herself. Perhaps she's found something of note.

We take our soup in the case room, where we find Penney borrowing Joe's desk. 'Gentlemen.'

We sit and give Lizzy our attention expectantly, leaving the adjoining door open so that we'll know if anyone enters reception from the street.

'Wulfric Hemings,' she begins, thumbing through her pocketbook and flattening out a page. 'Victim number five. Born into a noble family of bankers. A gifted student at school. Began a career in business management early in life. Progressed to politics over the years, becoming increasingly serious about it until running for MP in 1773. Represented Tower End for six years before moving to Holloway in 1779.'

'Interesting. Why the move?' I ask.

'It seems something of a demotion to me,' says Penney.

Lizzy nods. 'It certainly was. I'm not sure what happened or why exactly. I've been looking into it but have yet to discover the reason.'

'Pursuits?' I ask.

'Industry and commerce, mainly. He was involved in the reformation of import laws in '75 and became known as an investor and master of factories. Later on, he was in mining – was quite a commanding character, by all accounts. Made a name as a lawmaker and pocketed a fortune to boot.'

'Mining again,' says Josiah. 'It all comes back to mining.'

'Did Hemings have any direct connection with Wheal Berta?' I ask.

'Nothing I've found suggests so, but I'll check.'

'Enemies?' I start a new page on Wulfric Hemings in my pocketbook.

'Plenty. The Raggers all seem to have hated him, but then, he *was* a champion of the Silkertons, so…'

'The Raggers' is a term widely used to describe the left wing of parliament. It is said to have begun as a derogatory name for the more modestly dressed portion of parliament. The name 'Silkertons' refers to the right wing and originated in the prominent and bombastic sixteenth-century prime minister, Harold Silkerton, who was by all accounts, a flashy dresser.

'Yes, I see.'

Lizzy continues. 'There was a rather serious dispute back in 1780, mostly forgotten now. Hemings was fighting the Silkertons' cause when he was egged in the street just outside Parliament House. The Drakers failed to apprehend the perpetrators.'

'And the cause?' asks Josiah.

'The Raggers were pushing for shorter working hours. By all accounts, they were rather irked at the time.'

'Do you think the killings are political? Some vengeance-crazed Ragger?' I wonder.

'It's too early to say.' Lizzy closes her pocketbook. 'Of course, I'm still looking into it.'

'Very good.' I turn to Penney. 'Anything on Augusto

Ritcott?'

Penney reports from Josiah's desk. 'A similar story, though Ritcott's family were in manufacturing – cast-iron goods and cotton mills, mostly. At the age of twenty-three he went his own way, pursuing a career in politics. Used his business nous to climb the ladder. Became an acting MP in '74 and represented Southside until he vanished last month. Highly popular among the Silkertons.'

'I seem to recall he had something to do with slavers' rights,' I say.

'He pushed for the abolition of any rights for captive slaves,' explains Penney. 'Made it impossible for a slaver to ever be held accountable for any injury or death of a slave. He basically set back the Raggers' progress on that front by around two hundred years.'

'He sounds like a delightful fellow.' I finish my black soup and set the copper cup on my desk next to the old skull that I use as a paperweight.

'Well, the Silkertons loved him for it. He also personally funded the building of a dozen schools and successfully fought for the reinstating of poorhouses across Londaland. Now that he's known to be dead, there's talk of raising a statue in his honour.'

I nod. 'Popular indeed. Though, I imagine, as loathed by the Raggers as he was loved by the Silkertons.'

'Correct,' says Penney.

The jingle of our doorbell alerts us. When we glance from the case room into reception, Ebadiah is standing there, grimy head to foot with coal dust.

'I had to pay the driver extra on account of the filth,' he says, grinning mischievously. 'Got any grub? I'm starving.'

Josiah and I accompany Ebadiah to The Dog near Rook's Bridge and find a table. I order a ham and eggs breakfast for Ebadiah and we talk as we wait for its delivery. I tell Josiah, 'No, you can't have a pint,' before bringing Ebadiah up to date with the Sallow Grove investigation — and inform him of the new suspect, the hunched stranger — when he cuts in, wide eyed.

'Why, the innkeeper's a hunchback!'

'Innkeeper?'

'The man what runs the place where I'm staying. The one you told me about. They call it The Duke, though there ain't no sign. It's the only inn in Stonhaven. The innkeeper could be your hunched man.'

I take notes in my pocketbook. 'His name?'

'Mr Barronbrook.'

'And have you seen much of him?'

'I seen him as I come and go. I eat there most nights and sometimes he serves the pottage.'

'Sounds delicious,' says Josiah.

'Well, it ain't,' says Ebadiah, pulling a face. 'But his wife bakes bread fresh each day, and that's almost as good as Mrs Banyard's.'

'Is Barronbrook a scruffy sort, menacing?' I ask. 'Does he own The Duke? Is he a silker?'

'He's a threader, through and through. Ain't scruffy, though. No way he owns The Duke. I expect one of the local silkers does, someone like Forbes or Steverus.'

'Perhaps they're in it together,' says Josiah, wistfully. 'And Barronbrook is Forbes' man.'

I picture Forbes and a hunched figure hacking out graves in the gloom of the moonlit grove, but then my hopes unravel. 'Beyond his hunch, Barronbrook doesn't fit the description Larkin gave.'

Ebadiah shrugs. 'I can find out who owns The Duke if it helps.'

'Do that,' I say. 'What else have you learned in Stonhaven?'

'Steverus gave me a job haulin' barrows down the mine. Shift work, hard an' horrid. I don't much care for it.' Ebadiah watches the bar, expectantly.

'I'm sure. What have you found on Avory Steverus?'

'He's all right for a toff, I suppose. Can be mean when he

wants, though. You wouldn't know it at first. He's all smiles and polite. But he can turn like a whip.'

'I thought Forbes was the dodgy one,' says Josiah, his brow knitting.

'Forbes is no-nonsense,' says Ebadiah. 'A hard man, but fair from what I seen, and he knows mining better than any.'

Josiah grimaces at the unwelcome report. 'We'll see.'

'Perhaps we should be looking more closely at Steverus,' I say. 'Is there anything criminal going on at Wheal Berta?'

'No, but working down that mine is like torture. It's dangerous. People die down there.'

'Who died?' asks Josiah.

'I ain't got names. It's just the way the miners talk, like it's always happening. Like it could happen any time. That's just how it is. Most of the threader families have lost someone to the mine over the years.'

'Well, mining *is* a dangerous occupation,' I say. 'Always has been.'

'I guess,' says Ebadiah.

My concern for him deepens. 'I don't like the thought of sending you back there.'

'Well,' he says, undeterred, 'being a detective's dangerous, too.'

A serving girl brings his ham and eggs, setting the plate on the table before him and for a while our conversation is paused as Ebadiah eats. When he's finished, he looks up from his plate, which he's licked clean. 'Listen up. I came back to tell you two things. First, this afternoon at two is John Lancett's funeral. Thought you'd want to know.'

I frown. 'I didn't know Bretling had released the bodies. And second?'

'Lancett's arch-rival, Samual Frack, will be there.'

Josiah massages his temples. 'Not another poxy suspect.'

I smile and pass Ebadiah a bonus of two half-crowns. 'Yes. Mind-boggling, isn't it? Good work, Shoe Shine. Take a day off.'

John Lancett's *arch-rival*, Samual Frack, lingers towards the back of those gathered about the open grave as Lancett's coffin is lowered in. Standing at my right, Avory Steverus points him out to us across the crowd with a subtle gesture.

Stonhaven's only deadfield stands atop a wind-torn hill just south of the mine, beyond Stonhaven Hall and The Duke. To the south, west and north, the slopes are blanketed with pines. The eastern side is kept grassed to provide a sea view. The funeral is a grey affair, with a fine drizzle blowing sideways in from the sea and huddled figures wrapped in black against the damp. Dark umbrellas shelter the crowd like a crop of gothic mushrooms. A sign carved in stonewood over the lychgate arch reads, *Don't grieve – we are listening to the birds.*

But there are no birds today, not a solitary gull over the foaming sea.

Frack has a starkly pale face, presently expressionless. I try to deduce his thoughts as he observes his adversary's interment – wonder if he's pleased or in some way vitriolic – but I can't tell. He maintains a mask of neutrality. Perhaps he's simply contemplating life's brevity. He hasn't bothered with an umbrella so water pools in the brim of his stovepipe hat to drip from its lowest point, narrowly missing his long, aquiline nose.

Steverus looks dapper in black silk. It suits him well, but then, so does everything he wears.

'He has a coal mine a few miles south of here,' he explains below the hollyman's preamble, 'and an iron mine to the north. Natural competitors, I suppose, vying for the best prices at market. It's good of him to come, really.'

'Or is he here to gloat?' I ask. 'I'm told there was some animosity between them.'

'Oh, yes,' says Steverus candidly. 'You could say that. Frack and Lancett had many a run-in. That kind of thing was commonplace, but I'm sure it was nothing but business.'

'Do you think it might have led Frack into criminal action?'

'If you mean murder, then no. Their pugnacity was purely professional. More in a line of heated debates, I can assure you.

If it were not so, why is he here?'

'There are killers who cannot help but obsess about their victims.' I watch Frack through narrowed eyes. 'In their guilt they fear capture, pursue all knowledge of the aftermath and investigation keenly.'

'Not Frack. I won't believe it.' Steverus is adamant. 'You're looking in the wrong place.'

'Then where *should* we look?'

He shakes he head. 'I wish I knew. I could hold them to account for the death of my friend.'

Simon Forbes stands at Steverus' other side, while Josiah is to my left. Before us at the edge of the grave, Mercy Lancett weeps, the servants of her household aligned at her side. The rest of the crowd comprises mostly mine workers and a few other local threaders who've come to pay their last respects.

The hollyman concludes his monologue and signals the pallbearers to lower the coffin. I should probably explain that the man is not made from a prickly bush: a *hollyman* is a priest who oversees a deadfield that has a sentinary – the central, chapel-like building that's used by the hollyman and the gravediggers, and which presides over the hilltop. I'm no expert on the matter but I can only imagine the name began as *holy man* and has morphed over the centuries.

As the coffin descends into the pit, he makes the godly sign and then the sacred sign, respectful of both the popular silker and threader faiths. Josiah begins to make the sacred sign but quickly switches to the godly sign before resuming his look of boredom. There's a subdued atmosphere and a general sense that everyone is waiting to get out of the rain, mourning or not.

'I hate funerals,' mutters Josiah. 'Wretched things.'

'I quite agree. But they're necessary.'

People begin to drift away while we wait to give our respects to the widow and, among the shifting bodies towards the rear, a lone figure catches my eye, for he or she is standing stone-still, fixed as though staring in our direction. I can't really tell where the person is looking because of a deep hood that hides their features. For a heartbeat we seem to lock gaze but then the uncanny statue melts behind the other mourners to dart away, quick as a sprite. I crane my neck, peering, searching fruitlessly.

'Poor old Mercy. She really doesn't deserve this... Perhaps you and Josiah might like a warmer before returning home. A few of us will gather back at the mine head to drink a toast to old John. I'm sure you'd be welcome.'

I'm vaguely aware of Steverus' hushed voice but, with one foot already launching into pursuit, there's no time to respond. I leave the others peering after me with perplexed expressions and run, dodging mourners to weave my way, guided by a nebulous feeling that the figure may have ducked into the sentinary. I dash between graves and, reaching the end wall where a pair of arched doors leads inside, scan the porch recess before entering.

The inner space is dark, lit only by two small, high windows – one at each end – and smells of candle grease, dust, damp and death. At the centre of this gloom sits a set of trestles which recently bore John Lancett's coffin. A shelf holds an array of sacred texts. Old wooden chairs line a cold, tiled floor that's the colour of dried blood. The alter nook, the hollyman's office, the pillared wings with their niches and marbled remembrances: each of these I search with the speed of a puck — but my quarry is not here.

Retracing my steps, I skirt the building only to glimpse the figure disappearing into the woods of the southern slope and, gathering breath, I lengthen my stride to run full pelt. I leap gravestones, duck beneath low branches of the scattered yew trees and dash from the grey, wet light of the deadfield into the forest shadows. Mouldering pine needles are soft beneath my boots. Here I lose track of the figure and soon pause to listen for the tell-tale sounds of a fleeing soul. Below the thick canopy of fragrant evergreens, even the patter of rain is absent. Has the person stopped to hide? Are they lying in wait? Or did they already push so deep into the trees that they are beyond earshot?

I turn on my heel as a sense of dread befalls me, quickening my heart with a sudden chill. Panic and peril. The feeling is so overpowering that I abandon my search, leave the trees behind and hurry back up the slope to find Josiah and the others. It's a relief to get out of the forest. I'm breathless. A conviction remains: I have just encountered the killer, perhaps coming to within a few feet of death.

'What was all that about?' asks Josiah, looking miserable and soggy among the few remaining mourners.

'Chasing shadows.' I scan the treeline.

'Our favourite pastime.' Dejectedly, he kicks at a clump of grass.

Steverus leads Frack over to introduce us. Frack cuts an intimidating figure: broad-shouldered and tall, dressed in silker finery and using a silver-handled walking cane, though with no hint of a frailty. We are among the last to linger.

'Samual Frack, these are the gentlemen I mentioned, Michael Banyard and Josiah Mingle. They'd like to ask you some questions, I believe.' Steverus waits patiently while we talk.

'Delighted to make your acquaintance, gentlemen,' says Frack, offering a hand. I shake it while, a little further away and looking utterly unapproachable, Josiah simply nods. 'Steverus tells me this is about John Lancett,' says Frack. His face is clean shaven but for thick sideburns. His eyes, a cold grey-blue, meet mine confidently and without a trace of fear. 'Ask away.'

I begin. 'My questions are about your relationship with Lancett. He was a staunch rival of yours, was he not?'

'Yes and no,' says Frack, raising an eyebrow pensively. 'In business, we were indeed in direct competition, our mines being in proximity, our market likewise, though that is where the opposition ended. We tolerated each other with mutual respect.'

'I see. Did you have much to do with Mr Lancett in the months leading up to his disappearance?'

'Hardly,' says Frack. 'We sat in the same bidding chamber at the Guild Hall once or twice, though across the table. Beyond that, I doubt I saw him at all. We were not friends, you understand.'

'Do you know why anyone might want him dead?'

'As I understand it, he was doing quite well. I did wonder if he was robbed and killed in some back alley of Camdon, trying to defend the contents of his wallet. I hear he was last seen in the city.'

I turn to Steverus. 'Might John have taken something of greater value when he last went to Old Camdon, something about which we do not know?'

Steverus is quick to reply. 'Not to my knowledge. He would have had money in his wallet, of course, and his pocket watch, his wedding ring.'

'All of which were recovered with his remains. Very well, I shall keep you no longer, Mr Frack. Please contact me should you think of anything that might help.' I pass Frack my card, which he glances at before pocketing and, with a nod, moves on to offer his condolences to the widow.

Steverus waits until Frack is beyond earshot. 'Listen, Banyard. I for one do not believe Frack would have killed John Lancett, but you should know this. He lied just now. He and Lancett did meet up shortly before John went missing. They met at The Duke and talked over cups of rum. Though what was discussed, I do not know.'

I make a note in my pocketbook as Steverus leaves us.

Josiah looks glum.

'Cheer up. At least your feet are dry. What time is it?' I check the hillside. There's no movement between the firs or beyond the forest.

Josiah takes his pocket watch and flips open the lid. 'Half three.'

'Oh! We must go or we'll be late.'

'Late for what?'

An excerpt taken from the gawper file,
as written by Michael Banyard.

Gawpers move in a peculiar way, appearing to glide rather than walk across the ground, and it was not until recently that I learned that this is because, rather than visiting places, they 'conjure' places to visit themselves. It is therefore not so much that they move, but that in some peculiar way in space and time, they can move a location into their presence. I don't pretend to understand how this works or why. Indeed, they have other rather spectacular abilities that I have yet to fully comprehend: both telekinesis and a form of telepathy.

11

The Visitor

*In which Josiah gets a surprise and
Lord Draker offers a reward*

As our carriage trundles back up the coast and into Highbridge,
winter's early darkness descends over Camdon's skyrakers and
edifices like a cloak woven of shadow. Add a little of that close,
urban fog and it forms a murky setting where one might come
and go in relative obscurity. Perfect. The arrival of Willow
Buxton has been well thought out, long planned and
anticipated, and its imminence ignites my nerves as Josiah and I
arrive at Bunkin's Tea House. It's a respectable establishment
where respectable silkers often meet, respectably.

That, too, is part of the plan, for a lady of means would not
frequent some grubby Southside tavern, and a lady of means is
precisely how Miss Buxton must be perceived.

Spread throughout the main room are a dozen or so linen-
draped round tables – one of which we occupy. On the ledge
behind the counter, gleaming copper kettles, pots, cups and
utensils glitter in the lamplight. There is little natural light from
the mass of bullseye windowpanes that face onto the street.

When our refreshments arrive, Josiah sips his tea
indifferently and looks bewildered, childlike and lost. I lean

across our table to straighten his tie, feeling a pang of guilt for revelling in the moment. 'That's better.'

'Again, why are we here?' he asks, clasping and unclasping his meaty hands.

'You'll see,' I repeat, checking my pocket watch. 'Soon enough.' And that's when she floats in: crimson skirts of flowing silk, blonde curls alive with motion, her face held in a practised gaze that conveys a certain stature. All in all, she's a picture of sophisticated affluence, which is a far cry from the impression she made upon her first arrival in the city. Then she was bedraggled, thin, small and pale in filthy rags. She looked (and smelled) feral, for she had travelled rough for several days and had been drinking foul water straight from the Tynne, having escaped her owner in Loncaster. I smile at the transformation and watch Josiah's bemused expression morph into one of wonder. He stands: an involuntary reaction.

She glides across the floor and pauses before us, fixing upon him.

He opens his mouth to speak but she cuts in to prevent him from using her true name, just as my last letter warned her she must do. 'Why, you must be Mr Mingle,' she says with an Amorphian accent she's perfected over recent months. 'Mr Banyard has told me all about you.' She holds out a hand.

His jaw hangs slack. He stares, takes her hand and quickly releases it.

I rise to bow briefly. 'Miss Zadie Crawford, you are correct. This is Mr Josiah Mingle.'

'Pleased to meet you,' she says.

'Do take a seat, Miss Crawford. It's so very good to see you. I trust all is well.'

'Quite well, thank you.' She sits, pulling off velvet gloves that reach to her elbows. Josiah lowers himself onto his chair, breaking his stare only to glance at me.

'And how was your journey?' I ask.

'Without incident.'

'Did your escort treat you well? I trust your baggage has been

138

safely delivered.'

'All is well, thank you.'

'I believe this is your first visit to our fair city.'

Amusement flashes in her eyes, reminding me of an occasion when she first enjoyed a silker role. Back then, she helped us to dupe the registrar of Chantrees, the jewellers. 'That is so, and I'm very much looking forward to it.'

We are thorough in our detail for the benefit of the other customers scattered about the room. Should the identity of Zadie Crawford ever be questioned, we shall have witnesses to testify of her arrival in the city.

Josiah opens and closes his mouth and I'm reminded of the silver gulpers my friends and I used to net down at the weir as children. 'Does this mean you're here for good? You're staying?' he eventually asks.

'I am indeed,' says *Miss Crawford*. 'I'm renting a room at a house in Highbridge for a time—'

'Highbridge? But—'

'Though I shall be dining with you this evening,' she reassures him. 'Isn't that right, Mr Banyard?'

'Please call me Michael. Mother is at this very moment preparing a celebratory feast in your honour.'

'The honour is mine. If I'm to call you Michael, you must call me Zadie.'

'Very well. Will you take tea, Zadie?'

Our somewhat stilted conversation continues until, little by little, Josiah appears to revert to his usual self, albeit awkwardly, and I can't help feeling that what was meant as a grand surprise has transpired more as a cruel trick. After all the planning, I'm disappointed, and can only hope that by the end of the evening he may forgive me. In any case, he plays along and we get through the tea house meeting.

Things are a little more relaxed once we're back at 96 Bunson Street and can drop pretences. By the time Mother carries a large joint of roast aurochs to the table, Josiah's smiling and we enjoy several welcome hours of distraction from the Seraph case, dining, drinking wine and talking animatedly. And when the evening comes to an end, I send him to accompany Miss Zadie Crawford back to Highbridge in a carriage, telling him to see her safely home but not to linger. Society must become used to the idea of her presence before their association is disclosed.

I go to bed, content in my distractions, and listen for his return. He eventually arrives, singing to himself quietly as he climbs the stairs for his room.

The downside to all this (let's face it, there's usually a downside with Josiah)? It's likely he'll be a useless assistant for months. Hoping he proves me wrong, I take the gawper skull from its box under my bed and press its cold, bony surface against my forehead.

Magwitch is quick to answer my call.

Anything to report? I think.

All is quiet at the Sallow Grove, he replies.

Have there been any visitors at all?

Drakers gathered there earlier in the day, their leader among them.

Lord Bretling Draker?

This is the one. He means yes. *A learned man joined them there. He spoke of the trees.*

A man of science, do you think?

This is truth. The scientist left before dusk.

Lord Draker is researching the sallows, just as we have done. Interesting. Is their watcher alert?

He is. Michael Banyard, I bear grim news of my kind. Skallagrim is causing a rift among Dagomites. He professes all of your kind to be evil and has revealed a desire to eradicate them. He is lost. Unbalanced.

That sounds serious. The Dagomite king is on a quest to murder us all!

Skallagrim is serious and this may interfere with our communication. There is much unrest — are many disturbances on the planes.

Is he there still, in Mors Zonam?

Skallagrim has moved to a secret location for his security. Magwitch does not know where. Many Dagomites have departed with him.

But not you.

This is truth. Along with others, Magwitch has risen against his regime. Skallagrim and his captain, Tacitus, are fools. This will lead to a Dagomite war. Magwitch remains with his brothers and sisters, with Deadlock, Robespierre and Falstaff.

The news leaves me rather speechless and wondering what that might mean for humankind. After a pause I think, *Keep watching, Magwitch, and let me know of any news.*

Wednesday, 10th Elventide

'Good morning, Lizzy.' We enter the office at nine o'clock sharp without any real plan for the day, and hang our hats and coats on the stand. Wondering where to start, I go to consult the chart we have made, but opening the case room door, stop and stare curiously at a small, dark object on my desk. 'Lizzy?'

'She's not here,' says Josiah, glancing around.

'But the front door was unlocked.' I check the storeroom. Empty. And the concealed door to our hidden chamber behind the fireplace is closed, so she can't have discovered that. Or could she? I open the concealed door to peer inside and, finding that room empty too, close the door.

'Perhaps she's popped out for black soup.'

'And left the front door unlocked? Was Mardon in yesterday?' I ask, stepping closer to cock my head at the lump of coal that somebody has clearly left for me to find. My first thoughts are that it will leave dust on my desk and I don't want it on my clothes, but my mind soon turns to more sinister concerns.

Josiah peers into the case room through the open doorway. 'I don't think so. He's been spending an awful lot of time with the coroner. Why?' He spies the coal. 'What's that doing there?'

'I was hoping *you* could tell *me*.' Has an intruder been in here? I look around, wondering if anything else has changed. A new sheet of paper has been pinned up on the board; on it, a message scrawled in red ink. I read aloud. 'Woe is me, for I am undone.'

I'm still staring at the writing when Josiah notices the imographs. 'Look! Their faces have been scratched out.'

He's right. All of the victims' imographs have been defaced.
'Who would do all this?' asks Josiah.
'The killer.'
'You mean the killer was here?'
'In person.'
'When?'
I check the back door is locked and the rear window intact. 'It must have been during the small hours of the night. At any other time, he would've been noticed tampering with the door lock, and there're no windows broken. I wonder if the night watchman noticed anything.'
'He picked the lock.' Josiah looks worried.
'He must have. Both of them.' I examine the lock of the adjoining door. There's no sign of it being forced, no scratches on the brass facing around the keyhole. I glance again at the coal, the note and imographs. 'We must inform Lord Draker.'
Mardon arrives, cleanly shaven and looking dapper in a new long coat and a bottle-green silk scarf, which he hangs on the corner stand with his topper.
'Ah, just the fellow.' I usher him through and point to the coal. 'Take a look at this.'
'It's a lump of coal. So what?' he says distractedly.
'Somebody broke in and left it there. Well, not *broke in*, exactly – nothing's broken – but see here.' I gesture towards the pinboard with its alterations.
He takes a set of optical lenses from his surgeon's bag and examines the imographs. After a moment, he says, 'These scratches were made with a knife. The handwriting on the note is interesting.' He moves on to the note, passing a variety of lenses over the red letters. 'This has been written lefthanded to disguise the writer's true style.'
'What do you make of the coal?' I ask.
He moves to the desk, picks up the coal to give it a cursory glance. 'Anthracite, a fine grade coal. It's generally sold to silkers because it gives the best heat and less odour, but it's also used in iron smelting.'

'I thought coal was coal,' grunts Josiah.

'Far from it, Mr Mingle. There are four main types,' explains Mardon as Josiah rolls his eyes. 'Anthracite, bituminous, sub-bituminous and lignite. That's in descending order of quality. The threaders – those lucky enough to afford coal at all – use lignite, or brown coal as it's known. That's the poorest. What you have here on your desk is the best you can get, the sort silkers burn in their home hearths. Coincidentally, it's the same as the coal found in the mouths of the Seraph's victims.' He nods towards the defaced images.

'It's no coincidence,' I say. 'The more I learn of this case, the more I think Bretling might be right – we're hunting a threader who is trying to make a point. Any chance you can tell where this coal came from?'

'Afraid not, old boy. There is some variation of quality in every mine. I'm not sure it would help, anyway. I doubt very much that the killer is sourcing his coal directly. He'll be buying it from the coalman, like the rest of us.'

'You're right, of course.'

The girls arrive and we spend the next few minutes telling them what's happened.

'It's interesting that you think a threader is behind all this,' says Penney, her demeanour flat, bordering on cold. 'Lizzy and I were talking. We believe that, with everything we now know, there's a chance we might calculate a list of the killer's next likely victims. Might that be worth pursuing?'

I'm staggered. 'Sometimes, girls, you are really quite brilliant.'

Lizzy glares at me. 'No, Michael. We're brilliant *all* the time. It's just that mostly you don't notice.'

What *have* I done? They'll be asking for a pay rise next!

'We could do it now,' suggests Penney.

'I suppose you'll be wanting black bean soup before we start,' says Lizzy.

'And cake,' says Josiah. 'Don't forget the cake.'

Mardon glares at him, but nothing will dampen Joe's spirits today.

'It helps me think,' he says. 'What about Bretling?'

'Good point.' I grab my coat, wrap the coal in brown paper and drop it into a pocket. 'I'd better head over to headquarters. You'll have to make a start without me.'

Josiah and Mardon rearrange the case room, placing two desks back to back to form one large table around which we might brainstorm the problem. While Penney and Lizzy fetch the refreshments, I leave and ride out to Tower End.

Bretling is paging through reports at his desk when he bids me enter his office. With a twitch of his brow, he peers up at me expectantly. 'Well, what is it, young Banyard? You seem in a hurry.'

I take the parcel from my pocket, unwrap and present the coal. 'It's about this, sir.'

'More coal.' He huffs. 'Let me guess. Someone left this for you to find.'

'We had a break-in last night. This was left on my desk in the Mysteries Solved case room first thing this morning.'

He slides a drawer free of his desk and deposits it by his stack of papers, half a dozen lumps of coal tumbling around within as he does so. 'You're not the first.'

'Sir?'

'These are from my detective sergeants, each left in plain sight. Huntly found his on the breakfast table yesterday. Smeaton's was waiting for him on the nightstand by his bed! This killer is mocking us.'

'It seems he or she is a deft hand with a lock pick. I wondered if the night watch might have seen anything.'

'Indeed. I'll check.' He twitches again and takes a piece of coal from a shelf behind him. 'This one I discovered today on my doorstep.' He tosses the coal into the drawer with the others before wiping his fingers on a handkerchief. 'At this rate we'll all be murdered in our beds before he's ever caught. I swear, Banyard, I've barely slept for a month, and the 17th is looming. He will pluck another silker from Camdon and there's nothing we can do about it.'

'Are you convinced it's a man we seek? Might it be a woman, wronged by these fellows?'

'I've nothing to suggest either way, but let's face it, it's usually a man. And to kill so many? I can't see a woman doing that.'

'Well, I thought you should know about the coal. I suppose I should go.'

'Stay sharp, Banyard, and find me this killer. There's a bonus of a hundred guineas for the man who does.'

'We're trying, sir. Oh, there was one other thing. Can you be sure to tell your guard out by the grove to stay awake and focused on the job? It's imperative.'

Back at Mysteries Solved, I join the team around the desks where Josiah is slowly munching his way through a platter of honey cake.

'A hundred guineas,' I muse. 'Not a sum to be sniffed at.'

'I could use a hundred guineas,' says Josiah, spitting crumbs.

'Then let's be sure to win it!' I say, adding, 'Though we'll have to split the prize between us. Agreed?'

'Agreed,' comes a communal response.

The rest of the morning is consumed by discussion and argument as we consider each potential victim and debate the likelihood of their imminent death. Among our best candidates are five politicians, two mine owners, including Samual Frack, and several industrialists with strong links to the mining industry.

'Frack should be watched anyway,' I say, trying to narrow the field. 'He's also a suspect.' There's no way we can guard all ten of these silkers.

'Agreed,' says Mardon. 'These Silkertons also get my vote.'

'We should definitely watch the two who replaced Ritcott and Hemings,' says Penney.

Lizzy nods. 'They do seem to share the same political views. It makes sense that they might be similar targets.'

'That's it, then. We don't have enough agents to surveil more than these three. Josiah and I must remain free to investigate.' I bring our deliberations to an abrupt halt. 'Right. Who's going to watch Samual Frack?'

'I'll take Frack,' says Mardon. 'It makes sense for the girls to watch the MPs they've been researching. And with my recently acquired knowledge of the industry, I might easily infiltrate Frack's mining business.'

Penney and Lizzy nod their approval.

'It's agreed, then,' I conclude. 'There's a ramshackle inn in Stonhaven near Wheal Berta called The Duke. You'll find Ebadiah lodging there. I'm sure he'll help you make connections in the mining community. Keep an eye on the boy and the innkeeper, a hunchback named Barronbrook, also a suspect. Frack has a mine a mile or so further south.'

Mardon wastes no time, returning to 96 Bunson Street to pack a bag before setting off for Stonhaven in his Double Heart. Josiah and I watch the clockwork car rumble into the distance until its polished curves are swamped by the city traffic, and I'm pleased someone will be watching over Ebadiah.

Penney and Lizzy share a carriage bound for Parliament House in Old Camdon, leaving Josiah and I to mull over the case.

'I can't help but feel we're missing something,' I mutter.

'We're presuming this is all about mining,' says Josiah. 'But what if it's that woman from The Gunner?'

I do believe he's right. 'Good old Joe. How would you feel about a spot of luncheon?'

12

The Night Ghoul

*In which Banyard and Mingle take luncheon at The Gunner
and a leak becomes apparent*

The Gunner is bustling with customers when we arrive,
although we're fortunate enough to find an unoccupied
inglenook warmed by a meagre fire.

'Are you sure about this?' I ask Joe.

'She's held her tongue, hasn't she? Let's do it.'

We sit and watch through a smoky haze. Patty Primshaw is
a marvel to behold, juggling a multitude of jobs. Judging by the
appetising aromas wafting out from the kitchen, she's cooking
several options from the menu and, while a small crowd cluster
around waiting for their drinks, she splits her time admirably
between the stove and the bar.

On her third visit out to serve she spies us and soon heads
over to our nook. 'Yes, gentlemen? What's your pleasure?'

I smile at her. 'Two pints of Ruby's and bread and stew for
three, please.'

'But there're only two of you,' she points out.

'I'm *really* hungry,' says Josiah.

'Very well.' Patty taps off our ale and delivers it, slopping a
little froth from a tankard onto the tabletop. 'The stew will be a

few minutes.'

Joe leans closer. 'Listen, we can help you get away from here, but we need to talk.'

She draws away as though fearing a trap but, after a moment, takes a cloth from her belt and returns to mop up the spillage. 'Are you serious? You could get me in a heap of trouble, talkin' like that.'

'We're serious, all right,' says Josiah.

'We help people like you, Miss Primshaw. How does a wardrobe of silks, silker papers and a silker position in Rochington sound?'

'This some kind of jibe?' she asks. "Cause it ain't funny.'

'No jibe,' Josiah whispers. 'Can you keep a secret?'

'As well as any other.' She narrows her eyes sceptically.

'Swear you'll tell no one,' demands Joe.

'Very well. I swear.' She makes the sacred sign.

'My scars tell my story,' says Josiah.

'It's true,' I add. 'The scars on his back remain evident.'

She looks at us in turn. 'I have to get back to work but if you're on the level, meet me out back in five minutes.'

It's more like ten minutes later when she appears, watching us dubiously as she steps out from the rear door of the tavern into the alley, which is grimy and overshadowed by the surrounding buildings.

'It's not a trick, Miss Primshaw. You're safe with us,' I whisper, checking about to see that we are alone and not being watched. 'Indeed, we're risking much by approaching you at all, yet if we didn't, how could we help you?'

'Why would you help someone like me anyway?' she asks. 'You're silkers.'

'Yes,' I nod.

'And no,' says Josiah. 'Step closer and take a look.' He slips off his coat and lifts his shirt to reveal the ridged scars made from lashings he took as a threader.

Reaching out, she runs a hand over them as though to be certain they're real. 'You *are* serious.'

I pass her my card. 'Come to the office and ask for me. The first thing we must do is to take imographs and have your new documents drawn up.'

Slack-jawed, she takes the card and slips it into her apron pocket. 'I shall come at the very next chance.'

'Perfect,' I say.

With a nod, she re-enters the tavern.

Back inside, we're left alone while Patty serves other customers. A frown pre-empts Josiah's next words. 'Mr Banyard, I'm grateful that Willow–'

'*Zadie Crawford.* Get used to the name.'

'I'm grateful that Zadie is finally in Camdon. I'd like to do something to show my appreciation.'

'Like what?'

'I thought that perhaps I might cook us all a special meal. We could invite,' he pauses to be sure he has it right, 'Zadie Crawford – make it a party to welcome her to Camdon. With your mother, the widow, Mardon, Ebadiah – and we should invite Lizzy and Penney, too – there would be quite a crowd.'

'Mardon and Ebadiah may prove hard to reach but, other than that, I think it's a wonderful idea. One question. Can you actually cook?'

'Nothing to it.'

'Very well. We can do it tomorrow evening if we get the invites out today.'

He seems pleased and the lines on his forehead dispel as Patty delivers our food and drinks on a tray.

'Is Mistress Kenwigs here?' I ask. 'We have some further questions for her about the case we're investigating.'

'She's resting. Should be down soon, though,' says Patty. 'I'll tell her you're waiting.'

Josiah pushes one of his bowls of stew back across the table towards her. 'Do you know, I've quite lost my appetite. Please take this away.'

'Certainly, sir.' Patty takes the bowl and leaves.

We eat our stew and sup Ruby's from tankards while we wait

for Kenwigs to make an appearance. When she arrives, we watch her berate Patty, gesticulating aggressively, before the girl has a chance to inform her of our request. Kenwigs then waddles directly over to our nook with a look of contempt on her haggard, white-powdered face.

'Gentlemen.'

'Madam, thank you for attending our invitation,' I begin. 'Won't you join us for a moment?' We shuffle up to make room and begrudgingly she perches at the end of the bench. This near, we can see every detail of her bloodshot and bleary eyes, smell the powder and her sickly sweet perfume.

'I shall humour you, but be assured, I've told you everything there is to tell about Uriah Mumford, may he rest in peace.'

'You've heard, then.'

'That he's dead? Yes.'

'I'm afraid he's not the only one.' I watch her closely to gauge her reaction. 'There are a number of others who also frequented your tavern shortly before their demise.'

Her face contorts into a shocked, affronted expression, leaving me none the wiser. 'I do hope you are not insinuating—'

'I'm insinuating nothing, madam, but you cannot deny it's quite a coincidence.'

'Coincidence is what it is, sirs! An unlucky happenstance and nothing more!' She stands, the white lead unable to conceal a reddening of her cheeks. 'I've never been so insulted! I'll ask you to leave this instant and not return. You are hereby banned from these premises!'

'But it's a public house,' argues Josiah, in over his head.

'Madam, what was your relationship with the mine owner John Lancett? Did you know the industrialist Davey Brindle well?'

Eyes bulging, she shouts. 'Get out, you imbeciles! Before I call the Drakers!'

I deposit coins on the table, payment for the food and ale. 'Thank you, madam. You've been most helpful.' I rise, grab my hat to flourish it in a gesture of farewell, and we head for the door as she walks away.

'Good riddance, you old hag,' mutters Joe.

Kenwigs wheels about. 'I heard that, you cretinous oaf!'

He turns back to her as I grab his arm to pull him towards the threshold. He shouts, 'You were meant to hear it, trout!'

A pewter tankard sails by Josiah's ear and we make a dash for the door amid a hail of similar missiles, exiting to the sounds of smashing crockery.

This evening I write to my forger Ranskin, in Holloway, to order the necessary documents for Patty Primshaw's silker citizenship and new position, leaving the sealed letter on the hall stand where Mother will see it and post it in the morning. Ranskin is a secretive man I've rarely met, such is his cautious nature and secluded habit. He lives in a rundown shack not far from the Sallow Grove and, to those around him, presents the façade of a humble farmhand, though it's all a cover for his primary income, which is his business in forging documents of any requirement for a small and trusted clientele. For all his modest appearance, I suspect he has pots of gold hidden beneath his floorboards and he shall one day vanish, as though in a puff of smoke.

I find a folded copy of today's *Evening Herald* on one of the Grand Wexfords by the fireplace in the green room and pick it up to read. 'I think we might stay clear of The Gunner for a while...' I say absently.

'Probably wise.'

'Huh. The papers have at last cottoned on. The case has made the front page.'

Josiah appears lost in his latest penny dreadful.

I continue anyway. 'Bretling's twitch must be increasing by the minute. In the absence of any real information, they're running with *Night Ghoul Strikes Old Camdon.*'

'Very snappy, I'm sure.' Josiah turns a page.

'I suppose we'll not see these Silkertons naming him the Seraph.'

'Not a chance. Nor should they. He's no kind of angel.'

'Have you delivered all the invitations?' I ask.

'Yes. Though it's a shame Mardon can't make it. I'm just going out to visit Zadie,' says Josiah, rising from his chair.

'Not tonight,' I say. His face falls. He sits down. 'You must take it slowly. Allow her to become part of the scenery before you announce your undying love for each other to the world.'

'But–'

'But nothing.' I show Josiah the newspaper.

'I'd like to see Bretling's face,' he says. 'Wait a minute. What does it say?'

I read the report, blow by blow and realise it's not entirely uninformed. 'I thought Bretling put a gag order on the press.'

'He did,' says Josiah.

'Well, it's not working.' I read about the remains found at the Sallow Grove.

> Seven bodies discovered in shallow graves ...
> various states of decay, some now only bare bones,
> others still with rotting flesh adhering ... coroner
> states the victims were each killed a month apart.

I wonder how the information reached a reporter. Thankfully, details of the pierced eye orbits are not there. 'Oh dear. Lord Draker will not be happy about this.' My mock concern turns real. 'Wait a minute. *We* didn't leak this to the press, which means a Draker did. One of his sergeants, probably, or one of the officers present at the scene.' I recall the Draker guards stationed at the entrance to the grove, the sergeants, the diggers, the imographer – any one of them could have blabbed. In fact, the only people I'm sure would not talk to the papers are Myrah, Bretling and the Mysteries Solved team.

Josiah's not far behind me. His face creases with agitation. 'But Bretling will blame us! Hang on! What if Jinkers did it?'

'Either way, we're done for!'

Jinkers is a while in answering his door. I knock first and then

Josiah shoulders me aside to hammer so hard that the entire panel shakes. A pale face appears in a front window, peering out at us in fear. He waves to let us know he's coming and soon opens the door.

'What is it?' he asks, the whites of his eyes large. 'You nearly broke my door down. I thought I was under attack!'

'We might all be under attack sooner than you think,' I say. 'May we come in?'

'Of course.' Jinkers steps aside. We slip by and he closes the door. Gathering in his front room, I draw the curtains closed and he brings in another lamp. 'Now what's all this about?'

'*Night Ghoul Strikes Old Camdon.* Ring any bells?' asks Josiah, thwacking the newspaper onto the table before him.

'This evening's paper. Yes. Yes, I read the story.'

'Was it you?' Josiah glares.

'What do you mean?'

'Did you go to the press?' I ask.

'No!' says Jinkers, looking surprised by the allegation. 'Of course not. I'm working for you – sworn to secrecy – as you well know.' He taps his nose before gesturing towards the newspaper. 'Why would I go to the press? Do you think I'm short of money?'

'He's right,' I say. Jinkers has enough inheritance to see him to a ripe old age. 'He has no need to sell stories.'

'Well, someone has,' says Josiah.

'You haven't mentioned this to anyone?'

'No one. I swear.' Jinkers makes the godly sign.

Believing it was not his doing, we bid him goodnight and leave.

The Good News
None of us has leaked anything to the press.

The Not So Good News
Lord Draker doesn't know that.

No sooner have we returned home than Lord Draker is

hammering on our door, accompanied by a pair of officers, and a similar conversation ensues, except this time *we* are the suspects. Bretling twitches his way through the berating. We do all we can to assure him we had nothing to do with the story but it does little to abate his mood, which is foul to say the least. He leaves us shaken by his visit, with the threat of gaol, should it be proven that we have talked. I watch him from our doorstep in disbelief as he boards a Draker carriage and rattles away down the road, and wonder if we've been set up. It begins to snow again: large soft flakes, swirling in the cold blue glow of the iron watch-lamps. Retreating, I close the door.

I can't help feeling that this case is getting to me, that I might also develop a nervous twitch. Hoping for better news, I climb the stairs to seek the counsel of Magwitch and, placing the gawper skull against my brow, call to him. There's a sudden impact that throws me backwards and I drop the skull, reeling from an explosive flash and fusion of minds. I glimpse the burning eyes of a gawper, see his silhouette in my mind's eye, towering over me. Skallagrim. It can be no other. My head pounding from the unwelcome exchange, my temples sweating blood, I return the skull to its box and slide it back under my bed, not daring to try again.

Thursday, 11th Elventide

The morning begins with a ride down Bunson Street through a gentle yet seemingly endless fall of snow, our horses' hooves cleaving a layer that's in places two feet deep on the road, though increasingly trampled by traffic. Josiah and I arrive at Mysteries Solved to find a letter from Bretling that has been shoved under the front door, demanding our immediate attendance at headquarters. With a growing sense of doom, we leave Lizzy sorting her notes at the reception desk and ride out across Rook's Bridge. The snowfall has caused havoc with the traffic once more and we're forced to skirt a path around a steam truck that's stuck on ice, wheels spinning, a cart that's somehow managed to mount the pavement and turn onto its side, and a clockwork car that's crashed into a shop front. The horses, however, manage well enough and we're soon trotting west, edging the Tynne and then crossing Tower Bridge and on into Tower End where the road climbs steeply.

Bretling Draker spies us as we enter the City Draker Headquarters and waves us through. We ignore the desk sergeant who rises to question us and yet is robbed of the chance.

'This way, Banyard,' says Bretling, ignoring Josiah. 'We're in the morgue. The coroner's found something. Did you see this morning's papers? The *Herald*'s started a landslide.'

'We've not seen them yet. More of the same, I presume.'

'Along the same lines, yes. When I find who's responsible, they'll pay dearly.'

'I'm sure,' I say.

'It's the talk of Camdon,' says Bretling, striding ahead. 'Very unhelpful.' He pauses to take newspapers from a section officer's desk and thrusts them into my hands. 'Here. See for yourself.'

A cursory glance tells me our case has made every single front page. The *Camdon Herald* has gone for a similar headline to the *Evening Herald*, unsurprisingly, as they are run by the same silkers:

HUNT FOR THE NIGHT GHOUL

The *Jostler* has run with 'The Holloway Seven', and the *Tynne Side*, 'Night Ghoul: A Stalker of Gentlemen'.

Hoping we're not in for further accusations about the leak, we follow him through corridors to the morgue. The detective sergeants are already gathered, muttering among themselves around a disarticulated skeleton that's arranged in anatomical order on an old wooden gurney, at the head of which stands Myrah. Her hair is neatly bound up today, her facial features enhanced with make-up, an application unusual for her. She watches us enter with a half-smile that she abandons as though our presence is suddenly displeasing in some way. I'm left briefly confused until I realise she must have been hoping to see Mardon. Are her enhancements for his benefit? One can only assume.

'Coroner, I believe you've found something of interest,' says Bretling. 'This is the unnamed victim, is it not? By your reckoning, the first to be buried in the grove.'

Myrah nods. 'Yes, sir, as far as we can tell. I've boiled and cleaned the bones to make a thorough examination. What I've found may be significant.' She points to a faint vertical line on the right cheekbone of the skull before her on the gurney. 'At some point during the earlier part of his life, this man was injured. He suffered a downward cut to his cheek, a wound deep enough to score the bone. It healed long before he died, though I would have thought he'd have borne an obvious scar from that time on.'

'Very good, Dr Orkney. Is that everything?'

'Yes, sir.'

'Well, there you have it, gentlemen. Take a good look at that mark. It will assist you in finding this man a name. Now move yourselves!' Bretling strides from the room.

The sergeants hurry away as we, too, turn to leave, but Myrah takes Josiah's arm and thrusts an envelope into his hand. 'Please give this to Mardon.'

'What is it?' asks Josiah, accepting the letter.

'A personal note, from me,' explains Myrah, blushing.

'I'll take that,' I say, snatching it from Josiah's grasp and giving him a warning glare. 'I shall see this safely into my cousin's hands, coroner, although he is presently away on investigative business.' I pocket the note.

'Oh,' she says, sounding disappointed. 'He didn't tell me.'

'No, he wouldn't have. There wasn't time. Please accept my apology in his stead.'

As we leave the building, Josiah mutters in an amused tone, 'Well, well, Myrah and Mardon. At least we now know why we've barely seen him of late.'

'I'm cautioning you to leave it alone,' I say. 'You are not to interfere. Do you understand?'

'All right, all right.' He throws his hands up in mock defence. 'I get it.'

'I happen to think they'd make a great couple.'

'Hmm...' says Joe, smiling animatedly. 'They could wed and have little scientists.'

We return through the snowbound streets to Crowlands, where we take solace in cups of black bean soup at The Dog, amid a low rumble of gossiping voices. Among them we're able to discern a few lines on a topic of interest.

'Seven bodies in shallow graves, I heard,' says a portly threader, perched on a stool near the bar.

A slight man wearing a leather cap sitting to his left replies, 'I 'eard the same. Down Holloway, 'twas. A place the' call the Sallow Grove.'

'It's the Night Ghoul. They're saying he steals silkers from their beds on the stroke of midnight, cuts their throats and spirits them away before they've even bled out.'

'Nah. It's a soldier gone mad. That's what it is. All this talk of war's enough to drive us all barmy. It's a soldier who's terrified of going to war and has lost his mind. That, or perhaps it's a spy...' The thin fellow continues his speculations.

I'm mulling over the possibilities of the case involving an enemy spy, when a man in a long travelling cloak approaches our table, his face shadowed by a capacious hood.

'May I sit a while?' he asks, his voice deep. I realise I've heard it before, some months ago, soon after the Landsdale business. He found us in this very tavern, hoping we'd join the rebels.

'What business do you have with us, stranger?' asks Josiah, in a manner neither welcoming nor dismissive.

'The business of justice for Billy Landsdale,' he says, taking a stool. 'The business of justice for threaders everywhere.'

An excerpt taken from the gawper file,
as written by Michael Banyard.

It is common knowledge that many do not believe in the existence of gawpers. I do, of course, for I have now seen them on various occasions and so know them to be real. The first of these happened when I was but eight years old, when I met a gawper not far from our house on Bunson Street. I sweated blood on that occasion and have done so during every encounter since. It's inconvenient, to say the least, although it does serve as a warning that they are nearby.

An adult gawper is notably taller than a man. You will know one on sight. A ragged form will loom out of the mist or the darkness of night, its eyes of white flame will fix upon you with the 'gawper's gaze', a stare that you will feel penetrating deep into your soul. They have long been associated with doom, and surely have put an end to many, though it is my belief that they examine the minds of those they meet. If those minds are found wanting, a gawper can turn judge, jury and executioner in the space of a single breath.

They are, quite frankly, terrifying!

13

A Dinner to Forget

*In which Banyard considers a career in politics
and Mingle cooks up a storm*

The stranger takes a swig from his tankard and sets it on the barrel table. 'You may not know me, but I know all too well who you are.'

Irritated, I try to move him on. 'We've spoken before, sir. You're with the Landsdale Rebels. Our answer remains the same. We're not interested. Now, kindly leave us in peace.'

'I would, sir, though your actions lack the conviction of your words. Let me be clear. We know who you are. We know all about you and we know that we share the same leanings.'

'I agree in part, though that sounded a little like a threat, sir.' I lean forward to peer into the hood, trying to discern a face, glimpse a short beard and the hint of a wry smile.

'More an encouragement, I'd say.' He takes another sip of ale.

'To what end?' asks Josiah. 'To join you?'

'You would blackmail us into helping your cause?' I ask.

'Not at all. We share the same cause, do we not?' he says. 'There's no quarrel between us.'

I finish my black soup. 'Do what you will. We're not

interested.' Gathering our long coats and hats, we rise to leave.

At the door I glance back to see the man make a slow wave in our direction and sense he's laughing beneath the cowl. 'Really, the nerve…'

'Perhaps we *should* join them,' says Josiah, throwing on his coat. 'It sounds like they've enough to rat us out.'

'And lose all control of the successful operation we run? No. Where would it end? I'll not be forced into anything by these brigands. You know I'm against violence of any sort,' I add with a pang of guilt. It's a half-truth. There have been situations that have drawn me into violence of a kind, though I'm not proud of it. 'If they're truly onside with the threaders' cause, they'll let us get on with it.'

'But maybe we could help them. I doubt they have any silkers on board.'

'What do you mean?'

'We could guide them. Who knows? Perhaps they might even become part of our operation. You could educate them.'

'They're certainly in need of an education.' I button my coat, turn up the collar and don my tricorn. 'And they're not the only ones.'

'What?'

'They're not the only ones who need educating. Perhaps I've been looking at this from the wrong angle all along.'

'You've lost me.'

'I mean, perhaps I should be educating those who are already in power – the government – royalty, even.'

'You, an MP?'

'It's not so unthinkable, surely?'

'And who would run Mysteries Solved while you're away yacking with the toffs?'

'You.'

'Nah.'

'I'm serious, enough to give it some thought, at least.'

We cross the road and walk back to the office, trudging behind a company of infantry redcoats.

In the case room I find a few minutes to sit alone, reflecting. I drop my father's old tricorn onto the skull at the corner of my desk, for I feel a need to speak with him. He's not here, of course, not in any guise: the skull belongs to an unknown man. But my father's in my head. The hat was his and it comforts me to think I may know how he might answer the questions he can never hear.

'What would you have done?' I ask the hat.

Oh, you know me, Micky. I'm a pacifist at heart...

'But sometimes that feels like cowardice.'

You can't follow your convictions and be a coward. I believe that would be an oxymoron.

'But part of me wants to fight. Sometimes I wonder if the Seraph is on to something. This land is so very cruel. How can any of us stand idly by?' The simple truth escapes my lips with a passion that takes me by surprise. Whether or not it surprises the hat, I can't say.

And you will fight, my boy. You will. We all fight in our own way, do we not?

The hat's right. The hat's always right.

Within the hour I visit Parliament House to enlist as a *speculate*, which is a speculative burgess or representative of a Camdon City district. As a citizen of Crowlands, it follows that this would be the district I would represent in parliament, should I ever be successfully appointed. The registrar promptly provides me with a schedule of this month's parliamentary meetings that I'm invited to join, before waving me aside.

Josiah leaves the office early to prepare for tonight's dinner party. I sit alone in the case room and stare at the pinboard with all its images and notes, baffled by the case. Tavern words haunt me.

...he steals silkers from their beds on the stroke of midnight, cuts their throats and spirits them away...

...a soldier gone mad...

...or perhaps it's a spy...

If it does prove to be a spy, I'm going to hate myself for not taking the notion seriously. The realisation leaves me with but one conclusion: I must give the theory due consideration now to correct any oversight. So, how might a spy be driven to kill and dispose of a number of influential figures, including two politicians? And how or why might the mining industry be involved? I tumble the problem around in my thoughts, examining it from every angle. Perhaps the perpetrator is a sleeper hiding in plain sight: an MP moving in the circles of industry, someone who's been constant in their situation for years, just biding their time. But what secrets might they be stealing for our foreign enemies? What other goals may they be aiming for by infiltrating our systems of power? Truly, the possibilities are endless, and I'm left feeling more bewildered than before.

Hoping to regain some semblance of an ordered mind, I start a new list on the board, this one comprising slips of paper bearing possible motives for the murders, each of which I pin in place: financial gain, revenge, a deranged mind, hatred, blackmail, obsession. Beneath a new heading to the side that reads *Spy*, I pin more slips: *government secrets, foreign assassin, infiltration, finance, industry – coal and iron*. Every war machine needs its fair share of iron, of course, and enough coal to smelt it as needed. Guns, ships, armour, ammunition – they all need these key elements. Do our enemies seek to somehow cease our production and so subvert Londaland's industry? My final slip of paper reads *War Machine*.

At the end of the exercise I'm really none the wiser, though a single underlying motive looms in my mind: these killings might have been carried out simply to silence those who had learned too much. If it is a spy, it's a sloppy one – who makes plenty of mistakes which, by the very nature of the business, must be covered up and swept promptly beneath the proverbial rug. But what, then, of the regularity of the abductions? And why the coal? Was that merely a personal touch, meant to be a secret never revealed? Or perhaps meant to mislead? There was no mention of the coal or the orbital wounds in the papers. At least that's something that may help.

The dinner party begins with the arrival of Penney and Lizzy. Mother's in the kitchen fretting over the mess Josiah's making, and with Widow Blewett dozing in the sitting room, it's down to me to answer the door. The widow stirs as I sweep past and by the time I've welcomed the girls, she's awake and brightly alert. The girls hurry in from the blustery night to warm themselves before the roaring log fire, leaving their elbow-length velvet gloves on and their shawls about their shoulders.

In these social gatherings, small talk does not come easily to me. When your head is bursting with conundrums regarding the murders of seven men, it's hard to find energy for much else. Awkward in their presence, I'm relieved when the widow engages them with compliments on their gowns and Mother appears, dusting her floured hands on her apron.

'I thought Josiah was cooking tonight,' I say, raising an eyebrow as an ominous smell issues from the hallway leading to the kitchen.

'So did I,' she says. 'Miss Fairweather, Miss Danton, how good to see you.' She joins the conversation, which naturally enough is about the local carriages and the state of the snowbound roads, and I'm left standing to one side, feeling like a spare peg, though content to observe.

When Zadie Crawford arrives – or Willow Buxton, if you prefer – we greet her as the guest of honour and she plays her part well, curtsying. I gather everyone to make a formal introduction.

'Good friends, it's my pleasure to introduce to you a dear associate from across the sea, Miss Zadie Crawford. Miss Crawford is a very close friend to my departed uncle's surviving wife, who has chosen to remain in Mautusetts. In short, she's like a sister to me. I trust you will make her welcome and show her some good old Londaland hospitality while she settles in.'

'Oh, Michael, I'm so very grateful. It *is* generous of you boys to throw a party,' she says with her practised Amorphian drawl.

'Such a delight.' Behind the guise of a wealthy lady, I glimpse Willow's mischievousness, a glint in her eye that tells me she's revelling in her new role. 'I simply can't wait to get to know you all!'

Josiah leaves the stove to find us and he's a mess: flour and blood spattered all over the rolled-up sleeves of his shirt, his hands and bare forearms. His face is soot-stained and smeared with a black, burned substance.

'What *have* you been doing in there?' I ask.

'Cooking,' he says, through a forced smile. He lowers his voice. 'It's not as easy as you might think.'

We all laugh, but his attempts to make light of his struggle are thinly veiled. Zadie lays a hand on his arm. 'Oh, Josiah, you *are* a hoot!'

'Yes, well. It's good to see you, Zadie,' mutters Josiah. 'I'd best get back to work.' He checks the clock on the mantlepiece. 'Dinner will be served at half past six.'

My pocket watch reads nearly six o'clock, so we've not long to wait. 'Well done, Joe.' I try to encourage him, sure that we're merely off to a ropey start and that the evening is bound to improve. The girls talk and I listen. Notably, Penney makes no attempt to engage and I'm guilty of the same. Lizzy's smiles, on the other hand, knock me for six.

When there's no sign of Josiah half an hour later, I visit the kitchen to see how he's faring. The room's fogged with steam, condensation dripping from the walls. The smell of burning is stronger and a vast pile of pots and pans spills from the sink onto the benches, table and stool. The flagstones of the floor are slippery with spillages.

He spies me through the haze. 'Mr Banyard, can you spare a minute?'

'Would you prefer Mother?'

'I think she's given up on me.'

'Oh dear. Are we far from eating?'

'What's the time?'

'Almost six thirty.'

'No! Is it?'

'Yes.'

'Tell the others it's going to be a while longer.'

We repeat a similar conversation around seven o'clock and several times after that.

Eventually, we sit down to eat at precisely five minutes past ten. It's painful to watch. Josiah brings in six platters of bread, the mass of loaves in various charred states. 'They're not perfect,' he confesses. 'But we won't go hungry and there's plenty of butter.' He leaves. I take a loaf and give it a squeeze before knocking it against the tabletop. 'Like a rock.' I try to slice it but the bread knife makes little impact. 'I'm not convinced this is edible.'

He soon returns with a large tureen, which he presents in a grandiose fashion, lifting the lid to reveal a disappointingly small volume of blackened stew.

'You made stew?' I ask, surprised by both his menu choice and the time it's taken to prepare such a simple dish.

'Aurochs stew. It's a little overdone, I'm afraid.' He shrugs.

'It's burned.' I frown. 'How did you manage to burn stew?'

'It wasn't easy. Shall we eat?' He ladles out minuscule portions into bowls and passes them out, serving the ladies first. 'You won't need much. It's very rich.'

I sniff at my stew, which smells like cinders, and taste it, marvelling at the way he's managed to suffuse the dish so thoroughly with the flavour of what has clearly charred at the bottom of the pot. 'Hmm. Very good,' I lie, forcing a smile as the girls tentatively lift spoonfuls to their lips. Lizzy grimaces and shivers before ever sampling it.

Penney, as you might expect, eats some and smiles politely. 'Thank you for cooking, Josiah.'

'I'm sorry it's so late,' says poor old Joe.

'It doesn't matter,' I tell him, testing another of the half-cremated loaves.

Zadie takes a mouthful of stew and spits it back into the bowl, peering around the table apologetically. She starts to giggle. 'Josiah, you really are a terrible cook!'

I think they may see through her guise, but then Lizzy laughs next as Josiah nods acceptingly. 'I'm good at burning things,' he says with a shrug. Then Penney's laughing, and Mother too. Even Josiah laughs and I join them, happy as long as he's laughing along. I can only suppose that Zadie's Amorphian cover story is working in her favour.

'There's cake in the pantry,' says Mother, rising from her chair. 'I'll fetch it. We have cheese and biscuits, too. Come on, Josiah. You can help carry it. And later you can clean the kitchen from top to bottom.'

'Yes, Mrs Banyard.'

The laughter settles as they leave, though soon there's a commotion coming from the kitchen end of the house. Mother screams. Josiah shouts. The noise continues beneath a series of bangs and other noises. Around the table we look quizzically at each other before a burning smell pre-empts a stream of smoke that snakes into the room.

Baker begins to bay.

'Fire!' cries Mother, making a brief yet dramatic appearance in the doorway.

There's much running and shouting. In the kitchen, Josiah desperately tries to quench the flames that bellow from the oven with bowls of dishwater. The firebox in the range has grown so hot that a hole is melting in the top of the cast-iron flue, the metal glowing a vivid orange, the air being sucked in with a roar.

Lizzy runs out into the street to find a watchman, who raises the city fire brigade, who invade our house with hoses, soak the kitchen, climb long ladders and pump water down the chimney pots to be sure nothing else has caught alight in the old, tinder-dry house. With the flames out and the property safe once more, they clear away their equipment and leave.

Standing in the doorway watching them go, Mother tugs Joe's ear. 'Josiah Mingle, you shall *never* set foot in my kitchen again!'

He pulls himself free and rubs at his ear. 'Suits me.'

We gather again, though this time soot-stained, in disarray and more hungry.

'How about a glass of wine?' I collect the bottle from the side table, uncork it and circle, filling glasses. We're subdued when Mother and Josiah bring platters of cake, cheese, biscuits and cold meats into the dining room. I pour myself a goblet and retake my place at the table, standing to make a toast. 'To our new arrival – Miss Zadie Crawford.' I raise my glass with the others.

'And to…' For a moment I think Zadie will name him Silus Garroway and cause a whole heap of trouble. '… Josiah Mingle.' She beams. 'Chef extraordinaire!' We laugh and drink. Zadie continues. 'And to the distinguished Michael, to whom I owe a debt of gratitude.'

Lizzy and Penney look a little puzzled, not knowing the entirety of the help I have provided, but it passes without comment.

I'll say this much, Zadie's a deal sharper than Joe. Although uneducated in the official sense, she's learned quickly from her handlers in Rochington, mastering a believable countenance and an eloquent vocabulary. She's altogether impressive and, right this minute, casting Josiah in deep shadow – something that's not lost on him. I watch him as the night progresses, joking, laughing and cheering with the others, but there's also a sadness hiding in his eyes, one that's likely apparent only to those closest to him.

At the end of the party, when our three guests have left and the kitchen's restored to order – scorch marks excepting – Josiah and I take a glass of port in the green room, where Baker sprawls on a rug before the dying embers of the fire.

'Well, it wasn't too bad after all,' I say in a consolatory tone.

Josiah swigs port. 'It was *awful*. I'd be surprised if she doesn't find a rich silker to marry now.'

'She loves you, doesn't she?'

'She did. But why would she after *that*? I've made a complete fool of myself!'

'Perhaps it's for the best.'

'What do you mean?' He sounds genuinely upset.

'This will be a good test. If she's right for you, tonight won't matter. Won't matter a bit.'

'Do you think?'

'I know.'

'I was going to propose.'

'Propose what?'

'You know...'

'Oh! *Really?* It's a bit soon, isn't it? You know the plan. She needs to be seen around town, become part–'

'Part of the scenery. I know. But I want to marry her anyway. You see her as well as I. She's resplendent!' That's a big word for Joe! 'Magnificent.' Another. 'Why on Earthoria would she want to stay with an idiot like me?'

'I'm glad you didn't propose. It would have been a mistake. If she loves you, you have no need to worry. If she doesn't, you're better off without her.'

He doesn't get it but I don't push. Rather, I pour us both another nightcap and take solace in the fact that the house hasn't burned to the ground.

After my encounter with Skallagrim, it's with trepidation that I once more lift the gawper skull. My mind gate opens. Magwitch is quick to respond to my call. The rush of minds hits me hard and fast, leaving me reeling. On my bedside cabinet, a solitary candle flickers, casting the room in an eerie light as blood instantly beads on my temples and brow.

Skallagrim is causing mayhem, he thinks. *There is much disruption on the fourth plane.*

What of the Sallow Grove? I ask. *Are you still able to keep watch?*

Magwitch and Deadlock are watching, though there are moments of blindness that come and go.

Have you seen anyone visit the grove?

The farmer and his son gathered withies there.

Did you shriven them?

Deadlock shrivened them. He found nothing sinister. They are simple folk. Innocent folk. Deadlock let them live.

And half-terrified them to death, I think to myself.

It fits with Bretling's assessment. Did he shriven the entire family?

He did.

So, we can be sure they are not involved in the murders.

They are not involved in any way. Of this, Magwitch is sure.

Very well. An idea strikes me and I wonder why I didn't think of it before. *If I can arrange it, can you or Deadlock shriven each of those we suspect of the killings?*

We could, though this might result in the death of all.

Why?

Because when a Dagomite shrivens humans, a judgement he will make. Many times, the shrivening is enough to finish them. That way may not help, Michael Banyard.

I imagine a chamber full of dead suspects – among them those innocent of murder – and me left none the wiser. There might be no closure of the case, no court ruling, no proof of guilt, and who knows how many unnecessary deaths. Even if the gawpers were to name the murderer, we would lose important information that might have been gleaned. And how would I ever go about setting up such a scenario in the first place? I put the idea aside and wish Magwitch goodnight. Unfortunately, our investigation must continue the hard way.

14

The Safe

In which a drop of blood tells a story

Long days creep by as we hunt the killer. On Sunday the 14th of Elventide, Ebadiah pays a visit to report in. Sitting around my desk in the case room, we listen to his account of the last few days, everything he's learned that may be relevant to the case.

'I made sure to be around The Duke when Barronbrook was serving. Got to know him quite well. He's a good sort. Can't see him murdering toffs miles away in the middle of Camdon. He never leaves Stonhaven, for one thing. Though I asked him who owns The Duke.'

Josiah leans in. 'And?'

'Samual Frack.'

'John Lancett's rival,' I say.

'The very same,' confirms Ebadiah.

'That *is* interesting, though I'm not sure what it means to the case.'

'Perhaps Frack is the killer and Barronbrook is his stooge,' says Josiah.

Ebadiah continues. 'Mardon stayed at The Duke for a couple of nights but he's moved further down the coast now, to stay at a place closer to one of Frack's mines. Frack was pretty keen to employ him as a boss man.'

'Good.' I nod. 'We've learned little but the coroner's boiled the bones of the unnamed man and found a scar on his skull just below the right eye. She's convinced he must have carried a notable mark for some years in life. Ask around in Stonhaven. See if anyone remembers such a man.'

Monday, 15th Elventide

Bretling calls us in for yet another meeting and the sergeants and I report our findings. He's distinctly unimpressed with the general lack of progress, although I doubt any of his sergeants are bothering to investigate anything down in Stonhaven. When I mention the names Barronbrook and Samual Frack, he stares at me blankly, but then chalks them up on the board. It also earns me a scowl from Sergeant Goffings.

'This hunchback Barronbrook is a threader, I presume,' says Bretling.

'He is, sir.'

'And Frack is a mine owner, you say?'

'Correct.'

'Well, you can forget about him. We're not investigating silkers.' Bretling takes a cloth and wipes Frack from the board. 'Like I said, our man's a threader.'

'But, sir, Frack is the arch rival of the third victim, the mine owner John Lancett. Don't you think it's possible—'

'I do not,' says Bretling with a twitch. 'Sergeant Smeaton, get down to Stonhaven and bring in this threader Barronbrook.'

I attempt to intervene. 'But, sir, beyond his hunch, Barronbrook is an ill match for the description Larkin gave.'

'We'll bring him in anyway, just to be sure.'

I shudder at the abuse that I've aligned for Barronbrook, in all likelihood an innocent, hardworking man with an already crippling affliction.

'And what about this Sterling fellow, the one who's made a run for it? Any sign of him?'

Huntly shakes his head. 'We've sent likenesses out to every

Watch Station in the country, sir, along with the information we have on him. We learned from his owner that Sterling had a sister in Loncaster, so I've sent a man up there to investigate — see if he's hiding out there.'

'Very good, sergeant.' Bretling addresses the gathering. 'Gentlemen, we should have taken him by now. You're to double your efforts. If you find any suspect, arrest him. We'll hold each one until the 17th has passed. At least then we'll have an inkling if one of them is guilty. Anything new on our Tobias?' He means the unidentified victim. 'The one with the scarred cheek?'

Looking downcast, Sergeant Huntly runs a hand over his grizzled moustache. 'Nothing concrete yet, sir. We've narrowed it down to three possibles, though. I have men tracing them. All are believed to be out of the country and so may not have been missed. I've collected imographs of each man. They're with the coroner now for comparisons, so we should hear soon.'

Several other sergeants give further details of their enquiries — threatening interrogations, more like — although nothing of real value surfaces.

Inevitably, Bretling turns to the matter of the press. 'The papers are full of stories about the Night Ghoul. Silkers across Camdon are afraid to leave their homes. There's panic on the streets. Chivers Hapgood himself is demanding I stop these silker murders. Needless to say, when I catch the scoundrel who's talking to the press, I'll nail his wagging tongue to my office wall.'

'I wonder, is it not time to warn those we believe may be targeted next?' I say.

Bretling shakes his head. 'Do you know how many that would be? And how exactly might we do it without word getting out? It would only make things worse — cause mass hysteria, chaos.'

I take a folded page from my pocket and present it to Bretling. 'My team have made a list of likely candidates — MPs and prominent silkers in industry. Our best guesses. We narrowed it down to just forty-three. Ten of special interest.'

With a deep sigh he takes the paper. 'I'll think on it, Banyard. Can promise no more.'

I venture another suggestion. 'Sir, perhaps we might use the press to our advantage. The papers must be desperate for real detail on the murders.'

'And how might we do that, precisely?'

I feel the full weight of his scrutinising gaze. 'We could feed the killer information through the papers that would lead him. For example, we might influence him to act in a certain manner and so give himself away.'

'By Lychling, I like the sound of that,' says Bretling. 'Listen up, boys. This young man is using his head. Take note. Now, Banyard, how do you suggest we pursue the notion? You mean to lay a trap...'

I now rather regret suggesting the idea as I haven't thought it through. Think, man! My ideas clarify. 'I mean to bait the killer and be ready when he falls into a pit of his own making. We'd first need to establish the desired reaction. Do we want to anger him, drive him to make a mistake, or perhaps the opposite – we feed his ego, have the papers report that he's baffled all and must surely be a genius? If he believes himself sharper than others, in his arrogance he might also overstep the mark and be caught out.'

'We'll talk more about this, Banyard, you and I. Good work. Very good work.'

There's a sound at the entrance as the door opens and Myrah Orkney walks in to greet Bretling. 'Lord Draker.'

'Ah, coroner. Do you have news?'

'Nothing good,' says Myrah, looking haggard beneath her make-up. 'I've completed the comparisons from Sergeant Huntly. None of the three matches our Tobias. I'm afraid our mystery corpse remains a mystery.'

'That's a blow,' says Bretling, as Huntly shakes his head dejectedly. 'Well, boys, get back out there and catch me this killer before he strikes again.'

The 16th of Elventide passes without event, except to say that we all feel the burden of our charge and a quiet frustration at the lack of progress. I can only imagine that Barronbrook is in the hands of the Drakers by now, and being grossly misused, as is their way. Feeling a weariness over the whole thing, it's all I can do to draft a short note pleading my belief in the hunchback's innocence, and have one of Ebadiah's friends, a reliable street boy named Hicks, deliver it.

Wednesday, 17th Elventide

I've no idea what Bretling is doing with our list of potential victims, but Penney, Lizzy, Zadie, Josiah and I keep watch over a number of them, making an early start around seven in the morning. We even give Jinkers, Zadie and Widow Blewett fellows to observe. It's dark, of course, and we're hounded by a snowstorm, but we gather at Mysteries Solved to confirm our plans. There's a letter waiting for me from Ranskin, which I quickly open. Inside are Patty Primshaw's counterfeit identification papers, which I slide into a drawer of my desk before the girls can raise questions.

We set out soon after, each taking a list of endangered silkers. Penney and Lizzy follow half a dozen politicians, spending two hours on each one before moving on to the next, and taking notes of their movements so that, in the event of a disappearance or an attempted abduction, we might have an inkling about what has happened and where. To keep things simple for them, I brief the widow, Zadie and Jinkers to follow only one mark each. It feels like we're clutching at straws; in fact, I'm sure we are, but what else can we do? Today, it seems, someone will go missing and we're almost certainly powerless to stop it from happening.

Josiah and I follow a similar pattern to the girls, trudging through the snowy streets, wrapped in our winter long coats and scarves to watch wealthy silkers of industry, and meet up after each shift to exchange notes. Halfway through the afternoon, I'm alone and cold, and tired of watching people go about their everyday business when Josiah startles me, rushing around an Old Camdon street corner where I'm busy loitering and pretending to read a copy of the *Camdon Herald*. He slips and slides to a stop.

'Mr Banyard, there you are,' he blurts, his cheeks flushed, his scarf tails whipping in the wind. 'You must come at once. I've found something.' With that, he turns and hurries back the way he came. I abandon my charge – a silker entrepreneur named Manning, who deals mostly in the tin and iron trade – and follow. In any case, Manning looks set to be in his Tea House meeting with several colleagues for a good while yet, and he is a *very* slow mover, being rather corpulent.

Josiah runs down Market Street talking over his shoulder. 'I was trying to locate Mr Hanover and thought I'd start at his home.' He takes a left, soon stopping outside the entrance of one of the old townhouses that's managed to survive the encroachment of shops and businesses in Old Camdon. 'The residence of Mr Hanover,' he says, gesturing towards the door, which stands ajar. 'He was next on my list but I found it open. Had a quick look inside. No one home. Very suspicious.'

'I'll say.' I give the door a gentle shove and it creaks wide open to reveal a dim corridor within. 'Mr Hanover... Remind me...'

'He's Grand Master of the Mining Guild. The girls put him on the list because he's a prominent figure in the industry.'

'It seems they might have been right to do so.' There's a confusion of marks in the flattened snow leading to the door, but few distinguishable boot or shoe prints. In fact, the only ones I can discern look like they've come from Joe's new boots. I glance up and down the street and, seeing nothing out of place, enter Hanover's house. 'Hello!' I listen to the inner silence. 'Mr Hanover?' The hallway is cold, a chilled breeze flowing in from outside. 'What else do we know about him?' I ask.

Josiah slides a folded page from his inner coat pocket and consults his notes. 'Not much. Lives alone, has a housekeeper visit to cook and clean once a day. Keeps himself to himself beyond his work with the Guild.'

'There doesn't seem to be anyone here right now. Watch where you tread. There could be evidence to conserve.'

We walk further in. I peer up a bleak and barren staircase, sensing the place is not merely chilled because of the open front door, but that there is a deeper coldness, too: as though an emptiness of spirit. The impression unnerves me. 'Something has happened here,' I murmur, turning to open the nearest door and peering into a sitting room, the front room of the property. The curtains are closed, though they're thin, and traces of light and movement dapple through: people and traffic passing by on the street outside. I enter and stoop to lay a hand over the ashes in the hearth. Cold. Like the rest of the dwelling.

We visit the remaining rooms on the lower floor, four in all, and find each one similarly abandoned.

'Do you think the Seraph has struck again?' asks Josiah across the kitchen, his breath fogging. 'That he's taken Hanover?'

A clattering sound from upstairs startles me and I lead the way back out to the hall and toe my way up the first few stairs, craning to see what lies ahead. Climbing higher, an empty landing and several open doorways come into view. Josiah nods towards the rear of the property.

Reaching the top of the stairs, we turn to investigate the noise, only to find a window with a damaged latch that's open a few inches and clanging in the wind. The window is at the end of the landing and opens onto Hanover's cramped backyard, which is depressingly small. I peer out. There's no ladder or rope. No means of entry or exit to be seen.

'Is that how he entered?' asks Josiah, who, from where he's standing, can't see what I see.

'Perhaps.' I examine the sill but find no marks or scuffs to suggest someone climbed through, and no pry marks at the edge of the frame to indicate a break-in. 'Though I've a mind it is merely a window someone left open and on a catch that has since been broken by this morning's winds.' I close the window to stop the noise, latching it as best I can, before continuing into a bedroom, where a lump of coal greets me from the veneered top of a fine gentleman's cabinet.

'It's him, all right,' says Josiah.

'Check the other rooms. I wish to have a good look in here.' As Josiah leaves the bedroom, I add, 'This could be the very spot the Seraph found Hanover.' I sniff the air and catch a scent, soon locating the source: a shaving lotion in an ornate glass bottle at one end of the cabinet, next to a free-standing mirror. I replace the bottle and turn my attention to the rest of the room. The bed has been slept in and is roughly made. An empty cut-glass goblet sits on the bedside table. This, too, I sniff and detect a trace of brandy. The floor is clean and the room ordered, with only a gentleman's silk dressing gown in disarray, slung casually over the iron railing at the foot of the bed.

Josiah calls from the room next door.

'Mr Banyard. Look at this!'

I hurry back to the landing and on into the neighbouring room, where Josiah stands, his head and shoulders lost inside a wall safe. There's a lighter shade of wall in an oblong around the safe's door, and a painting that presumably covered the safe is upended on the floor. I take in Hanover's study: a writing desk bearing quills, ink pots, two glasses smelling of brandy, and a bottle-green reading lamp; shelves of leatherbound volumes and accounting books; an intricately patterned Morracibian rug on darkly polished floorboards and several seascapes hanging on oak-panelled walls. 'Two glasses. He had a guest.' My gaze falls back to Josiah and the safe. 'Was that open when you found it?'

'Yes,' he says. 'And there are still things inside. Documents and bank notes. Perhaps it was a robbery. But then, why would a thief leave the money?'

'Don't touch anything,' I caution him and he steps away from the safe. 'The Drakers will want to see everything as it was found.'

'Blood!' he points at a solitary drop of blood on the floor. 'Should we fetch them now?'

An excerpt taken from the gawper file,
as written by Reginald Francis Banyard.

Recorded on the 4th Trimoon, in the year 1769.
An account by Thomas Winter, clerk of the Dockside coopers,
Dandies Oaken Kegs.

Thomas: I was working late in the Dockside office when I saw lights flickering beyond the window. It was gone eight o'clock in the evening and already dark, so the lights caught my eye. The weather had been stormy and I thought that some rascals were out there causing trouble, or even stealing barrels from the workshop or the warehouse. You can get in through the upper loading bay from the outside, if you know the pulley system, you see, and a few nights before, a watchman caught a pair of rogues lighting a fire in the yard and—

Reginald: Mr Winter, please keep to the relevant facts. I'm only interested in your encounter with the gawper, or was it gawpers?

Thomas: Yes, of course. Gawpers, sir. Three of them.

Reginald: Very well. Did you go outside to see what the lights were?

Thomas: I did, though by the time I'd found my pistol and opened the door there was no sign of anyone.

Reginald: So, what did you do?

Thomas: I took a lantern and walked around the outside of the warehouse, just to be sure. Found nothing, but when I came back around the side, I saw those lights again.

Reginald: Can you describe them?

Thomas: They were strange, sir, like nothing I'd seen before, like fire lights or candles, though they wavered in and out, and were attached to nought, just floating in the air. It was impossible, what I saw, ghostly. They were there one minute and gone the next. Do you see?

Reginald: I do, indeed.

Thomas: Then, quite sudden-like, the first figure appeared as though from thin air.

Reginald: Can you be any more specific? How exactly did it appear?

Thomas: It's hard to say, sir. It was like a shimmer in the night that grew from one point. Not slowly but in a blink. There came something like a ripple through the air and there it was, gawping at me, and all I could see was those burning white eyes.

Reginald: Where did this gawper appear?

Thomas: Out by the barrel ramps. I can show you if you'd like, sir.

Reginald: Please, Mr Winter, lead the way.

15

Sapphires

In which Mingle tells of his brilliant *idea*

Bretling's response is prompt. Arriving some twenty minutes after receiving my note carried in haste by Hicks, he towers over the crimson droplet with a grimace while Sergeant Goffings lurks at his shoulder. 'What do you think, coroner?'

Myrah kneels to examine the blood stain, which is around half an inch in diameter with a roughly egg-shaped outline. 'It's completely dry. All I can tell you is that, given the temperature of the room, this probably fell to the floor two hours ago or more. Michael, was it dry when you found it?'

'It was,' I say. 'Or, at least, so it appeared.'

Myrah removes her spectacles to polish them on her scarf. 'Then perhaps three hours or more.'

'So small an amount,' says Bretling. 'It could be from a nosebleed or a minor accident. I'm not sure we can read anything macabre into this.'

'Not in the blood alone,' I say, 'but together with the missing man, the open door…'

'Yes, I see your point.' Bretling lights his pipe and smokes. 'If this is a sign of murder, it's a perplexing one. What kind of killing leaves behind a single drop of blood?'

'A very good question,' ventures Josiah.

'A single stab wound to the eye with a narrow dagger, perhaps.'

'You could be right, Banyard,' says Bretling.

'Certainly, if the blade remained in place,' adds Myrah. 'Otherwise I would expect to see a quantity of blood.'

'You say you've touched nothing in the safe?' asks Bretling.

'Nothing, sir,' says Josiah. 'It's exactly as we found it.'

Goffings takes a keen interest in the safe, removing the documents to examine them and then counting the money before announcing, 'A hundred guineas in used notes, sir.'

'Log it,' says Bretling. 'It's evidence.'

'Why would the safe be left open and yet nothing taken?' asks Josiah.

'Something may have been taken,' I point out. 'We've no way of knowing unless we can prove what was in the safe beforehand.'

'With no body as evidence, we can hardly presume he's dead.' Bretling jabs the stem of his pipe at Goffings. 'Sergeant, head over to the Mining Guild Hall and find Mr Hanover. If he's not there, I want to know when he was last seen and by whom – and find out what his usual haunts are and what was in his safe.' Goffings takes several steps towards the door. 'Oh, and sergeant,' says Bretling, 'it goes without saying – not a word to anyone about our findings here.'

Goffings nods determinedly and, narrowing his eyes at Josiah and me, leaves.

While Bretling and Myrah are occupied discussing the safe, Josiah heads for the landing, catching my eye and nodding towards the door.

I follow him out and whisper, 'What is it?'

'There was three hundred guineas in that safe when I counted it,' he states.

'Goffings pocketed two hundred? It's *were*, by the way. Not *was*.'

He nods. I consider informing Bretling of this development,

but Goffings has left and, when he returns, it will not be with the incriminating bank notes upon his person. 'Do nothing. There's no way to prove him a thief. Not yet, at least. It would be your word against his.'

'As you say.'

While we await Goffings' return, the four of us walk through the entire house again, seeking evidence or signs of a struggle – anything that might tell us what took place – yet finding nothing. We end up back in the study. 'A diary would be useful,' I say, rummaging through the drawers of Hanover's desk. I close them. 'Nothing.'

'Someone at the Guild may know of his appointments,' says Bretling.

'Let's hope so.'

Goffings eventually returns, red-faced and breathless. 'Lord Draker, sir, Hanover has not been to the Guild today.' Bretling's eyebrow twitches at the news as Goffings continues. 'He should have attended a committee meeting late this morning. The chair of the committee tells me Hanover mentioned a collection of sapphires that had recently come into his possession, gems valued at more than five hundred guineas. Said he would expect them to be in the safe, although he mentioned there's a chance Hanover had already taken them to be securely stored at Yorkson's.' Yorkson's is a bank on Quaffer's Row in Old Camdon.

Goffings nods towards Josiah and me. 'As the sapphires' whereabouts are presently unknown, I suggest we search these two before they're allowed to go.'

Bretling looks surprised by the idea. 'You think I've employed a couple of thieves to help with our enquiries?'

Goffings shrugs. 'All I'm saying is we should check, just to be sure. I mean, what do we really know about these outsiders? They ain't Drakers. Never will be.'

Bretling turns to us, a glint of mild amusement in his eyes. 'Gentlemen, my sergeant would like to search you. Do you object?'

'Not at all!' I'm quick to say.

'Go ahead,' says Josiah, looking bored.

We hold our arms out at our sides to make the job easier and, after a good pat-down, yet empty-handed, Goffings narrows his eyes. 'I don't trust either of these two.'

'You don't have to trust them,' says Bretling, refilling his pipe with tobacco. 'You *do* have to work with them.'

We leave, glad to be shot of Goffings. The afternoon has darkened and we're done with spying for the day. Walking back to find our horses tethered two streets away, Josiah starts to limp.

'Are you all right?' I ask.

'It's the new boots. I need to wear them in.' He hobbles on, the affliction increasing. Only when we mount the horses to ride home do the pained lines on his face ease. 'I'll be glad to get these off and have my feet up, warming by a fire.'

'Very well. I think a glass or two of spiced wine is in order; that should ward off this winter chill, don't you think?'

'I do indeed!'

It's not until later that I realise I should have found his lack of objection to Goffings' searches ominous. I'm already installed in a Grand Wexford before a blazing fire in the green room and pouring a goblet of spiced wine, when Josiah staggers in, still in his new riding boots. 'Why on Earthoria are you still wearing those?' I ask.

'Fancy giving me a hand?' He drops into the chair opposite to offer up his left boot. As he does so, the boot rattles softly. I lean in, meaning to take hold of the heel and pull the boot off, but stop and look him in the eyes. 'You have sapphires in your boots, don't you?' It's not so much a question as a statement.

'Do you have a small bag or pouch I could borrow?' he grins.

I take the boot by the heel, pull and watch a cascade of sparkling cut sapphires spill over the rug as his foot slides free. The gems range in colour: blues, violets, yellows and greens.

'Oh, that's much better,' he laughs the words. I feel my face contort into a scowl. 'Now the other one,' he says, swinging his right leg up.

'Do it yourself.' Astounded, I turn away but circle back to lean in close as though listening and knock twice on his skull with a knuckle.

He recoils. 'Ow! What d'ya do that for?'

'Just checking it's not hollow. You've jeopardised our standing with the Drakers. These will be missed! Bretling will have already visited Yorkson's and will know the sapphires were never banked. Who else will they think took them?'

'The Seraph, of course. It's the perfect crime. We've already been searched and they didn't find anything.' His annoying smile returns.

I consider punching him. 'We don't even know if it was the Seraph.'

'I couldn't help it, Mr Banyard. I found the stones and had a brilliant idea.'

'It was a *stupid* idea! When they've figured this out, they'll come looking for the sapphires.' My statement is closely followed by a stout hammering at the front door. 'They're already here! You fool. Hide them! I'll buy us some time. Here.' I take a pouch of marbles that Ebadiah has left on the mantlepiece, empty it out onto the rug and toss the bag to Josiah. 'Where's Baker?'

'I let him out into the back garden.'

I head for the front door but Mother gets there first, and meets me in the hallway.

'Michael, there are Drakers at the door asking to come in.'

'Don't worry, Mother. It's about the case we're investigating. I'll handle it.' I pass by to meet Goffings at the doorstep, who looks rather pleased with himself. Behind him, five hulking officers carrying lanterns await his command.

'Ah, Mr *Barnyard!* Good. We're here to search your property.' He shoves me aside with his considerable weight and pushes his way into the house. His officers follow, tipping their hats as they pass.

'Sergeant Goffings, if I may have a word?' I call, tagging

along behind. 'I have some matters of the case I wish to discuss... Sergeant! Sergeant Goffings! I demand to speak with you this very minute!' My pleas go unanswered as the Drakers storm quickly through the house, turning out everything as they go: drawers, cupboards, shelves. The furniture is upturned and left in disarray. Mother and Widow Blewett stand aghast, yet know better than to intervene. It doesn't take the Drakers long to reach the green room door, where Goffings pauses, turning to me. 'Where's your ape, Mr Mingle? Is he hiding somewhere, or has he finally fled the nest?'

'He's—' I give up as Goffings opens the green room door to reveal Josiah standing with his back to the fireplace, his hands clenched behind him, a tight expression on his face. I have a bad feeling in the pit of my stomach. The Drakers give the room the same treatment, turning over furniture, emptying the corner cabinet, searching everything and everywhere. They take pocketknives and slice open cushions, carving up the old, polished leather of our beloved Grand Wexfords. I fully expect them to uncover the sapphires at any moment, but then another dreadful thought occurs to me: if when they are done here, they have found nothing, they will move on to the upper floor and find the gawper skull tucked under my bed in its hat box. It would no doubt, at the very least, be confiscated and never returned. I might then be arrested on any number of charges and *interrogated* by the authorities. Nothing good would come of it.

Goffings kneels to examine the loose marbles on the rug, picking one up to turn it in the firelight. 'A bit careless, don't you think? Someone might slip on these and fall. You should keep a safer house, *Barnyard*.' He glances at Josiah's nearby riding boots and wrinkles his nose. He tips each one upside down and peers inside before replacing them. 'Check outside.'

The officers unlatch and lift the windows, leaning out with lanterns to examine the immediate grounds. Goffings sends a pair out to roam the garden but they soon head back in when Baker bounds at them, barking. They eventually quieten, their hunt exhausted. Straightening, Goffings approaches Josiah. 'Gibbs, Torby, search these fellows. Step away from the mantle, Mr Mingle, if you'd be so kind.'

'Oh, come on, sergeant,' I object. 'You've already searched us once today.'

A bead of sweat runs from Josiah's brow. A few cinders rise up the chimney from the fire. 'Gladly, Sergeant Goffings.' He steps aside and again we stretch out our arms to allow the officers to pat us down and delve into our pockets. I watch Gibbs or Torby – I'm not sure which – search Josiah and expect him to discover the gems any minute, but the moments come and go and still they find nothing.

'Gentlemen, your neckties…' says Goffings, looking smug. We oblige, removing our cravats and dropping them to the floor. 'Your boots, *Barnyard*.'

I remove my riding boots and sit them on the floor next to me. Goffings takes and upends them to be sure nothing is hiding within. He turns back to the mantle and studies every item upon it: candles in brass holders, a box of Sulphurs, a cast-iron statuette of a noble lantern dog, the polished brass carriage clock set in marble. When he seems convinced the sapphires are not in the room, he stoops to warm his hands by the fire, gazing into the flames. 'Enough, gentlemen. What we are looking for must be hidden elsewhere. Do you have a cellar, *Barnyard*?' he asks as Josiah and I slip our boots back on.

'Of course. This way, gentlemen.' Thinking desperately, I play for time and, waving a hand towards the door, lead the Drakers out of the room and around the corner to the cellar. 'Help yourselves.' I open the cellar door for them and stand aside as they file past. 'You'll find a nice claret down there and we've a fine collection of port. You should try the Fitz Gerald '62. Full-bodied with an exceptional bouquet.'

Goffings glares. 'Be quiet.' He waits with Josiah and me as the officers take their lanterns down the worn stone steps and into the dank darkness below. After a few minutes they reappear from the gloom to ascend.

'Nothing, sir,' reports the first man out.

'Upstairs,' says Goffings.

This I cannot allow. 'Sir!' I begin, without really knowing what I'm to say next. Inspiration strikes. 'I'd be terribly obliged if you'd allow me to retrieve what you so clearly desire and bring it to you. It might save us all a great deal of time.'

'You'll fetch them for me?' Goffings asks, narrowing his eyes with suspicion.

'I will, indeed.' I nod. 'If you will but wait here, I shall deliver them to you promptly.'

'Very well. We'll wait. But no funny business. I'm warning you, *Barnyard*.'

'Of course, sergeant.' I head up the stairs and hurry directly to my room, draw out the hat box and carry it through to Josiah's room at the back of the house. There, I open a window and lean out to drop the box into a tall bush in the back garden. Baker barks at me. 'Shush!' I tell him before closing the window. That will have to do for now. Returning to the stairs, I descend, slipping my notebook from my jacket pocket.

'Here they are, sergeant, as promised. All my notes on the Night Ghoul. You may of course borrow them, although I would appreciate their safe return.' I present the notebook.

'What's this?' His face contorts.

'Why, it's everything I have on the Holloway case, of course.'

'I don't want your pocketbook, you imbecile! We're looking for Hanover's missing sapphires!'

'The sapphires!' I feign surprise. 'I'm afraid we know nothing of the sapphires. They're in Yorkson's Bank, surely? Perhaps you should look there.'

'Upstairs, men!' he barks, fuming. 'Tear the place apart! I want those jewels found!'

They continue the search, leaving a wake of destruction and disorder, but inevitably return to us at the foot of the stairs.

'I found these, sir,' says a hapless Draker holding up two necklaces, one of rubies and the other amethyst.

'I think you'll find your officer has been in Mother's jewellery box.' I watch the Draker sag as my words take hold.

'Put those back, Officer Gibbs.'

While Gibbs returns Mother's jewels to their rightful place, Goffings fixes upon Josiah, jabbing a finger at him. 'There's something off about you – don't think I don't see it – and when I find out what, you'll be in trouble.' Without another word, he leads his men back through the house and out into the street, emptyhanded and thwarted. I close the front door, glad to be rid of them.

Back in the green room, I turn to Josiah. 'So, what *did* you do with the sapphires?'

With a mournful look, he squats on his haunches to stare into the shimmering flames of the fire.

16

The Phantom Carter

In which Josiah is dismayed and Magwitch reports

Josiah holds his head in his hands. The flames dance. 'I'm sorry, Mr Banyard. The sapphires are gone.'

'Are you telling me you threw them into the fire?'

He nods, miserably. 'I thought with five hundred guineas in the bank we might better help Kenwigs' girl, and others, of course. But it was all for nought. The Drakers came and I'd only just collected up the stones. I was standing by the fire and, well… They're burned. Ruined!'

I stoop next to him to see the gems blackened and gleaming, scattered about the hot orange glow of burning logs. 'They're not ruined. They'll be fine. Fire doesn't damage sapphires. It just turns them black for a while. I'm not sure how you managed it, Joe, but you found the perfect hiding place.' I take the fire shovel from the wood basket and give the burning logs a nudge, knocking a handful of gems to the bottom of the hearth. These I scoop up in the shovel. 'They'll be fine, but we do need to find a better place to hide them while we think this through. Goffings might well be back.'

'I thought you'd have me hand them in anyway.'

My anger towards Josiah cools. 'We'll see. I'd like to know

how Hanover acquired them.'

For now, I decide the safest place to store the stones is in our secret chamber, behind the fireplace of the case room at the Mysteries Solved office. While Mother and the widow do what they can to put the house back in order, Josiah and I extinguish the fire to reclaim and clean the sapphires. Once cooled, they take on their old colours and sparkle brightly. We find a leather pouch in which to keep them. I throw on my long coat and trudge to the office through the bitterly cold and foggy night.

With the gems safely hidden, I return to 96 Bunson Street, pass the stable and slip through the side gate into the back garden. The hat box has not fallen far into the bush but is out of reach. I'm forced to climb several branches in discomfort, snagging my coat and scarf, and wedging a foot painfully in a fork. My head, too, begins to hurt. Halfway up, a flicker of light further down the garden draws my eye. Freeing my foot, I climb down and work my way clear of the foliage as a pair of shimmering white eyes fix upon me from out of the haze. Around them, the form of a gawper materialises. My heart jolts but steadies as I realise it's Magwitch. He's found me, even without the gawper skull in my hands, just as he said he would. It's not the first time he's sought me out this way. Without thinking, I go to him as he closes on me, his lower half intangible, melding into the night. A dewy dampness forms on my brow.

A visitor has approached the Sallow Grove, a man driving a cart and horses. He thinks the words into my head, although we are but three feet apart.

I subdue the urge to verbalise my reply. *A carter! How long ago?*

Not long. Magwitch was delayed. With Skallagrim disturbing the fourth plane, it was no small task to find you.

I see. Tell me everything. What happened?

The carter drove in towards the grove. Drakers were lying in wait. They blocked the road. The carter fled.

Did you trace him? Can you name him?

I cannot. The fourth plane—

Skallagrim...

This is truth. Magwitch can show what was. He reaches out a clawed hand towards my head. The lights of his eyes blink out.

A trickle of cooling blood runs from my temple as a living picture begins to manifest in my mind's eye: a thousand fragments like wind-blown sand coalescing to form one whole. In startling clarity, I see and hear all that Magwitch witnessed: the ditch-edged road with its overreaching ashblacks, nearing the field and the grove, disappearing into the murk of night; above, the bright half-moon shimmering down, transient behind folds of drifting, moon-shot cloud; and there, a figure violently lashing a pale pair of cantering horses from the bench of a juddering cart, cleaving the fog.

I watch the scene play out. Bretling must have posted a larger guard today, expecting the doom of an eighth unlucky silker and therefore an attempted burial at the grove. Ahead of the cart, a single rider breaks from the shadows of the trees that edge the way, his horse clip-clopping to a halt at the centre of the track. Soon a second rides out, and a third. They keep coming until the way is blocked by a half-dozen, each man armed with a blunderbuss levelled at the oncoming driver. Moonlight glints from the silvered handguards of rapiers slung at the riders' waists. The driver sees the blockade and tugs hard on the reins. The carthorses whinny and reel. The foremost horseman fires, the shot ringing out across the night, exploding with a plume of smoke: a miss, or perhaps a warning shot. In a wild manoeuvre, the driver brings the cart about, almost toppling as the wheels strike a ditch. He regains control of the cart and the Drakers give chase as he flees, unharmed.

So, he turned back, towards the city?

Magwitch's eyes flicker open. *This is also truth.*

Did they catch him?

They did not. Magwitch closes his eyes again to conjure a second vision in my mind. I see the same driver flailing his horses with the reins, the cart dashing away upon another stretch of moonlit country road. The load bed is covered by an oilcloth that's roped down tightly. Presumably, Hanover's body lies beneath, cold and dead. From the front, the driver throws a ceramic grenade, which trails a thin line of fume before detonating loudly on impact with the road. There is much fire and smoke. Others streak the air in quick succession, bursting around the hooves of the Drakers' baulking horses. They whinny and rear, turn and scatter, the pursuit in sudden chaos. Through the thinning sulphurous haze, I glimpse the rear of the cart as it's swallowed by the night.

So, he could be still on his way back to Old Camdon! It's my theory that, because all the victims were taken while in Old Camdon, the killer himself most likely resides there.

Magwitch seems to read my thoughts, although I did not mean to voice them. *In that case, we should go now with all haste!*

He's right. What's more, the most direct road from Holloway to Old Camdon is Bunson Street. *Our* street. Magwitch vanishes in a swirl of mist, leaving me alone in the garden. I forget about the gawper skull and hurry inside to raise Josiah, but not before glimpsing a startled face at my neighbour's window. Jinkers! He'll have a field day with this!

Throwing on his hat and coat and buckling up his gun belt, Josiah hurries with me to the stables. We quickly saddle the horses, mount and clatter out onto the ice and stone of the frosty road. We turn about, squinting up and down the street, our breath misting.

'Has he passed already?' asks Josiah, checking his pistols are loaded and returning them to their holsters.

'Who knows? North or south? Take your pick.'

We stare as a tall figure coalesces on the crest of Rook's Bridge, hazy in the fog.

'That's Magwitch,' I explain. 'Seeking the carter.'

Josiah steadies his dappled mare before wheeling her about to head south, towards Holloway. 'Good hunting!' he calls back to me, coaxing the horse into a trot.

When I glance back at the bridge, Magwitch has gone. I dig heels to set Blink moving but, unsettled by the gawper, the coward stalls, refusing to budge. I stroke his neck and whisper soothing words to calm him. Whinnying, he settles, and soon we're crossing Rook's Bridge and entering Old Camdon. Instinctively, I bend our path east towards The Gunner but find Firth Lane like a graveyard, not a soul in sight. I've no need to draw on Blink's reins to halt him. He stops of his own accord, as though unwilling to proceed. I listen, studying each twisted-timbered building of the lamplit lane, every shadow and the marks left by traffic in the trampled snow – though there are too many tracks, and they are too confused and interwoven to be easily read. I dismount to examine them more closely, leading Blink a short way by the reins. At the back of the tavern several horses are tethered, but there are no carts or their wheel tracks.

Through fern-frosted windows I watch drinkers carousing in the tavern, their faces bathed in the amber light of storm lamps, their chatter and laughter muffled by the leaded glass. Yet another sound reaches me from a street nearby: the clamour of a coach and horses, or is it the Seraph with his cart? Sensing he's somewhere in my wake, I turn Blink, heave myself up into the saddle and coax him on, retracing my path back into the heart of the old town. He bears me down Westerly Road, Shoe Lane and into Market Street, where the phantom noises distance and dispel without ever a glimpse of the vehicle or its horses. I'm left straining for any whisper or footfall in the despicable city smog, follow several such sounds, but at length abandon my search, stopping in the middle of Drapery Lane. A lone tabby pads across the road before me. All is quiet. If the Seraph brought a cart through Old Camdon tonight, he has escaped and made it safely home.

My mind turns to Josiah. Wondering what he's found, if anything, I return to Rook's Bridge and ride down Bunson Street. Perhaps a visit to the Sallow Grove is in order. With luck, I'll meet Joe along the way.

After a long ride I find him sitting on the banks of the pond by the grove, tossing pebbles into the misty water and watching ripples shatter reflections of moonlight. Willie stands nearby, tethered to a tree.

'Find anything?' I ask, dismounting to loop Blink's reins over a neighbouring branch.

Josiah shakes his head and casts another stone. 'Not much. I followed a set of cart tracks that became obvious a mile or so down Bunson Street. They led to the trackway back there...' He gestures towards the far side of the grove. '... the place where the carter was turned back by the Drakers. There are pieces of grenade scattered on the road.'

'I saw. Did you check the grove?'

'There're no new graves. The only tracks were mine. I guess the Drakers messed it up again.'

Something drifts out on the water beyond the pond's frozen edges. Josiah throws: the pebble speeds into the depths. Bubbles rise to the surface.

I recall his comment about the Seraph choosing to use the grove when there's a perfectly good pond a few yards away. 'What's that?' I ask, pointing out over the water as an ill feeling sends a shiver down my back.

Josiah stands for a better view. We skirt the pond to close in on the floating object and see it more clearly.

'Just a fallen branch,' he says.

But the idea won't leave me: the suspicion that there are bodies lurking beneath the water's surface, perhaps weighed down with stones. 'I'm going to request that Bretling has the pond dredged.'

We ride home and stable the horses. I leave Josiah blanketing them and slip into the garden to retrieve the box containing the gawper skull. Longing for my bed, I hurry inside, only to be seized by Jinkers as I'm closing the back door.

'Micky! A word if I may...' He releases me but holds the door open, thrusting his face into the house. 'May I come in? There's something rather important I'd like to discuss.'

'Can it wait?' I ask. 'It's late and it's been a rather taxing day.'

'No. It can't.' He pushes his way in and, wearily, I show him through to the green room and place the box upon the table.

194

'Take a seat.' I gesture towards a Draker-sliced Grand Wexford and he stands by the chair, eyeing the damage yet choosing not to mention it. Josiah arrives and sets an iron pot heating over the fire.

'Good evening, Mr Jinkers.' There's an awkward silence as Jinkers watches Joe add cloves and cinnamon before pouring dark rum from a bottle into the pot to warm. A pleasing aroma spices the air.

'Good evening, Josiah.' Jinkers looks at me quizzically. 'Is it all right... to talk? In front of *him?*' He throws his head towards Josiah.

'Mr Jinkers, I presume you refer to the encounter earlier this night in the back garden. The one you overlooked from an upper window of your house.'

Jinkers nods apprehensively. 'That's right.'

'In that case you may indeed talk freely. I hold no secrets from Josiah.'

Joe fetches goblets and ladles out three servings. 'Here, take one against the cold.' The drinks delivered, he takes a seat by the fire.

'I saw a gawper,' he begins. 'A gawper and you. As though meeting.' Jinkers' gaze jumps back and forth between Josiah and me as though seeking reassurance or perhaps looking for a shocked response. 'You don't deny it?'

'I don't.' At least his attention is not on the box. 'I did indeed meet with a gawper. My father began a study of their kind before I was born. I am continuing his work.'

'You know all about them, then?' His jaw hangs loose. His eyes bulge.

I confess. 'More than most, perhaps.'

'Will you tell me? Tell me everything?' His eyes plead with me. 'You know I have a natural fascination of them. Now I'm beginning to see you've been holding out on me all this time!'

I tell Jinkers the basics of my knowledge of gawpers and he listens attentively, seeming awestruck, if not embarrassed by his history of constant hearsay and the regalement of fairy tales about gawpers he's maintained over the years.

'*Dagomites...*' he says, repeating the new term over and again when I use it, as though afraid he may forget. He eventually sits down to take it all in. My discourse lasts around half an hour, at the end of which Jinkers nods acceptingly. There is one detail I'm happy to omit, however: an account of the moment when Magwitch handed me the skull of an ancestor through which I might communicate with him more directly.

When at length Jinkers runs dry of questions about Magwitch and his involvement in our investigation, he yields a report of his own, which mostly consists of more overheard snippets of tavern talk and gossip, all spawned by the latest barrage of newspaper stories. At each mention of death or murder – or, indeed, any relating word – he makes the godly sign, standing to turn thrice upon the spot after every third sign, until at last, the rigmarole of it all gets to me.

'Listen, Mr Jinkers, you can't make all this fuss every time someone mentions death. We're investigating a string of murders. There's simply not the time for it!'

Sheepishly, he nods. 'I'll try, though it's hard breaking old habits.'

We part on good terms, wishing each other goodnight, and I finally climb the stairs for bed, put away the hat box and collapse onto my mattress. Magwitch appears in my room, startling me.

Did you find him? I think hopefully.

Magwitch shakes his head sombrely. I hear his gravelly voice in my mind.

The carter has escaped.

Thursday, 18th Elventide

'Is this man still under suspicion?' Outside Barronbrook's holding cell, deep within the Draker Headquarters, I glare at Lord Bretling Draker. 'No?' He lights his pipe, humouring me as I rant. 'And has he been extensively *questioned*, as his bruises suggest? Yes? Then might I suggest he be released?' I didn't come here for this but Bretling's had it coming.

On the other side of the black wrought-iron bars, the poor hunchback from The Duke, Mr Barronbrook, is slumped on the stone floor in a dank corner, bleeding from several cuts to his swollen face where Drakers have *pursued* their enquiries. His patched clothes are filthy and I'm not sure he can even stand after the treatment he's endured.

Bretling picks a speck of dust from his otherwise pristine uniform and expels a large cloud of smoke that smells of sweet liquorice and cedar. 'Very well, young Banyard. Have it your way. He *has* been questioned, after all.'

'By Sergeant Goffings?'

'A lucky guess, Banyard.'

'Did he learn anything pertinent, I wonder?'

Grimly, Bretling shakes his head and gestures for the lantern-jawed guard to unlock the cell door.

'What happened last night?' I ask as the guard releases Mr Barronbrook. 'Presumably you had extra guards set on the road to the grove.'

Bretling seems reticent, exhaling something close to a sigh. 'I believe my men intercepted the killer en route to the grove where he intended to bury Hanover's body. They gave chase when he bolted.'

'And?'

'They lost him. He was prepared for them. Was armed accordingly. His precautions worked.'

I act as though this is news. 'That's a shame.'

'Yes.' Bretling rubs at his twitching brow as though he might smooth away the irritation. 'My watchman also reported two other visitors to the grove. Why were you there?'

'We followed a hunch,' I explain. 'Thought the killer might try something. Though we ended up by the pond, which brings me to the reason for my call. I suggest you have it dredged for bodies. After all, it would be a more conducive place for one to dispose of a corpse.'

A glower overshadows his face. 'I'll do no such thing. Are

seven not enough for you? If more are found, it will only serve to make my life harder.'

'Not necessarily. More bodies could mean more evidence. It could aid the investigation.'

'I doubt it.'

'If you don't dredge and later it comes to light there are more bodies in the pond, it would look bad for you.'

'You're not going to let this go, are you?'

'No.'

'All right.' Grudgingly, he nods. 'If it will shut you up, it may be worth it, although bodies in water tend to surface. You should know this, Banyard. That fact alone makes the pond rather less *conducive*.'

Barronbrook limps from his cell, pausing before me to bow his head. 'Thank you, sir.'

The gesture leaves me uncomfortable. 'I'll have a coach take you home,' I say. 'Allow me to accompany you from the building.'

He stumbles and I rush to support him.

'Lend a hand,' says Bretling to the guard, who swiftly obeys, and between us we help the hobbling man.

'Be at the Sallow Grove tomorrow at ten if you want to see what's in that pond.' Bretling stalks away.

The guard and I assist Barronbrook through the corridors and out onto the front steps, where the guard leaves us.

'Do you swear to me that you had nothing to do with these bodies at the Sallow Grove?' I ask Barronbrook, seeking assurance.

He fixes upon me though the slits of his swollen eyes, and the mere effort of standing seems to cause him pain. 'I swear, I've killed no one, master. Not now, not ever.'

'I believe you.' I wave a carriage over from across the street and help Barronbrook up into the cabin. With instruction to seek the care of a doctor, I push a guinea into his hand, direct the driver to The Duke in Stonhaven, and pay the fare. The driver drops the coins into a pocket of his coat and calls the horses into action. I watch the carriage jostle away down the road until it passes out of view.

An excerpt taken from the gawper file,
as written by Reginald Francis Banyard.

Recorded on the 4th Trimoon, in the year 1769.
An account (continued) by Thomas Winter, clerk of the
Dockside coopers, Dandies Oaken Kegs.

Thomas: This way, sir, if you will. (At this point Mr Winter leaves the chair at his work bench in the counting room to lead me out into the front courtyard of the premises, an open area surfaced with worn cobbles and patched with pitted flagstones. We cross this to follow a broad track that drops down to a loading area near the waterfront. Here, iron runners are set into the stones: presumably the forementioned barrel ramps. Beyond lies the stone edge of the quay and rows of iron mooring posts. All manner of ships and boats rise and fall on the turbulent sea.) It was right here, sir. The lights started here and then the gawper appeared. They continued to flicker around the figure and it looked like a hole in the sky! As though I was peering through into a different world! And then the others came, as though through their own hollows in the air, and I was faced with three towering figures all with glowing white eyes fixed upon me!

Reginald: What did these figures do?

Thomas: The one in the centre — that was the first to appear — approached me, its eyes boring into mine. I felt a terrible pain, like a pressure building in my head and I can recall no more after that. I must have passed out and, when I awoke, they'd gone, leaving no trace. I checked my pocket watch and found that more than an hour had passed.

17

Bones

In which Bretling Draker has the waters dredged

At Mysteries Solved, Penney greets me with a furious look. I think she's upset at my lack of attention until I see that Josiah and Lizzy look much the same, and then I wonder if I've walked in on a row. 'What is it? What's the matter?'

'Goffings,' growls Josiah. 'He was here with a half-dozen of his idiots. They forced their way in, turned the place over.'

I tense because there were documents in the drawers of my desk that could land us all in a mountain of trouble, among them Patty Primshaw's fake identity papers. 'But–'

'Don't worry,' whispers Josiah, while Lizzy moves around the reception room righting chairs and putting paperwork back into order. 'He was after the sapphires, of course, but Lizzy stalled them long enough for me to empty your desk and stow everything in the hidden room. They didn't find that.'

'That was quick thinking, Joe.' I walk into the case room and find the pinboard untouched. The drawers and the contents of Josiah's desk lie scattered across the floor. Mine are open and empty. 'He had a good look at this, I suppose.' I gesture towards our display on the wall.

Lizzy joins me. 'He did, Michael. He stared at it for a time.

He made notes.'

'Oh, well. I don't suppose it will help him very much. They're only allowed to investigate threaders and every one of our suspects is a silker. He'll report it to Lord Draker, of course.'

'Of course,' agrees Josiah.

'It doesn't matter.' I feel violated by Goffings' visit.

'How did your meeting go?' asks Lizzy. Today she looks stunning and smells of lavender and mint, and her presence is distracting. 'Will he dredge the pond?'

I force myself to focus. 'He will. We're to join him there tomorrow at ten in the morning.' Again, I picture the carter pursued by riders in the fog on the road. 'After last night, our Seraph – wherever he is – now has a problem on his hands, a body he can't dispose of by his usual means.'

'I was thinking the same,' says Lizzy. 'He'll have to get rid of it somewhere else.'

'So, how? Where?' asks Josiah. 'The river?'

'Possibly. We should have the Drakers watch the bridges and every bank of the Tynne where access is not overlooked. Where else?'

Josiah shrugs. 'If it were me, I'd dump the body in a hedge or ditch somewhere.'

'He may have already done so. A ditch. A hedge. The river. We should have checked last night as we rode home.' I'm angry with myself. 'We must have the hedgerows between here and the grove searched. The riverbanks too.'

'He may have chopped the body into pieces and dumped them in any number of places,' says Josiah. 'Or burned it to ash on a fire.'

'Let's hope not.' I draft a letter to Bretling suggesting he set a watch on the river and make a search of the hedgerows and ditches along the Holloway end of Bunson Street and the surrounding roads and lanes. Folding and sealing the note with wax, I stamp it with my signet ring before finding the street boy Hicks to deliver it.

Penney comes to me in the case room. 'Michael, what would

you have us do?'

'I need Lizzy to keep shop. I wondered if you would visit Zadie and see that she's settling in. Perhaps you might show her the sights of Camdon City.'

'Certainly.' Penney rests a hand briefly on my arm. Our eyes meet, but again I sense a sadness when she withdraws.

As she leaves, the sudden roar of my cousin's Double Heart heralds his return. Through the frosted windows of the case room, I see the hazy silhouette of the clockwork car as it draws up outside. Mardon enters Mysteries Solved, dumps his surgeon's bag on Lizzy's desk and hangs his hat and coat on the corner stand.

'It's been a devil of a drive,' he says, pulling off his fine leather gloves and dropping them on top of the bag. 'The road's solid ice and I'm half-frozen to death.' He rubs his hands together, attempting to warm them. 'Lizzy, I don't suppose you could fetch a cup of black bean soup? Or something stronger if available. I'm all out.' He taps the chest of his waistcoat to emphasise the emptiness of his hipflask. 'Don't worry. I'm leaving the car there for the near future.'

'I'll see what I can do.' With a glimmer of irritation, Lizzy leaves her desk and heads out, muttering below her breath, *'Good day to you, Miss Fairweather. How are you, Miss Fairweather?'*

'I do hope you have better luck with the coroner.' Grinning, I take Myrah's note from my coat pocket and hand it to Mardon. 'Myrah passed this on for you, soon after you left for Stonhaven.'

He takes the letter and sits in the visitor's chair by the fire to read it, his expression clouding.

'Oh dear. It looks like bad news,' I observe.

Crestfallen, Mardon crumples the letter into a ball and tosses it onto the flames. 'Well, no one likes a rejection, do they?'

'I don't understand. She looked so disappointed when you didn't arrive with us.'

'I swear I shall never understand the female persuasion.'

Lizzy delivers a half-bottle of whisky and a copper cup of

steaming black bean soup. 'I've brought you both, though you deserve neither.'

Mardon takes the drinks and tops up the copper cup with a measure of the spirit before taking a sip. 'Just the ticket. Thank you, Lizzy.'

'Did you learn anything while away?' I ask.

Mardon stokes the flames with a fire iron and adds more coal. 'Nothing you're going to like. I wasn't sure about Frack at first, but the more I get to know him, the more amiable he is.'

'He offered you a position?' I pull up a chair and sit down.

'He did, indeed. You're looking at the new head of operations, though not my usual kind, of course.' He snorts at his own joke, takes another sip and stretches out his legs before the fire. 'I've to return tomorrow afternoon.'

'So, you took a shine to Frack.'

Mardon nods. 'He's a fine sort, Micky. Not a murderer, unless, of course, he has a fractured mind and the wherewithal to hide it, which is not impossible, I suppose, but in this case I'd say unlikely. He's a gentleman.'

'Avory Steverus thinks the same.'

'It doesn't surprise me. My opinion? We should be looking elsewhere.'

'What about the lie that Frack told at Lancett's funeral?'

'I spoke to him one evening after work over a few drinks. It wasn't hard to get him talking. It seems to me that Frack simply forgot about the meeting with Lancett. The exchange was a simple discussion about territories. Each man had wondered the same – would their profits be better if they agreed upon independent trading zones? In the end they decided the idea involved too many complications and limitations and didn't change anything. I suppose such a meeting, which ventured little and had no impact upon any party, soon slipped from memory. What would you have me do, stay under his employ until the case is solved?'

'Return as expected. Give it a few more days just to be sure. I shall send a note to advise you after that.'

He accompanies me into the case room where I draw a line through Frack's name on the wall. 'Tomorrow morning they're dredging the pond by the Sallow Grove. I thought you might accompany us before you leave.'

Mardon walks home and Lizzy soon leaves to meet up with one of her political contacts, and so for a while Josiah and I are left alone to ponder the case. I'm lost in thoughts about the Seraph's methods when Josiah disturbs me.

'She's here,' he says, watching the street from a window in reception. At fifteen minutes past three, Patty Primshaw arrives at Mysteries Solved. Josiah opens the door for her. Glancing furtively over her shoulder, she slips inside and looks nervously around. I'm glad the girls are out. I'm sure Lizzy, in particular, would be outraged by our lawbreaking if she ever found out.

'Ah, Miss Primshaw, do come through.' I direct her into the case room where she stands, gawking at the gruesome imographs on the wall as I close the door. She turns, startled. 'Never fear. You are free to leave whenever you so wish. We need imographs for your identification papers, but before we go any further, I must have your word that you'll hold all that takes place here in the strictest confidence. You can tell no one. Do you understand?'

'You can trust Mr Banyard,' says Josiah.

Patty nods. 'I swears, your secrets is safe wiv me.'

'Your new identity will be Cristina Longarton, of the Ashgrove Longartons. You must memorise the name and learn to respond to it.'

'Cristina Longarton,' she repeats, 'of the Ashgrove Longartons.'

'Very well, then.' I walk to the fireplace and press the hidden button beneath the end of the mantlepiece. There's an audible click and a panel set in the wall swings open. 'Please.' I gesture to the chamber within where all manner of disguises and silker clothes are arranged on hangers. There is also a dressing table complete with mirror, a collection of wigs and make-up. 'I'm sure you will find something complimentary that fits.'

Dubiously, Patty peers into the secret room.

'When you're ready, come out. I'll be here to take the imographs.' While Patty selects a silker's dress and ostentatious wig, I take my box camera and tripod and set it up in the case room, pointing it at a stretch of wall that I keep clear as a featureless backdrop.

When she's dressed, she opens the hidden door to poke her head into the room. 'I need help with the paint. I ain't never used it before.'

'Of course.' I'm a dab hand with disguises and have her looking like a powder-faced lady of standing in no time.

We have her stand against the wall, so that the location of the image cannot be traced, and I take several imographs until I'm sure I have one or two that will work. Back in the secret room, Patty changes back into her threader clothes and wipes her face clean before leaving, her entire visit taking less than twenty minutes.

In the shadows of his doorway, Jinkers nods as I go over the details of the carter and last night's fruitless search.

'So, we know the killer drives a cart,' he says when I'm done.

'Yes. At least, if that was indeed the killer, trying to take the latest victim to the Sallow Grove as we suspect.'

'If it was not the killer, it was some other criminal in fear of the Drakers. Otherwise, why run?'

'It does seem too large a coincidence,' I agree. 'The Drakers believe it was him.'

'I shall look into it, Micky. Leave it with me.'

Friday, 19th Elventide

The pond looks different this morning in the frosty daylight. The sun is low and pale in a sky of white and grey, the air crystalline in clarity. Our figures cast five long shadows at the edge, where bullrushes and boarwort rise in clumps, and the water's surface is crusted with encroaching ice. Bretling, Myrah, Mardon, Josiah and I watch as a dozen Drakers wade through the pond in a line, stirring up mud and detritus with pitchforks. In places the numbing water reaches to the dredgers' chests and I'm glad I'm not among them. The pond is large, its footprint comparable to that of six or seven reasonably sized townhouses combined. The Drakers will be at work for a while.

Beyond a brief and rather cool greeting, Mardon and Myrah have not spoken. They remain taciturn in each other's company.

Bretling plants his hands in the pockets of his coat. 'I received your note, Banyard.'

'And...'

'I'll do as you ask. It seems a reasonable course of action and I agree. The banks of the Tynne and the ditches and hedgerows must be searched, the bridges and roads watched.'

'Were your men able to give a description of the carter or the cart?' I ask.

'Nothing of any real value. The man was heavily wrapped against the elements, a scarf around his face. From the tracks we know the cart wheels span precisely seven feet. Low back. An oil cloth roped over to cover the cargo.'

'Speaking of which, is there any more information on Hanover's last movements?'

'Nothing new. He's disappeared like the others. The only difference is that single drop of blood and an open door.'

'What about the Sallow Grove Tobias?' asks Josiah. 'Do we have a name yet?'

'Sergeant Huntly assures me he should be hearing from his journeymen very soon. Two have gone to Amorphia and one to Gandinka.' Gandinka is an island off the coast of Urthia, a voyage of a week or so – a perilous one, considering the recent turbulence of political relationships.

'Gandinka? Have you considered the Seraph might be a spy?' I ask.

'Believe me, I've considered everything,' says Bretling.

'And what about the runaway, Sterling?'

'The sister in Loncaster swears she's not had contact, though she *would* say that. We have a man keeping her under surveillance in case Sterling makes an appearance.'

The dredgers work their way slowly across the pond and for a time we watch, listening to the liquid sounds of their movements as they stir the waters. They're less than halfway across when a man brings his pitchfork up to examine a find.

'Bones!' The cry goes up. Crowlings in the nearby field scatter into the sky.

We follow Bretling's lead as he skirts the edge, closer to the find. Those around the finder congregate to scrape the pond's floor and in ones, two and threes, the greenish-brown bones are gradually brought to the surface and gathered in, until the area renders no more. At the bank, we stand over the grim offerings as Drakers lay them out: a random arrangement of human ribs, long bones and, most notably, a skull.

'It's male,' says Myrah, turning it in her hands. 'See the prominent brow ridges.'

Bretling fails to suppress a twitch. Facing the dredgers, he tells them, 'Continue.'

Shivering, they re-form the line to resume their work.

Myrah replaces the skull. 'The small bones are lost to the mud as you'd expect, but there's enough here to suggest a whole body was once placed in the water.' She and Mardon continue to study the bones, looking for any sign of injury that may have caused death. 'There are no obvious marks. A more thorough examination will take time.'

Bretling says what we're all thinking. 'If there was coal present, that too would be lost to the mud.'

'What about a dragnet?' asks Josiah.

Bretling twitches again and reaches into a pocket for his pipe. 'Thank you, Mr Mingle. I shall have a net sent for.'

I leave the bank and wander a short way across the field, stop and peer at the treeline of the woods. Bretling follows me to stand at my shoulder. 'Don't even think it,' he says. I presume he's pre-empting what would have been my next suggestion: that we dig the woods for bodies, too.

Another shout rises from the pond. 'Here!' Again, the

dredgers gather to focus in, turning up bones and collecting them on the bank as we watch.

'This is definitely a second individual,' says Myrah unnecessarily, as a Draker brings in another skull. 'They've been here quite a while, more than six months, I'd say, by the staining. The flesh decomposed long ago.'

My stomach turns as I consider what the fish in the pond have fed upon, then to be consumed by farmer Tinlock and family, or sold to others at the local marketplace.

'Can you calculate an approximate date?' asks Mardon.

Myrah seems reticent. 'I'll take a closer look back at the mortuary, but don't hold your breath.'

Drakers blanket the bones and carry them away.

Before we part, I turn to Bretling. 'Listen. I'd be much obliged if you'd keep your man Goffings out of my premises.' I walk away before he can answer and feel his gaze burning into the back of my neck.

Mardon leaves Holloway for his job at Frack's mine while Josiah and I return to Mysteries Solved. From there I head into Old Camdon to attend my first-ever meeting of parliament. Nervously, I enter Parliament House and take a seat towards the back on one side of the benches, which all face in towards the centre of the historic chamber. The chair soon declares the meeting open and a number of discussions arise, the first, a lengthy and laborious debate about the tax on various imported goods. The second is equally as tiresome and ends with a vote by the established MPs to agree upon the content of a trade treaty with Urthia, the latest in a long line of peace-seeking manoeuvres, doomed to fail like those before.

My interests awaken upon the opening of the third, however, as the chair introduces a new theme, that being the general welfare of threaders and related laws, offering opportunities for individuals to challenge the government in the seat of power. Chivers Hapgood skirts questions infuriatingly, and various members of parliament wrangle to win arguments either for or against the protection of threaders and their few remaining rights. Feeling timid and out of my depth, I listen – all the while growing increasingly indignant – until stirred into action by a particularly cruel-mouthed Silkerton, who rants on and on about the 'inferiority of the underclass' and 'undeserving nature of all threader bloodlines'.

'Such physiological differences set them and us apart,' he states with conviction. 'And so our laws should differ accordingly. The threaders are of a hardier stock. They need less food to survive, less heat to stay warm. In short, they need less, and less they should have.'

Those on the surrounding benches applaud and fill the air with 'hear-hears', while those opposing jeer.

'Silkers pay their fair share of tax,' he continues. 'Why, then, should they be honour-bound to provide any guarantee of well-being or surety to these rapscallions? They would, after all, slit our throats at the first opportunity.'

A volley of agreement rises from the surrounding ranks, encouraging the man.

'You Raggers in dissent, are you blind? Have you not seen our newspapers, full of stories about a threader who is systematically murdering silkers in their beds? Or have you not yet learned to read? Perhaps a little more schooling is in order!'

The room erupts into disarray – with laughter from the Silkertons and derisive cries from the Raggers – until the chair calls everyone to order. In the ensuing silence, I stand, barely aware of what I am doing or about to say. It is as though I have stepped outside of myself, and my words, when they eventually eject, sound as though they spring from another.

'Threaders are every bit the same as you or me. There is no difference. They bleed when cut, feel pain, suffer the elements, just like us. They are not of hardier stock nor changed in body or soul, nor in any other aspect. There is absolutely no difference between them and us excepting for a chance of birth. One might compare it to the fall of an autumn leaf, which itself has no influence on what it is or where it lands. Sir, I suggest it is you who is blind! You are *certainly* in need of education!'

A similar chaos ensues during which I am simultaneously laughed at, mocked and verbally abused, yet also, by a small minority, applauded. The reaction is so severe that a full three minutes pass before the chair manages to establish order, and by then there seems no need for any to respond directly to my words. Reeling, I spend the rest of the meeting in something of a daze, glad when it is over so that I may leave the chamber.

Outside, a gentleman tarries me with a hand on my shoulder. I turn to see who it is and recognise him as one of the few who applauded my valiant, if foolish, outcry.

'You are new to the chambers, are you not?' he asks, offering a hand, which I shake.

'I am. A naïve speculate, sir. I should thank you for your support, though I feel politics is not for me after all.'

'Ah, don't be so easily dismayed. You're the new man from Crowlands.'

'That's correct, sir, Michael Banyard. And you are...?'

'Lord Henry Price. I liked what you said in there, Mr Banyard. Brave. Very brave.' Henry Price is a serious-looking fellow with a ready smile. His hair is greying, styled in short waves and combed back away from his cleanly shaved face. His ensemble is as neat as his grooming. I take an instant liking to him.

'It's a pleasure to meet you, Lord Henry.'

'I do hope you give it another try. The first time in chambers is a trial for the best of us. Don't let it put you off. That's what they want, you see. To bully us out of there so they might have their way without confrontation. We need more fellows like you. Do you see? People with a mind to bring about change.'

'I see.'

We talk for a few minutes about the lacking rights of threaders and it's clear we share common ground.

'Listen, Banyard. Forgive my forwardness, but perhaps we should meet up. I'm always on the lookout for another collaborator.'

'I shall give it some thought. Thank you. Until next time.' I tip my hat and walk on.

18

The Symbol

In which plans come to light,
and Banyard and Mingle descend into darkness

Josiah seems pleased with himself when I arrive at the office after midday and toss my coat, hat and scarf onto the corner stand.

'What are you so happy about?'

I greet Lizzy, busy writing up notes in reception, and walk through to sit at my desk in the case room.

Josiah follows me in. 'I just turned down a job. A trivial matter of a missing will. We don't need it.'

'As in last will and testament?' I think his pleasure comes from an inflated sense of power, having been in charge for a matter of hours during my absence. Again, I regret attending the chambers and add another black mark against my political idea. 'Were they paying?'

'I told him we should take it,' says Lizzy from reception. 'But does anyone listen to me?'

Josiah closes the case room door. 'Oh, yes. They offered a tidy sum.'

My face contorts. 'Rule number one, Joe – never turn away an honest job. That's the ruin of any business.'

'Well, I forgot rule number one and you weren't here to remind me.' He drops the grin and reaches for his latest penny dreadful, a story about a gigantic morh-beast loose in the city.

'It sounds like Lizzy reminded you.'

'How was parliament?' He sounds disinterested. 'Have you fixed the world yet?'

'No. And to answer your question, it was dreadful, except for a lord named Henry Price.' Telling him about my encounter with Price, I recognise an inner hope, albeit small, that an alliance between Price, myself and perhaps a few others might lead to change.

Josiah, on the other hand, appears unimpressed by my account. 'Give it up,' he says, flipping through pages to find his place. 'You'd make a terrible politician anyway.'

'Do you think?'

'I do. This Price fellow is probably as rotten as the rest of them – an aristocrat, born and bred.'

'He seemed different.'

'Of course he did. He wants you to back him.'

He may have a point but I argue anyway. 'You should be his biggest fan. He's fighting to better the rights of threaders. He's probably the best hope for threaders everywhere.'

The jingle of the doorbell interrupts our rather painful discourse and I open the case room door to peer through. Ebadiah enters the reception room, a copper cup of steaming black bean soup in one hand and a half-eaten meat pie in the other. He perches at one end of Lizzy's desk and takes a huge bite of his pie, which prevents him from talking until he's chewed and swallowed. As before, he's soot-stained and filthy, head to foot.

'Any news?' I ask while we wait.

'Aye,' he eventually says. 'News of your scar-faced dead-un.'

That gets our full attention.

Josiah puts down his illustrated novella. 'Oh?'

'Yeah. You know Steverus, the foreman of Wheal Berta? Well, he's only been foreman for seven months or so. Before him it was another, a man with a scar on his face – a dead ringer for your Tobias. Name's George Berringford and he ain't been seen since Steverus took over.'

'Well done, Shoe Shine.' Returning to the case room I write out the name to label the first of the cadaver imographs, adding a question mark and pinning it to the board. The others follow me through. 'Anything else?' I ask Ebadiah.

He shrugs. 'Just that George Berringford was known to have been unhappy with his pay. When he didn't turn up for work one day, no one thought twice about it. Everyone expected him to quit anyway.'

'When you've finished your pie, I want you to find Lord Draker and tell him exactly what you've told me.'

'Right you are. Wait, there was something else. There've been rumours of a secret down the mine.'

'What, Wheal Berta?' asks Josiah.

'Aye,' says Ebadiah. 'Rumours of gold.'

'Does that happen?' asks Lizzy.

'I don't know everything about it but yes, I believe gold has previously been discovered in coal.' I scribble a new note – *Wheal Berta gold?* – and pin it to the board. 'What's the source of these rumours, I wonder. Is there any truth in them?'

'Some of the miners are saying it's the reason for John Lancett's murder. That someone wanted the gold and tried to make him talk. Ain't no one allowed down that lower level. They say for safety reasons, but I suppose there could be gold down there and that's why.'

'Could be anything down there,' says Josiah, enlivened by the mention of gold. 'We should investigate.'

I ask Ebadiah, 'Did you tell anyone about the body with the scarred face?'

''Course not. I just asked if anyone knew a man with a scar on his right cheek. Didn't tell them why.' Ebadiah chomps down the last of his pie and wipes his mouth on his sleeve.

'Good,' I say.

'Oh, yeah,' he continues with a wink. 'There's this, too.' He pulls a flattened scroll of paper from inside his waistcoat pocket. 'Thought you'd want to see this for yourselves.' He hands over the scroll, which I unravel and flatten out upon my desk, weighting it down with my pistols, an ink pot and the old skull that usually sits on the corner. We gather round to view the schematic.

'This is the winch room,' says Ebadiah, pointing. 'And that's the downcast shaft.' Running a finger down the drawing, he indicates a half-dozen horizontal tunnels leading off from the vertical shaft on both sides. 'These are the levels and this is the forbidden one.' His finger stops on the lowest tunnel. Across the plan are marked twenty or more small symbols, at first meaningless to me. Although each is repeated in a key at the base of the drawing, the cursive hand is all but illegible.

'What do these represent?' I ask.

He points in turn. 'These are jenkins. Those are pillars. These cup shapes are blinds. That'll be shale, mudstone or clay overlaying the seam...' He continues to explain each of the strange symbols. At least, that is what I think, until Lizzy sets me straight.

'What's that?' She points to a symbol towards one end of the lower level: a small circle with dot at its centre and a spike leading upwards from its outer edge, like an hour hand at two o'clock.

Ebadiah peers at it. 'You got me there, Lizzy. *That* I don't know.'

Josiah leans in for a closer look. 'A secret symbol, suggesting what? Hidden treasure? Gold?'

'What do you think, Shoe Shine?'

Ebadiah shrugs again. 'You ask me, there ain't nought down that mine but coal and misery.'

'When are we going, then?' asks Josiah.

After a moment's consideration, I say, 'Tonight.'

The place looks abandoned and it's the first time I've seen it without the usual bustle of industry. Crouching behind a rise of prickly gorse, Josiah and I watch the mine head, cast in moonlight and shadow. 'They say there used to be twelve months in a year,' I whisper over the moan of the wind as it plays against the stones of the tall smokestack. 'Did you know?'

Josiah shrugs apathetically and adjusts the long rope coiled over his shoulder.

I continue. 'Some say the Old People built huge flying machines that travelled beyond the sky, that they brought back valuable minerals from other worlds, but something went wrong. Others say that land was being lost to a rising sea, and that the miners brought back vast quantities of dust with which to make islands. The celestial miners were too greedy, and afterwards...'

'Only eleven months.'

'Yes, though perhaps we shall never truly know why.'

He peers pensively up at the bright moon. 'Strange, isn't it?'

'What?'

'That we know so much and yet so little.'

I realise this is perhaps the most profound thing I may ever hear Josiah say, take a moment to appreciate it and think, yes; Mardon – with all his learning and apparent wisdom – is a blip in the immense span of our seemingly never-ending universe. After everything, our finest scientists, who think they know so much, have barely scratched Truth's surface.

'You know, you really surprise me sometimes.'

'Why? What have I done?' he asks, shifting his gaze back to Wheal Berta and scratching his armpit.

And just like that, the moment passes. 'Never mind. I think we're alone.'

'Will the horses be all right?'

We've left Blink and Willie tethered in a small patch of scrubby ashblacks nearby.

'They'll be fine.'

'Can we get on with it, then? I'm freezing.'

Ebadiah has informed us of the shift work rotation and assures us that tonight the mine will be unoccupied for eight hours, its doors locked, production paused. We find it so and, while Josiah keeps watch, I pick the lock of the main door before slipping into the first and largest of the chambers, the winch room, where the steam-driven wheel system hauls the cage up and down the vertical shaft. Besides that, there's the lamp room where the lamps are maintained and stored, and lastly the foreman's office, which we've seen before. Josiah slips the heavy rope from his shoulder, dropping it by the cage, while I take a Grindel lamp from the lamp room and raise its glass shield and the fine, wire sieve, which prevents the flame from passing through to ignite combustable gases. He strikes a Sulphur and lights the wick. The acrid scent of burning whale oil rises into the air. Hoisting the lamp to guide our path, I cross the main chamber – lamplight throwing long shadows from the furnace, cage and wheel – and we creep into Steverus' office.

In the half-light of the Grindel lamp's feeble glow, the room seems smaller than I remember. Several charts are displayed on the bare stone walls. We quickly find one that is a close match to ours and compare the two, Josiah holding the lamp so that I can take out and unroll our chart.

'They're different,' I say.

'How?' He squints at details in the gloom.

'Here and here.' I indicate several points. 'Some symbols are missing. I think ours is an older drawing. Look, these shafts are shorter.'

He nods, his expression bewildered. 'Does that help us?'

'I don't know.'

'What about the extra symbol – the one not shown in the key?'

'That's missing, too. Search the room.' I roll and pocket our chart.

'For the missing symbol?' His brow wrinkles in confusion as he raises the lamp to better see my face.

'I don't know what we're looking for, but if it's here we must find it.'

Another Grindel lamp sits on Steverus' desk. Josiah lights it and, with a lamp each, we make a slow sweep of the room, examining everything as we go. There are surveying tools in the desk drawers: measures, plumblines, angle gauges, unused paper, drawing and navigation compasses, a setsquare, a magnifying lens and a brass-ringed telescope. Ink pots and quills are arranged on the far-right corner of the desk. Towards the back sits a stack of business letters and reports on the quality of the mine's load; to the left, a set of weights and scales. Shelves host a further collection of documents, yet nothing here indicates a find of gold or hints at treasure of any kind. I return to Ebadiah's chart, flattening it out upon the desk.

'The answer must lie here. Why would an older drawing, which clearly depicts the mine at an earlier stage, have the new symbol? It makes no sense.'

'You've got me, Mr Banyard. Does that mean we have to go down there?' Josiah's uplit face is grotesquely unsettling, though the thought of descending the mineshaft more so.

Leaving the foreman's office as we found it, we walk to the cage that's suspended on a chain over the enormous iron wheel. There's a clearance gap between the cage and the shaft on all sides, which means one slip and a man might tumble down the mine as his weight pushes the cage aside. We need it out of our way and so I loop one end of the rope through the cage bars, drag it aside and tie it off around the stonework base of the wheel engine.

Josiah's brow wrinkles. 'Why can't we use the cage again?'

'Because to do that we'd need to fire up the furnace and run the steam winch, which would alert every soul for miles around. I'm afraid we'll have to climb.' I kick the remaining coils of rope over the edge and watch them tumble into obscurity. 'Would you like to go first?'

'No. Nor second.'

'Come on. Where's your sense of adventure?' When he offers no reply, I add, 'Very well. Stay here and keep watch.'

Josiah glances around at the wavering shadows. The wind moans. He shivers. 'On second thoughts, I'll follow after.'

'You can lose your guns. We won't need them in the mine. One spark and the place might explode. We'll need more light, though. The Grindel lamps are safe down there.' I shrug off my long coat and ditch my hat and gun belt on the flagstone floor to perch on the edge, hook my Grindel lamp onto my belt and test the rope with a tug.

'We are going to die.' Josiah brings a third Grindel lamp, which he lights, and I hook this onto the underside of the tilting cage.

'Undoubtedly, but not today.'

Of course, I could be wrong. Lamplight illuminates the top of the shaft and a fall of some thirty feet or so before petering into darkness, although the charts show the downcast runs for around two hundred. The thought brings little comfort.

Reluctantly, Josiah unbuckles his gun belt and deposits it along with his hat and coat next to mine. I grip the rope and heave my weight onto it, sliding from the stonework at the edge of the opening. Hand over hand, I lower myself, bracing my legs against the stone facing. Some twenty feet down is the first dark opening on one face of the shaft, directly opposite another. I work my way towards the entrance on my side of the shaft, glad to swing myself into it and stand on the damp floor, resting my cramping arms. Josiah's form peers down over the top edge, framed in the square opening. I call up to him. 'Your turn.'

He lumbers down the rope to join me and I help him into the side shaft. This, however, is merely a resting point. We have no interest in this level. When we've recovered from the climb, we descend to the second shaft, and repeating this lengthy and exhausting process, work our way down to the very lowest of the tributary shafts. Standing in the entrance, we raise our lamps to peer over into the downcast, which continues beyond this level. Below us, lamplight shimmers on a liquid surface.

'Water,' says Josiah.

'We're below sea level. One open fissure and the entire mine could flood.'

'May I suggest we hurry.'

We turn back to the horizontal shaft and walk, examining the support beams as we go, all the while searching for a glimmer of gold in the grimy stone. There are remnants of coal everywhere, the air thick with a damp, oily smell. From somewhere beyond view comes a repeating *drip* of water. The shaft is long and meanders, following wherever the coal seam has led the pick men. In places it broadens out, in others it narrows. Several times it divides and we are forced to choose one route and track that to its end before returning to check the other.

We're still exploring the tunnels when a distant echo alerts us: a sound like a brick falling from a faraway table.

'Did you hear that?' asks Josiah.

'Yes.'

'What was it?'

'I don't know. Listen.'

We listen. 'It was nothing,' I say, but then another similar sound rebounds from somewhere above.

'There it is again!'

I turn back for the entrance. 'Come on!'

An excerpt taken from the gawper file,
as written by Michael Banyard.

From where did these strange and frightening beings stem? Since the age of eight, the question has plagued me. It is one not easily answered, although I have, over a period of recent weeks and months, gleaned a little insight from my meetings with Magwitch. I shall here attempt to lay out my findings, compiled as they are from a number of exchanges.

First, I should note that Magwitch himself has not communicated with absolute certainty on the matter but has conveyed the following in a speculative tone.

The Dagomites believe they were once human, before the cataclysm, to which they refer only as the clysmus. This fits with our own understanding of a devastating event that took place thousands of years ago. The dates are unknown and can only be guessed at by today's finest scientific minds. Yet Magwitch professes with more certainty that the Old People, from whom both humankind and gawperkind are perceived to have descended, somehow managed to ruin the world and, for a great expanse of time, life was altered. There were, of course, survivors, all taking human form in those early years, although the subsequent tribes followed their own paths.

At least one of these tribes endured in a ruined wasteland, forsaken by all others. I can only conclude that by telling me this, Magwitch was suggesting the Dagomites were then people and have since become something different in nature, by means of a deviation caused by their cruel and poisoned habitat. I surmise that they adapted to survive, either by chance or design, to become what they are today.

19

Cold

In which Barronbrook starts a fire and funerals are attended

A new noise reaches us: a rushing, slithering, whipping sound.

'The rope!' I cry.

We run, only to see our escape route plummet in snaking loops past the tunnel's entrance before plunging with a splash into the dark waters below. As the echoes abate, we glare upwards in time to glimpse a dim figure drop something else into the shaft. There's an ominous silence as the thing falls towards us, trailing a fine grey line of smoke. My gut twists in fear.

'Run!' I scream. We bolt back down the tunnel.

Somewhere behind us, a deafening explosion strikes, the shockwave knocking us to the floor with a burst of fierce orange light and an all-enveloping heat. This is quickly replaced by a backdraft of chilled air. The ground shakes beneath our feet and there comes a rush of water as our level begins to flood.

'We need to get out of here now!' I say.

Our boots pound through a streaming inch, a foot and then three feet. Racing the rising threat, we fight to reach the down shaft before the torrent drowns us and, in a moment, we're pushing against an unstoppable tide. I glimpse Joe swirling away from me, and then he's gone as the tunnel turns utterly dark, our Grindel lamps extinguished. The icy sea overwhelms us. Hurled this way and that in the eddies, I try to swim against the flow with no clue which way is up, nor where Josiah may be. I hold my breath and, peering blindly, swim in what I think is the right direction. The water ceases its invasion, its swell slowing, and from the darkness springs the faintest of watery lights. I make a new push towards the glimmer, my lungs bursting. Clamping my mouth shut, I refuse my body's inner screams for air. There is no air to be had. Instead, I begin a slow exhale, which brings little relief, and just when I know I must breathe a lungful of sea, I feel the grasp of a large hand on the scruff of my shirt and I'm heaved upwards. I burst from the water, choking on a half-breath of liquid and air that seems to lodge in my throat.

Josiah clings to a crevice in the shaft wall with one hand. The other is tucked beneath my arm to keep me afloat. He draws me in towards the wall where I grip the edge of a stone, and for a few minutes we stay there, just catching our breath as I cough and splutter and tread water.

'I didn't think you could swim,' I say.

He glances around uneasily at the rippling surface that appears to have stopped rising. 'I can't.'

I blink away the water to peer up the shaft and see what I first believe to be our executioner, watching his work play out from the safety of the winch room floor, but as my vision clears, I recognise the figure and wave to him.

'It's Ebadiah, come to help.'

'Get us out, Shoe Shine!' shouts Josiah.

Leaning out, Ebadiah calls down to us. 'There's no rope.'

'Try the lamp room!' I shout.

He leaves our view briefly, returning to drop a new length of rope over the edge, though it's way too short to reach us. 'That's all there is,' he explains.

I reply. 'Can you drop the cage? We can climb the chain.'

He disappears again and we crane our necks to watch the

Grindel lamp swing as he starts to release the winch brake. No power is needed for the heavy cage to fall.

'Wait!' I scream. 'You'll kill us! We need to get out of the way.' Around eight feet above our heads is the entrance to the next level. I nod towards it. 'We have to climb.'

Using every nook and cranny available, we claw our way up the pitted stone surface to heave ourselves into the tributary entrance. Once we're clear, Ebadiah gives a warning cry. 'Look out!'

With an almighty clamour, the cage drops on its chain. The pulley wheel gains speed until the iron floor hits the flood, sending up a great spray of water, and the cage sinks.

'Now lock it off,' I tell Ebadiah.

A moment later the chain grinds to a halt, the cage now fully submerged. Josiah goes first, taking a running leap from the tunnel to grab at the chain. He catches it well and climbs, but this time there is no respite. No resting every fifteen or twenty feet. And it's harder work heaving yourself *up* a slippery, iron-cold chain than it is *down* a dry rope. I follow, and before we're halfway up we're both feeling the strain. Our muscles scream. Our fingers are numb.

At the top there's a further complication: the chain runs directly down the centre of the downcast, nowhere near the edge, so we're forced to climb a further twelve painful feet up to the great wheel and manoeuvre onto its spokes and rim, before dropping to the floor, shivering violently.

I glance at my hands and then at Josiah. We're as pale as ghosts.

'D-d-did you s-see anyone?' I stammer through chattering teeth.

Ebadiah runs to us from the wheal house entrance. 'They're coming. The explosion has brought them. Go! The window!'

We hear voices approaching from the track outside. Ebadiah waves us on towards a hinged window in the lamp room and we fling it open to drop our effects through. Josiah climbs up and jumps from the sill, releasing a muffled yelp as he hits a bank and rolls the rest of the way into a ditch below. I soon follow, and then Ebadiah, balancing on the outer sill, nimbly draws the window closed before making the leap. We gather our hats, coats and gun belts and, with them piled in our arms, follow Ebadiah around the edge of the mine. Beyond, a coastal path runs down to a cove and then up to a stretch of wave-worn steps. It's a long way around but the route is sheltered from the mine by a cliff edge and, as far as we can tell, we're not seen.

Before long we're standing outside the back door of The Duke, soaked, exhausted and freezing as Ebadiah throws grit up at Barronbrook's first-floor bedroom window. The hunchback swings the window open to peer down at us.

'It's me, Ebadiah,' the boy whispers, waving his arms.

'What time do you call this, lad? And who's that with you?' asks Barronbrook, irritated by the disturbance.

'Some friends of mine, in need of help. Can we come in?'

'I suppose.' Barronbrook closes the window and retreats, appearing again behind the opening back door to thrust a lantern in our faces. 'Be quick, then.'

He recognises me as we enter through a porch and his frown eases. 'Well, if it's you, I don't mind so much.' His cuts and bruises are healing well, the swelling around his eyes greatly reduced.

'You're very kind.' I wave my hat in a bedraggled sort of way. 'Mr Barronbrook, this is my associate, Mr Mingle.'

Barronbrook nods. In the kitchen he raises his lantern to take a good look at Josiah and me. 'What have you been up to? You're wet through.'

'Investigating,' says Josiah, holding out his hands to warm them on the stove that's been curfewed for the night.

'Oh, don't use that. I'll get a proper fire going in the main room.'

It transpires that the main room is the same chamber in which we first questioned Avory Steverus over brandy, although now, instead of finding it coldly basic, it feels warm and entirely comforting. Barronbrook ushers us onto a large rug made from rags that spans the width of the broad fireplace. 'You'd better get out of those wet things before you freeze.' Stooping over the fireplace, he clears away the evening's ashes, arranges kindling and brings in a shovel loaded with glowing coals – presumably from the kitchen stove – to spur the fire into life, then heaps on split logs from a stack that sits to one side. 'I'll fetch you something to wear. Won't be much, I'm afraid, but it'll have to do.' He hobbles away as we strip, dumping our wet clothes and riding boots onto the floor.

Ebadiah makes a poor attempt at stifling a laugh. We quickly cover up by wrapping ourselves in our long coats, which are mostly dry. Our shivers slowly subside and we're delighted when Barronbrook returns laden with some of his old britches and shirts.

'You showed me kindness at the gaol,' he says.

The clothes are ill-fitting, to say the least, and Josiah splits several seams as soon as he sits before the fire, but it doesn't matter. We're growing warmer by the minute, and several cups later – Barronbrook's mulled wine is the best I've ever tasted – we're becoming rather merry.

I don't know if it's the drink or the cold that has addled my mind, but Josiah gets there before me. 'Wait a minute. Where did you get that map?' He rounds on the boy.

'What map?'

The firelight casts Josiah's contorted face in shades of orange. 'The map! The chart of the mine you gave to us.'

I catch up. 'It was a trap, set for us! We were meant to go down there. Were meant to die down there.'

'Which means someone's been following us, seeking the opportunity,' says Joe.

Ebadiah's eyes widen in horror. 'I didn't know. Someone slipped it into my bag.'

'Who?' we ask in unison.

'It could've been anyone. I thought it might be him.' Ebadiah points to Barronbrook, who looks surprised. Josiah and I glare at the hunchback.

He puts his hands up defensively. 'It wasn't me, Shoe Shine. I can promise you that.'

'Then who?' fumes Josiah.

'I ain't a clue,' says Ebadiah. 'I've asked a lot of folk a lot of questions about the mine. I thought it were just one of them being helpful.'

Confounded, I check the pockets of my long coat, only to find them empty. 'Whoever it is, they have my notes.'

We attend several funerals over the course of the next few days, as the six other individuals recovered from the Sallow Grove are laid to rest. Most pass in sombre monotony with all the attendees one might expect, though an event of note occurs at the closing of Uriah Mumford's interment, which takes place at the already overcrowded cemetery in Old Camdon. It's the ancient city's oldest deadfield, originally outside the residential limit, now fully absorbed after hundreds of years of expanding districts. The morning is crisp and bright; the atmosphere anything but.

Uriah Mumford was popular among his family and friends. The event draws quite a crowd, though whether the cause is the character he possessed or the wealth, I cannot say. The ceremony drags on until eventually – thankfully – the hollyman, presiding at the foot of the grave, concludes his sermon. The widow, Victoria Mumford, the bereft sons, Jethro and Samuel, and Uriah's business associates, Ranalf Harmon and Otis Jacks, take turns to cast soil over the lowered coffin.

The toymaker Stanley Larkin makes an appearance, approaching the widow soberly, his arms laden with an object hidden beneath a cloth. I had not noticed him until this moment, and so presume he has been here throughout the ceremony, hidden among the mourners.

'What's *he* doing here?' asks Josiah.

Intrigued, I press through the dispersing crowd to listen in.

'Mrs Mumford, my deepest condolences,' says the toymaker, cradling the object in one arm briefly to remove his topper. 'I do hope you'll forgive my intrusion. Your dear departed husband commissioned this for one of your sons, shortly before his disappearance. It was to be a birthday gift, I believe.'

'Oh,' says the widow with a perplexed expression. 'And who might you be?'

'My name is Stanley Larkin, madam, a toymaker.' In a fluid motion he sweeps the cloth covering aside to reveal his creation, the Wheal Berta automaton. Now he bows his head in a humble gesture and presents the model. 'If it is acceptable, I should like to gift it to your family, since it is completed and I have no use for it. I thought you should have it.'

In a state of morbid distraction, she says nothing but receives the model with an almost imperceivable inclination of the head.

'A noble gesture,' I mutter to Josiah as we watch the mourners leave.

George Berringford's interment is a different matter. By the lack of mourners, it appears he was either something of a recluse or deeply unpopular. It takes place on the hilltop in Stonhaven at a burial plot not far from John Lancett's. Apart from Josiah and me, there are but two present to hear the hollyman's address: Avory Steverus and Simon Forbes. Inescapably, we find ourselves conversing after Berringford's bones – scarred skull and all – are in the ground.

'He was a solitary soul,' says Steverus, as we stand around the graveside.

Forbes remains silent and I wonder if he's refusing to speak ill of the dead, as tradition dictates.

'I have the impression he was disliked,' I say, hoping to learn something about the mysterious loner who was foreman at Wheal Berta before Steverus.

Steverus deliberates. 'I think that perhaps life had been mean to him.'

'And in return, he was mean to life?'

'He was a hard man,' admits Steverus. 'He did his job. There was a little kindness in him.'

At this, Forbes smiles wryly and I discern that *a little kindness* likely means *none at all.* 'He was hated, then?'

Forbes speaks. 'By some.'

'What about family?'

Steverus shrugs. 'He never spoke of any. I rather think he was alone, perhaps an only child, his parents passed.'

'Do either of you know any reason why someone would want him dead?'

'He was unpopular,' says Steverus. 'It's no easy task, keeping order among the common rabble.'

'How did it happen that you took on the role when he disappeared?' I ask.

'I was already a good friend of John's. When he thought Berringford had abandoned his post, John bade me step in to help.'

'And you learned the trade?'

'There was little to learn, Mr Banyard. The Steverus family has been in mining for centuries, and I since my first step.'

'Is there gold down the mine?' asks Josiah.

Steverus and Forbes exchange amused glances.

Forbes stares down at the coffin. 'I wish there were.'

Josiah persists. 'If not gold, then some other treasure?'

Forbes replies soberly. 'There's nothing of worth down that mine but coal.'

'Of course,' says Steverus, 'there's less accessible coal now that the lower shaft is flooded. Did you hear? Someone broke in to sabotage the mine, dropped a stick of pyronitronite down the main shaft. Who knows why?'

'Do you know who did it?' I ask.

Steverus frowns. 'I'm afraid not.'

At my second parliamentary meeting, I enter the great chamber to find my new acquaintance, Henry Price, awaiting my arrival. Seeing me, he waves and gestures keenly towards the seat next to his. I join him, glad of a friend. The session begins and it's not what I'd hoped for. It's long and boring with little if any opportunity to speak about anything relevant to my cause. Price seems to nod off at one point, but perhaps he's only resting his eyes. To be honest, the entire thing feels like a complete waste of time.

I leave the session, wearied by the experience and jaded about my wonderful future in politics.

On the steps outside Parliament House, a fellow surprises me by laying a hand on my shoulder in much the same way Price did when I was last here. I turn at the touch and recognise the hooded man from The Dog, though now his hood is withdrawn and a ragged scar running down the side of his face is clearly visible. Twice now, he has attempted to entice me to join the Landsdale Rebels. Cautiously, he draws me aside from the steps and the busy square below as though we should not be seen together out in the open. Behind a stone column of the portico, he looks around to see if we've been noticed.

'Mr Banyard, you are launching into a sea of untold treachery. Take a word of warning, abandon ship before it's too late.' His message delivered, he slips his hood up and leaves, quickly lost in the milling crowd.

The Feast of Elventide will soon be upon us. I have things to prepare, presents to buy! Colourful decorations go up in the streets around us: garlands, strings of lanterns, and bows of holly and fir all tied up with bright ribbons. Outwardly, the atmosphere is merry and nostalgic, although not far beneath the surface lurks a darker mood, one that broods in fear of a sinister presence. Silkers feel it most keenly, while threaders leer from the shadows and doorways of hovels, many of them enthralled by the thought of their masters' night terrors. As Elventide Day approaches, silkers across Old Camdon lie awake in their beds, watching for the pallid face of death at the window.

Relief comes in the form of an unlikely threader, upon the morning of the 23rd Elventide. The first I know of it is from a rather vitriolic note, delivered into my hand from an aloof Draker, who seems underwhelmed by his role as messenger boy.

'It's from Bretling.' Noting the seal, I tear open the envelope as the Draker leaves Mysteries Solved to retrace his steps along Bunson Street's bustling pavements. Lizzy and Josiah listen, our other operatives being elsewhere engaged.

> *Mssrs Banyard and Mingle,*
> *I'm delighted to inform you that we have at last taken the*
> *Sallow Grove murderer as our prisoner. The threader*
> *concerned is at this very moment behind the bars of a Draker*
> *holding cell while we document his confession. I'd like to take*
> *this opportunity to thank you and your team for the services*
> *you have most loyally provided and hereby close the contract*
> *held between us. You are to cease all further investigation into*
> *the matter. Final settlement shall be forthcoming.*
> *Yours sincerely,*
> *Lord Draker*

I fold the note. 'It has the Draker seal. It's official, then. We're off the case.'

'It can't be,' says Josiah, astounded. 'Perhaps the letter's fake.'

I pass it to him. 'It's in Bretling's own hand. See for yourself.'

He stares at the cursive script. 'I don't believe it. I just don't.'

'I'd have thought you'd be pleased,' says Lizzy, watching us wrestle with the news. 'At least we can all stop worrying.'

Josiah paces, scrutinising the note.

I'm not entirely sure what my plan is but I can't stay in the office. 'There's something wrong with this. Why would he confess? It doesn't fit with the killer we've come to know.' I collect my coat and slip it on, take my tricorn and put that on too, before taking Josiah his topper.

'He can't just cut us out like this. After everything we've done!' He looks up from the note to his hat and then to my face. 'Where are we going?'

'To see this killer for ourselves.'

20

Mandola

In which Banyard and Mingle confront Lord Draker

We ride swiftly to the Draker Headquarters – keen to know the truth behind Bretling's claim, one way or the other – and every minute my intellect searches for answers that just don't seem to be there. Has the Seraph achieved his final goal and so relinquished his life into the hands of the law? He will surely be hanged, or banished to Mors Zonam for a less merciful death. And his crimes against the pride of the silkers are so great that he will surely be extensively tortured long before any such sentence is passed. Why, then, would any man, guilty or not, confess? But one course of action may quell my turbulent mind, and that is to question this confessor myself.

By chance, we meet Bretling on the steps as he's leaving his headquarters. He sees us tethering our horses and looks surprised, though for once he's smiling and without his recent tic.

'Gentlemen.' Pausing, he tips his hat. 'What brings you here?'

This irritates me. 'You know very well why we're here, Lord Draker – to see your prisoner.'

'Ah, you received my note. Good. Well, I'm afraid that won't be possible. The prisoner is under strict guard – no one except the investigating officers permitted entry. I'm sorry but you've had a wasted trip.' He nods. 'Good day.' And he walks on.

We continue up the steps, all the faster when he turns.

'Did you hear me, Banyard? You can't go in!'

We go in. At the reception desk, the duty sergeant is busy talking with an officer. We would usually submit to procedure, but today we march through, indifferent to the objections that follow, and stride down a corridor that leads to the holding cells.

There's a commotion behind us and Bretling bellows. 'Stop them, sergeant!'

Ahead, the sour-faced Sergeant Huntly steps out of the gaol room to block our path. 'Now, where might you gentlemen be going in such a hurry?'

'To see your prisoner, of course.' I wave my tricorn in an *out of my way* motion.

Huntly plants his feet and draws a pistol, levelling it at us. 'Oh no you're not.'

'This is absurd!' I say. 'Have we not worked this case together? We're on the same side, man! Now, don't be ridiculous. Lower your gun!' Out of the corner of my eye, I notice Josiah's hands move to his own pistols, as yet holstered on his belt.

Wavering, Huntly drops his aim but immediately raises it again at the sound of Bretling's commanding tone. 'Hold them, sergeant.' Bretling joins our little gathering in the passageway.

I argue our case. 'Lord Draker, the least you can do is allow us to see this man you claim is the killer. It would take but a minute.'

He looks us over and checks his pocket watch, deliberating. At last he relents. 'All right, then, Banyard, though I shall be present for the duration. And I don't have long, so make it quick.' He nods to Huntly, who holsters the gun and steps aside. We enter the gaol room, congregating around the bars of a cell that's guarded by a pair of bulky watchmen. Bretling's taking no chances. 'This is the man. Calls himself Mandola, though we're not sure if that's his surname or a nickname. The fellow's deranged.' Bretling digs in a pocket for his pipe. 'Not everything he says makes sense.'

'So how can you be sure he's the one?' asks Josiah, peering through the bars at a scruffy threader who looks to have been sleeping rough for some time. 'He doesn't fit the description Larkin gave.' The man's face and manacled hands are coated with filth, his hair matted. A rank odour emits from the cell.

Bretling lights his pipe with a Sulphur and smokes. 'That doesn't matter.' His words issue with plumes of smoke.

'His confession was irrefutable,' says Huntly. 'And witnessed by a dozen officers.'

'What did he say, exactly?' I ask.

Bretling crosses to a desk opposite the cells to collect the transcribed statement. 'I quote: *It was me killed them toffs. I did for them, all right, all seven. They had it coming.* When asked why, he said, *Them gents was a bad lot. They deserved to die. They crossed my path and, well, a man's got t' live, ain't he?* He then rambled on about how life's not fair and how he was hungry and killed them for money just so he could eat. It's all rather solid, wouldn't you say?'

'But the victims were all found with their personal possessions,' I point out.

'Perhaps he only took their money,' suggests Huntly. 'He doesn't seem to know what he's doing or saying half the time.'

'You killed all seven?' I ask Mandola, who nods emphatically. 'Seven and no more?'

'Now, hang on a minute, Banyard. We've no evidence to suggest the others were killed by the same hand.'

'Strip him,' I say.

The others look at me as though I'm insane.

'What?' asks Bretling, his mouth gaping.

'Strip him! Let's see the build of this killer who, one after another, singlehandedly killed seven strong and well-nourished gentlemen and moved their bodies. Let's see the muscle behind the hands that did it and managed to cut all those graves through sallow roots. I'm serious!'

'By Lychling, I believe you are,' says Bretling, taking a long draw on his pipe. He points the tip at me. 'I knew no good would come of this. Should have trusted my instincts. You mean to prove him innocent. Why must everyone be innocent, Banyard? It's always your way.'

'I only seek the truth.'

Bretling's twitch returns as he gives me a withering look.

'And where's his cart? Was he found with a cart? A horse, even? I think not. Look at him. He barely owns a pair of shoes!' The man's shoes are in tatters and if I were to meet him on the street, I would – at one glance – be inclined to buy him a new pair.

'Just because my men encountered a carter near the grove, doesn't mean it was the killer,' counters Bretling, gesticulating angrily with his pipe.

I continue to rant. 'The killer had to transport the bodies somehow. Or did this man happen upon each one at the grove itself? Some coincidence, wouldn't you say?'

Silence.

And then Bretling begrudgingly gives the order. 'Strip him. Curse you, Banyard. Must you always be right?'

'Sir,' Huntly interjects. 'Might not the man have killed the victims at a time when he was stronger and owned a cart, and since then fallen upon harder times?'

'Why, yes!' says Bretling. 'What do you say to that, Banyard?'

'It's nonsense,' I say. 'The last victim was taken just six days ago.' Though, for all concerned, the notion is rather eclipsed by the sight of the naked prisoner, who is skin and bone. To compound the absurdity, I suggest, 'Shall we give him a spade and watch him dig a hole? I think we might forgo the roots...'

The question is unnecessary. The poor man is so malnourished that he can barely stand. 'I killed those men,' he says, defending his position. 'I did it. You should hang me, sirs. Get it done.' His words falter into a confused string of nonsense.

'He's a real pocket of frogs,' mutters Josiah.

'How does he profess to have done it?' I ask.

236

'He says he stabbed them,' says Bretling. 'A detail he could not have gleaned from the papers.'

'I stabbed them!' says Mandola, grabbing the bars of his cell. 'I stabbed them all over.'

I turn on Bretling. 'Which doesn't fit with Coroner Orkney's findings. And you believed him?'

'I did. Now I'm not so sure.'

'I presume you asked him about the coal?' I say accusingly.

'What coal?' asks Mandola before Bretling can answer.

'He's innocent, at least of the crime to which he's confessed.' I'm convinced of it and I can tell by the faces of the others that their convictions falter. 'What you have there is a homeless man who has been driven to the brink of insanity by dire circumstances and hardship. He wishes to die but lacks the courage to kill himself. He should be pitied and helped, given shelter and food. That man needs hope, not a noose!'

Bretling avoids my gaze when he says ominously, 'Our questioning of this suspect will continue. If he is our man, we'll find out for sure. And if he's not, I've a plan in mind.'

We leave the Drakers mulling over their challenged theories and return to Mysteries Solved, where my mind soon turns to other pressing matters. Patty Primshaw will be rescued from her situation at The Gunner this very night. I leave the office to arrange a coach for Josiah and myself, and a second to arrive at the back of The Gunner at precisely ten o'clock in the evening. From there it will carry Patty and her suitcases of new silker clothes and accessories away to our friends in Rochington.

Our plan is simple: the boy Hicks and his cohorts are primed to cause a disturbance at the front of the tavern. While Madam Kenwigs is busy chasing them from the premises, Patty will flit from the back door and into the coach. Josiah and I will oversee the transition and give Patty enough money to see her well provided for, until she's properly set up in her new role (yet to be determined).

As is so often the case, the escape itself is not the hard bit. That comes later when the runaway is hunted like an animal.

Our hope, then, lies in a swift and clandestine journey to Rochington followed by several weeks of hiding before Patty – appearing as her new identity – will again see the light of day.

I visit Yorkson's Bank on Quaffer's Row to withdraw the last of our funds and gaze sadly into the empty lock box before closing its drawer and turning the key. If it were not for Josiah's ill-conceived and yet fortuitous theft of Hanover's sapphires, our illicit threader rescues would grind to a halt. Which reminds me: I must take the gems to Ranskin soon. He'll know someone who will for a small sum provide a valuation, no questions asked. Perhaps I'll do that after Elventide Day, that celebration marking the turn of the year. For now, they're safe enough from Goffings' grasp in the secret room at Mysteries Solved.

I browse shops in Old Camdon, buy black bean soup from a street vendor and drink it in the street, select presents for Mother, Widow Blewett, Zadie and every member of the Mysteries Solved team, including each of Ebadiah's street urchins. Though a strange thing happens when I come to browse for Penney's and Lizzy's gifts. My inclination is to spend rather more on them than anyone else, which I could understand for Penney's part, but for Lizzy? In a jeweller's, I find myself drawn to a rather spectacular diamond necklace that would suit her splendidly and, once I've visualised it sparkling about her neck, I can see it on no other, though I can't afford it, of course. Not with everything else we're funding.

The event leaves me confused. I'm supposed to be with Penney, have been besotted since I first ran into her on Bunson Street at a young age. Why, then, this new obsession with Elizabeth Fairweather? Perturbed, I purchase silver bracelets, rather modest by comparison, though attractive and well made – one for each of them.

For the rest of the afternoon, I'm plagued by the unsettling incident and Lizzy's face sweeps mercilessly into my mind at every opportunity. What she's doing there, I can't say, though she refuses to leave and I'm forced to admit a certain indescribable feeling that dwells in the pit of my stomach each time. I have to wonder: was there something other than black beans in my soup?

I visit a cobbler's shop to buy a dozen pairs of children's boots. He looks me up and down, but doesn't ask why I want them as I pass a list of the various sizes I need. I pay and leave, loaded down with bags.

Several torturous hours later, I conclude Lizzy is haunting me! I make a concerted effort to banish her from my mind and, upon my return to the office, offer her a bemused, 'Good afternoon.' She greets me, frowning as I pass her desk on my way to the case room. Once inside, I quickly close the door between us, so desperate am I to be out of her presence.

At my desk I have a little more success and wrestle my thoughts back to the Seraph case. My concerns are that, with the easy confession from Mandola, Lord Draker and his sergeants will prove him, by any means, the murderer. If subsequent evidence is not forthcoming, it shall be in some way created, the truth twisted to suit the facts. The Drakers themselves may end up believing they have the right man, which I'm sure would end badly. For one thing, the search for the true killer would end and his murderous reign continue.

Well – I vow to myself – *I for one, will not stop until the real Seraph has been caught.*

The Gunner: five minutes to ten

Icicles hang from the eaves to glint in shimmering lamplight. The thatches and tiled roofs are powdered with snow, the cobbled pavements, too. It's a frosty night, not a cloud in the sky, and the waxing moon shines brightly. The overall effect is a scene of peculiar and unsettling brightness. Tonight, darkness would be our friend, shadows our retreat.

But there are none.

In the back road behind The Gunner, Josiah and I climb down from our coach, our faces swathed in scarves below the eyes. The driver knows he will be well rewarded and so he waits, the horses resting. We have funds for this, but little more.

Our breath is spectral in the chilled air.

'What do you think?' asks Josiah, peering up at the moon between the tall rooftops and then into the tavern through its small, icy rear windows. 'The moon looks big tonight. Perhaps we should call it off, do it another night.'

'It's a Tuesday,' I say. 'The moon's always larger on a Tuesday. Didn't you know?'

'No. It's bigger on a Tuesday?' He looks at me, amazed.

'No, of course it isn't. Don't believe everything you're told, Joe. Anyway, it's too late to call it off. Hicks and the street urchins are already in position.' I wish I could see through the walls and doorways, watch the boys and girls at work out on Firth Lane. I glance up the road. 'Where's the second coach? If it doesn't arrive soon, Patty will have to take ours.'

'What about us?'

'We'll walk home.'

'But it's freezing.'

'You've grown soft since becoming a silker.'

Josiah shrugs. 'Maybe.' The coach rounds the corner at the end of the road. 'It's here.'

The coach approaches, passes and turns awkwardly in the narrow road, before drawing up opposite the other.

'Get the bags.' I lead the way, open the door of our coach's cabin compartment and pass out leatherbound suitcases befitting a silker lady – hat boxes and a vanity case among them. Josiah loads them into the coach, and not before time. A shout rises from the other side of the building. It sounds like the start of a fight and I'm not entirely sure what Hicks and company are doing, but I picture the picking of pockets, the knocking over of tankards and a general turn of unruly behaviour. If one were to scrutinise the scene, one might comment on the chances of these homeless children sporting such new boots. But no one will remark, for no one cares.

It doesn't take much to wind a silker up. They are this very minute joining forces, as is their way, to combat the threader miscreants. Along with the boots, I gave them free rein to run

240

amok, yet with one all-important rule: 'Under no circumstances are you to allow yourselves to be collared.'

The baggage transferred, we listen to the rising noise of the scuffle, watching for movement at the back door of The Gunner. A moment later it bursts open. Patty Primshaw steps out, closes the door and hurries to us.

'I'm ready.' She looks nervous but also determined.

'Your carriage awaits,' I say, waving a hand towards the coach. 'Once inside you must get changed immediately. You are?'

'Cristina Longarton,' she says, 'of the Ashgrove Longartons.'

'Very good.' I thrust an envelope containing money and her new identification papers into her hands. 'All is prepared. Your driver will deliver you safely to your destination. Now go!'

Patty climbs into her coach, glancing back briefly. 'Thank you.' She closes the door, draws the curtain closed, and that's the last we see of Patty Primshaw. The driver flicks the reins and the horses pull the carriage away. We quickly follow in our carriage and, beneath the bold light of the moon, we trundle contentedly from our crime scene.

Later, when most others have made for their beds, I answer a quiet knock at the front door of number 96 Bunson Street. It's a knock I've stayed up for. Hicks stands there, cap in hand. The distant peals of Draker whistles pierce the night as they continue their search for the runaway girl. No matter. She should be halfway to Rochington by now.

'Is all well?' I ask.

'All is well,' he confides in a lowered tone. 'No arrests, Mr Banyard.'

I slip him an extra half-crown for a job well done and close the door.

An excerpt taken from the gawper file,
as written by Michael Banyard.

I have learned that the gawpers' telepathic abilities stem from a purely physiological or biological phenomenon — that is to say, there is nothing ghostly involved. The gawpers have a bone-like organ that we humans do not possess, located behind the forehead and set between the brows. For the sake of reference, I have named this the trilobe, owing to its shape, which is almost triangular in form, with three lobes or chambers that meet at the centre. Whether or not this organ is also responsible for the telekinesis I have witnessed, I have yet to discover.

Ultimatum

*In which Josiah laments and a fateful day
begins to unfold*

Wednesday 24th, Elventide Eve

The day begins with our usual brisk walk up Bunson Street to
the office of Mysteries Solved, though the events that follow are
far from usual, and steal the festivity from an atmosphere
heightened by excitement and fear. First, I buy a copy of the
Camdon Herald from a paperboy as we pass by, trying not to slip
on last night's snowfall, instantly gripped by a concerning
headline:

A MESSAGE FOR THE NIGHT GHOUL

'What's this, now?' I unfold the paper and read the article to
Josiah as we walk.

> *In assisting our fine institution of watchmen, the Camdon
> City Drakers, the* Herald *is hereby printing at the request of
> none other than the esteemed Lord Draker, a direct message
> meant for the murderer of silkers, popularly known as the
> Night Ghoul. To date, the killer has cruelly taken the lives of
> seven men of standing from our fair city.*

'There's no mention of the two from the pond,' I note.

> *It is thought he calls after midnight, stealing silkers from their beds, to do away with them as is his wont, before burying them in shallow graves in the southern district of Holloway.*

The article then revisits previously revealed details of the case. I skip ahead to the bold text lower down the page.

> *Lord Draker's message to the killer: To you, who has performed these most vile acts against the city, I say this:*
> **'Cease and desist your activities, and hand yourself in to the nearest Draker watch station. If you should fail to do so, and it is discovered that another silker has been taken, reprisals shall follow.**

With deepening dismay, I pause on the pavement to read the rest.

> **'For every victim you have murdered, a threader shall be selected at random, thereafter, to be hanged by the neck until dead. This shall take place at the gallows in Old Camdon before a public crowd. The first shall be hanged at midday, upon the Feast of Elventide.'**

I'm staggered by the man's callousness.

Josiah frowns. 'But that's tomorrow! He's going to start killing threaders on Elventide Day?'

'That's what it says.'

'He's insane!'

'He's desperate.'

And next, we find the front door to our office locked, which tells us only that we have beaten Lizzy to Mysteries Solved – in itself an insignificant detail – though upon unlocking and entering, we quickly find that another has been here before us.

The case room door is closed; this we see as we hang our hats and coats. Josiah sets about lighting a fire in the reception room's hearth while I enter the case room, only to stop and stare as an involuntary sound of disappointment escapes my mouth.

'Oh…' Before me, the frosted glass of the back door lies scattered in a thousand shards across the floor. The door itself leans open, an icy draught blowing in. In the fine frost that has collected through the gap are several small shoe prints leading out into the snow.

'What?' asks Josiah from the other room.

'We've had another visitor,' I say, noting with despair that the door to the secret room is hanging open an inch. 'I should have known. Everything went way too smoothly last night.'

Joe reaches the doorway, sees the state of the case room. 'The sapphires!'

'Taken, I imagine. We seriously need to improve security around here.'

We search the secret room to confirm it: the gemstones are gone. Back in the case room I stoop to examine the boot prints that lead outside.

'Nothing else has been touched,' laments Josiah. 'It's as if whoever did this knew exactly what they were looking for.'

'Because they did,' I say, straightening and trying to subdue my frustration. 'It was Patty Primshaw. It can have been no other. She had opportunity to find the sapphires when changing for her imographs.'

'If she found them then, why didn't she take them then?'

'Because she wanted the documents, the wardrobe and the other money we promised. She got them, too. She's cleaned us out.'

'That rotten, thieving…' Josiah spouts an inventive string of expletives and slurs on Miss Primshaw's name. He punctuates this by thumping a fist down onto his desk before heading for the door. 'We'll go after her!'

'There's no point,' I tell him. 'She'll be miles away by now.'

'But the safehouse in Rochington… We know where she's

going!'

'She's chosen her own path, Joe. No use fighting it. She's paid off the driver to take her elsewhere, pocketed everything we've given, and disappeared. We'll not see her again.'

The news hits Josiah like a speeding steam truck. He slumps onto his chair and, with his elbows on the desk, holds his head in his hands. 'My sapphires!'

'I think you'll find they were Hanover's sapphires.'

More expletives follow, delivered with undeniable passion.

'Can you see to this mess?' I fetch my coat and put it on before sitting at my desk. 'I have but half an hour before I'm to be in parliament and the window must be quickly replaced.'

While Josiah fetches a glazier, I ride to Parliament House in Old Camdon, tether Blink in the overcrowded stables block to the rear of the building and take a seat next to Lord Price, who today is looking tense and alert.

'Michael.' He greets me with a nod and leans close. 'This should prove a more interesting debate than the last.'

'Oh?'

'You'll see.'

The chair calls the meeting to order with all the usual pomp and ceremony, and soon the gathering is embroiled in an argument about the rights of threaders and their working conditions. I don't know enough to understand everything that's said – there are mentions of unfamiliar terms, laws and sub-laws – but Lord Price was right. It *is* much more interesting than the last, and within half an hour I'm engrossed and fascinated by the procedures. When the chair calls for the Right Honourable Lord Henry Price to take the podium, I'm enthralled and impatient to hear him speak. He doesn't disappoint. His preamble is brief and soon he's into the meat of the matter.

'The commissioned report on threaders' rights clearly states that more than 70 per cent of workers are underfed, if not utterly malnourished, and living in a state so poor that no self-respecting silker would deem it fit for his livestock.' From there he rambles a little but quotes specific facts and figures, demonstrating an extensive knowledge of the report which, he reminds parliament, was ordered three months ago and has only recently been made available to the fully fledged MPs. Being only a junior speculate, I was not eligible for a copy.

It matters not. Price has singlehandedly turned my thoughts on politics upside down. An hour in and I'm in awe of the man. As I listen to him, a strong sense of hope rises in me that no amount of nay-saying from the opposition can dampen. Perhaps I *will* go into politics after all!

Another hour of debate passes and, having answered many questions and skilfully combatted several arguments, Price retakes his seat. It is with pride at our association that I nod to him and smile, whispering, 'Well done, Lord Price.'

A few minutes later, a steward quietly enters the chamber to stand briefly at the edge, searching for someone as the discourse continues. To my surprise, his gaze settles upon me, and he works his way over, between the benches. He leans down and in a lowered voice says, 'Speculate Banyard?'

'Yes,' I reply, wondering if I've unknowingly made some error of etiquette.

'A man is asking for you on Parliament Steps. He says it's of extreme importance.'

I frown. 'Who?'

'He wouldn't give a name.'

Thinking that Josiah or perhaps even Bretling needs me, I lean in and whisper to Henry, 'I'll be right back.' I rise and make my way through the building. On the steps outside, I stand, looking about for the mysterious caller, but see no one who shows the slightest interest in my presence.

Most odd, I think, and supposing I should probably wait for a moment or two before giving up, I tarry there, watching people pass by.

A hooded figure to one side of the steps catches my eye and I recognise the man as he glances at me over his shoulder. He departs, slipping beyond view around a corner, but the look was enough for me to know. It was he who called me out.

The very next moment, a sudden and ear-splitting explosion at my back blows me from my feet. The ground seems to liquify and I'm thrown, tumbling down the unyielding steps, enveloped by a cloud of dust and falling debris. Pieces of rock and grit strike me as I roll to a stop on the pavement, deafened and disorientated. As though from a mile off, screams fill the air, soon to be followed by the anguished cries of the injured, though for several minutes I can see no one through the haze.

The air slowly clears. I try to rise and find myself remarkably – surprisingly – unharmed beyond a few cuts, grazes and bruised bones. Several others further up the steps and therefore closer to the explosion have not fared as well. I limp to their aid, rip makeshift bandages from my shirt and tend to wounds before straightening to see the full extent of the damage to the building. Parliament House is half-blown to smithereens.

'Lord Henry?' I work my way up the remaining steps to pick my way through rubble, try to find where the chambers began and so estimate the location of Henry. Some are bleeding, dragging themselves free of the collapse. Others are beyond saving, their bodies broken. Rescuers work across the site, silkers and threaders among them. I am but one of many. Most of the dead lie scattered beneath tons of stone. The grand pillars, walls, upper floors and ceilings, exquisite mouldings, chandeliers, porticos and oak-panelled rooms and corridors – all of it has descended to crush and maim those unsuspecting unfortunates below. Alas, Lord Henry Price is surely among them. I find the spot where he must have been seated when the detonation struck. It is piled high with vast lumps of walling. He didn't stand a chance.

When Bretling learns I was on site as the explosion took place, he summons me to his office at the Tower End Draker Headquarters. 'Come in, young Banyard. Take a seat. Tell me what happened.'

In my account I'm guarded, wondering if I should give the Landsdale Rebels up, for I'm convinced they orchestrated the attack: one I consider to be cowardly and senseless. But Bretling soon puts my mind at ease.

'We know it was perpetrated by a group who call themselves the Landsdale Rebels. They've made it perfectly clear. Wondered for a time if you might be one of them, in fact,' he says candidly, passing a note to me across his desk. 'This was mailed to the Prime Minister within an hour of the explosion. He's presently recovering in Quirkstone Hospital.'

I glance at the note, which simply reads:

Farewell to Parliament House, courtesy of the Landsdale Rebels.

Bretling pockets his pipe and, with elbows on the desk, interlinks his fingers. 'What do you know of these people, Banyard?'

'Very little, sir, though I believe I was approached by an associate of theirs.'

'Oh?'

'Apparently, they wanted me to join their ranks.'

'That's interesting. You refused?'

'Of course, sir.'

He gives a mirthless half-smile. 'Do me a favour. If they ask again, take them up on the offer, but let me know.'

'You wish me to be your spy.'

'Astute as always, Banyard.' He leans back in his chair.

'I'll give it some thought, sir.'

'Did you see this morning's papers?'

'I did.'

'Well? What did you think?'

'I rather thought it a bad idea, sir.'

'Duly noted. Thank you. You may go.'

Before I leave the office, Sergeant Huntly pokes his head into the room to address Bretling. 'I've a message from one Stanley Larkin, sir. Says he has information about the Night

Ghoul and wants to pass it on in person. Asks if you could come to his shop for two o'clock this afternoon, sir.'

'Really,' says Bretling. 'Who does this fellow think he is? Tell him I'm busy. At two o'clock I shall be at the Sallow Grove going over everything. If it's that important, he can find me there.'

'Very good, sir.' Huntly leaves and I soon follow.

'It was the Landsdale Rebels,' I tell Josiah after luncheon, when I'm recovering at home in the green room and have washed and dressed my assortment of minor wounds. 'I know it.' I explain about the fellow who had me leave the meeting moments before the strike, and about the note to the Prime Minister. 'Do you now see why their way is no good? They killed Price, their only real hope of change. All they've achieved is to feed the hatred these silkers already feel for the threader population.'

Josiah remains subdued, allowing me to rant. 'Here.' He pours another brandy and slides the glass towards me. 'I'm sorry about Price. Will you stay in politics?'

'I don't know.' I take another sip of the warming spirit. 'The problem is—' I stop talking because Jinkers is at the rear windows again, looking ridiculously furtive. He peers into the room, presumably checking to see if we're alone, before knocking on the glass. Josiah raises a sash to let him in and I gesture to the Draker-slashed seat opposite mine. Outside, the sky has turned a dreary leaden grey and an icy wind has risen. Josiah closes the sash.

'What happened to you?' Jinkers sits, leaning forwards to scrutinise the grazes on my face. 'I heard there was a bomb in town. You weren't...?'

'There? Yes, I was. Do you have something to report?' I dab at a wound on my cheek with a handkerchief.

Jinkers nods. 'I've done some digging into the cart situation for people connected to the case who live in the city. Thought I'd start local...'

'Who?' Josiah pulls a chair closer to sit down.

Jinkers takes out a notebook and flips through to find the relevant page. 'Madam Kenwigs of The Gunner, the toymaker Stanley Larkin, Victoria Mumford, Jethro and Samuel Mumford, Ranalf Harmon, Otis Jacks, Master of the Dockside forges, Markus Hinton, and the head tailor at Thackory's, Zachariah Sterling.'

'That's a lot of work,' says Joe, sounding mildly impressed.

'I said I would help.'

'And what did you find?' I ask.

Jinkers closes the notebook. 'None of them owns a cart...'

'Well, that was a waste of time,' says Josiah, frustrated.

Jinkers finishes his sentence, '... except for Stanley Larkin.'

Now he really has my attention. 'Why would the toymaker own a cart?'

'I don't know,' shrugs Jinkers. 'To make deliveries, I suppose. Some of his toys are large – rocking horses, dolls houses and such.'

Josiah shakes his head. 'You must have it wrong. We've seen Larkin's place, been there twice. He has nowhere to keep a cart and horses. He lives above a little shop with nothing much out back.'

I picture Larkin's rear workshop where we sat to talk, recall the double doors that open onto an empty cobbled area and then a back lane.

'He doesn't keep it at the shop,' explains Jinkers. 'It's in a storehouse further down the road.'

I stand. 'Show us.'

'Do you really think it could be Larkin, the gentleman toymaker?' asks Josiah sceptically, as I wave down a coach to take the three of us into Old Camdon.

'I don't know, but we'll look at this cart, and if it's the same as the one the Drakers encountered, we'll find Larkin and have it out with him.'

A coach pulls over to let us board. I recognise the bristly, weather-worn driver.

'Old Town Way, if you please, Mr Fletcher. There's a place we must find.'

With a nod and a lash of the reins, we're off, rattling up Bunson Street and over Rook's Bridge. We bear west along the banks of the Tynne for several minutes before bending north into Old Camdon's labyrinthine streets. Before long, Fletcher slows the horses to a halt.

Fletcher leans down from the driver's seat. 'This is Old Town Way, sirs.'

'We're in your hands, Mr Jinkers,' I say.

Jinkers hinges open the window to call out. 'It's further down that way, beyond Larkin's, the toy shop.'

'Right,' says Fletcher. There's a clopping of hooves and the coach lurches onwards. As we pass, I study the toy shop with its impressive window display, and note the door sign has been turned to *closed*.

A few moments later, Jinkers knocks on the cabin ceiling and calls out. 'This is it.'

Fletcher reins in the horses and we dismount from the carriage onto the pavement. The storehouse is the third in a row of terraced buildings, all with large double doors in the style of a coach house, and each is set back from the road where the kerb gives way to a slope for access. Jinkers leads us to it. 'It's in there.' He points to the doors, which are old and flaking with paint, though still solid and strong, and bolted and padlocked with sturdy ironwork.

'Have you actually seen the cart?' asks Josiah.

Jinkers frowns. 'Well, no, but his neighbour said he keeps it here.'

I kneel to study tracks on the icy slope, and find the marks left by wheels that I estimate to be around seven feet across. 'This could be it, Joe.' Between the wheel lines are a scatter of horseshoe prints. Pedestrians walk the pavements and the road is busy with carts and horses, barrowmen, carriages and even the odd steam truck, so I can't stand here and pick the lock – or have Josiah break the doors down. Instead, I rattle them in frustration and try to peer in through the tiny gap where the doors meet, though all I see is darkness. Either the way is blocked beyond the doors or the storehouse is lightless.

'Is there a back way in?' growls Josiah.

'Follow me.' Jinkers sets off down the pavement. We follow him to the end of the row, where he turns left down the lane that hooks around to the back. 'There.' He stops, gesturing towards a similar set of double doors at the rear, which are also chained and bolted shut. A single high window sits over the broad oaken lintel, but it's small and boarded up.

'That's my way in,' I tell Josiah. 'Can you get me up there?'

22

The Room

In which Banyard and Mingle...
and Jinkers... investigate

Josiah makes a cradle with his hands and, using that as a foothold, I reach up for the boarding. He hoists me higher until it's within reach and I work my fingertips in under one edge, eventually managing to pry a plank loose. I wrench it free, drop it to the ground and move on to the next.

'Is he allowed to do that?' Jinkers asks Josiah below me.

'No, but who's going to stop him?' growls Joe.

Before long the boards are gone and I'm left with an open frame edged by broken glass. Wrapping my scarf around my fist, I knock out the shards and listen to the tinkle of them hitting the floor inside.

'Take me up, Joe,' I say, gripping the sill for support. Hauling myself up with some help from Joe, I pull my body in through the window head first and clamber down into the dim interior. The light from the window cascades down the rough stonework of the rear wall, doing little to illuminate the rest of the room, but by its glow I make out the shape of the cart and, as my eyes adjust, it becomes clearer. This is indeed the same sort of cart that I saw in Magwitch's shared vision. I recall it dashing away from the mounted Drakers, see again the grenades fly from the driver as the scene replays in my mind. Untying the ropes, I throw back the oilcloth to reveal an empty load bed. I dig out a box of Sulphurs from my coat pocket and strike one, holding the small flame over the grimy wooden boards and stooping close to examine them. The trace of a rank odour hits me. There are darkly stained patches on the surface of the planking where, at some time, the cart's cargo has leaked. I sweep the match closer, see blotches that could be dried blood, or perhaps oil. By matchlight it's hard to tell. The flame burns my fingers. I let it drop and blow it out where it falls on the cart.

Walking around to the driver's bench, I half-expect to find a store of grenades, though it's clean and empty. A quick sweep of the remaining space tells me little. There are the kind of objects one might expect to find in such a place: a well-worn broom, a few tools hanging from nails on the wall. Nothing much. No blades. Not even a spade, which may have raised an eyebrow. I clamber up the door joists and out of the window to rejoin the others.

'It could be the cart, or one very similar,' I tell them. 'We must inform Bretling and have Myrah take a look.' I lean the window boards against the wall. 'She'll tell us if that's blood in the cart.'

'What, now?' asks Josiah as we walk back to the street.

'First, I have some questions for Larkin.' We stride briskly to the toy shop and, finding the sign unchanged, I hammer loudly on the door. When there's no response, I take hold of the doorknob to rattle the door. 'Larkin! Are you in there? Larkin!' The shaking of the door sets the bell system jingling.

The more I dwell on it, the more I think Larkin's cart is the one the Seraph drove. I turn to Josiah. 'I have a bad feeling about this. Joe, break open the door.'

Josiah wraps a hand around the doorknob and, bracing himself against the frame, rips the metalwork clean out of the door, lock and all. The door swings open with a further jangle of bells. 'After you.'

Inside, the shop is unlit and, once the bells have stilled, it's eerily quiet. 'Hello?' I call, feeling the hairs rise on the back of my neck. Puppets and dolls are like leering daemons, hanging from the ceiling and loitering in corners. Automaton figures are lifelike statues, watching us move with malicious envy. 'Larkin? Are you there?'

'The place seems abandoned,' says Jinkers, creeping along behind me, the whites of his eyes large in the shadows.

We move through the gloom, past the counter with its silent till and on into the passage that leads to the workshop at the back, lit softly by a meagre light from the rear windows. A cursory search assures us that this, too, is unoccupied. I glance out of a frosty window at the wintery back lane before heading for the stairs. 'We'll check the first floor. Mr Jinkers, perhaps you should remain here and keep watch. Let us know if anyone comes.'

'As you wish.' Jinkers puts his hands in his pockets and looks around nervously. Josiah and I, ears straining for any sound, slowly ascend the narrow stairs, where each tread creaks at our shifting weight. The landing leads on past several doors into an ominously dark passageway. I call out again and open the nearest door: the bathroom, empty. We enter what, by its unused appearance and lack of clutter, must be a spare bedroom and move on into a second room, clearly kept by a gentleman – presumably Larkin. A cabinet sits to one side of the bed and gents' clothes hang in a wardrobe.

'Check the floor for droplets of blood.' I close the wardrobe doors, scanning the carpet around me.

'You think the Seraph has taken Larkin?'

'I grow convinced that he's somehow involved. Perhaps he's allowed the Seraph to use his cart and has been silenced. Be careful what you touch. This could be a crime scene.'

Josiah judiciously replaces a hairbrush on the surface of Larkin's cabinet, next to a cutthroat razor, shaving brush and bowl. 'Why would Larkin be involved? Why use Larkin's cart?'

'I don't know. There could be a connection we've missed.

Something other than Mumford's automaton. But what?' The question hangs in the air, remote and unanswered.

There's no blood in the bedroom that we can see, nor anything out of place. In fact, Larkin keeps his room impeccably tidy, though I recall he has a housekeeper who visits, so perhaps this is her doing. His razor is the folding type and is very clean: not the sort of blade that could be easily used as a dagger.

Three doors down; two to go.

The next opens onto a study, small but ordered and well furnished. Larkin even has a Grand Wexford at his desk, the desk itself being inlaid with matching deep-green leather. Books line the shelves, the titles in keeping with the interests of a creative toymaker. There are manuals on metalcraft, woodworking, clockwork mechanisms, and novels of an adventurous nature, nothing suspect. I pull one from its shelf and pretend to read the cover. 'How to dispose of a body without getting caught.'

'What?' Josiah's head spins in my direction.

'Just a jape, my friend. Perhaps our humble toymaker is just that – a humble toymaker.' Resignedly, I slide the novel back between its fellows.

'He's a very fine toymaker, in my opinion,' says Josiah.

I move on to the four drawers of the desk. The uppermost holds paper and some sheet parchment; the second, pencils, a penknife, ink and quills.

Josiah takes a narrow letter opener from the top of the desk. 'This could do the job.' The opener is in the shape of a thin, silver dagger. He simulates a stab to an imagined victim.

'Any blood?'

He peers closely at both sides of the blade. 'None *I* can see.'

'Leave it there. We'll inform Bretling later.'

Josiah replaces the letter opener on the desk where he found it – next to a large glass paperweight – and crosses to the fireplace to peer into a brass coal skuttle. 'There's coal!' he says.

'Well, that proves it!' I mock him. 'He *must* be the killer!' In a more reasonable tone I add, 'Really, Joe – every household from here to Scolanda has coal.'

'It's the good stuff, like the coal the killer used – the stuff your cousin was droning on about.'

I open another drawer, this one full of diagrams, drawings and notebooks. I scan through a few of them. All are plans and schematics of toys that Larkin has designed. 'He really is a clever man, this fellow–' I freeze as my eyes fix upon a familiar notebook, one that is smaller and thinner than the others. One that I recognise as my own. 'What's this doing here?' I lift it out to show Josiah before slipping it into my pocket.

'Your pocketbook! Larkin was at the mine!'

'And he tried to kill us. But why?'

'He's the Seraph!' says Josiah.

'I still don't believe it. I can't see Larkin killing seven – perhaps nine – silkers.' The final drawer is disappointingly empty. I slide it closed and we move on to the last of the doors. This one is at the end of the passage and is locked.

Jinkers calls up the stairs to us. 'Micky, it's Mrs Figgins, the housekeeper. She wants to know who broke the door.' He sounds worried.

'Do send her up, Mr Jinkers,' I call back before turning to Joe. 'A most fortuitous arrival.'

We hear her outraged tone long before she rears into view at the head of the stairs. 'Sirs, what do think you're doing, invading a gentleman's home like this? Why, when Mr Larkin sees what y–'

I try to settle her. 'Calm yourself, dear lady. We're investigating the Night Ghoul murders. Pray tell, when did you last see Master Larkin?'

'Yesterday afternoon when I called by to clean, of course. Now, what's all this about? I've a good mind to fetch the Drakers!'

'Really, Mrs Figgins, that won't be necessary,' I say. 'Please tell us what lies behind this door. And do you have the key?'

She glares at us, one after the other, but decides to answer. 'I don't know what's in that room. Master Larkin keeps it locked.'

'The key?' says Joe impatiently. 'Where does he keep it, woman?'

She shakes her head and takes a step away from him. 'I don't know, I swear! He told me that what's beyond that there door was none of my business. I've minded my own ever since.'

'Thank you, Mrs Figgins. You've been most helpful.' I gesture towards the stairs, hoping that she'll take the hint and leave. I turn back to Josiah. 'Open that door.'

Josiah shoulders the door several times under the housekeeper's disapproving gaze, and when that does not work, he charges it, to throw his full weight against it. There's an explosive, splintering sound as the inside frame splits apart. Ripped from its hinges, the door thunders to the floor. We enter as Mrs Figgins heads for the stairs, shaking her head in dismay.

Gazing around at the walls, my perception of Stanley Larkin instantly changes.

'What do you say now?' asks Josiah.

We're faced with a barrage of images, nailed, pinned and glued. The walls are covered with them. To one side sits a table, not tidy but awash with papers. I find a wall lamp, turn on the gas and ignite it with a Sulphur, and adjust the flame. The amber glow illuminates the details of old imographs, yellowed and faded, at the far end of the room. I approach them to see the faces of a family, each person close in resemblance to the others.

'What is this?' asks Josiah, peering around. 'Who are all these people?' From the table, he takes an imograph, lifting it to the light. Across one edge, sections have been cut away. He lets it fall back to the table where other similar imographs lie.

The family comprises a father who is clearly a coal miner, blackened from the pit. The smiling woman on his arm must surely be his wife and the mother of the four children. There are others, too. I spot a man similar in age and appearance to the father, another miner – a brother and uncle, perhaps? The faces repeat from image to image, the ages and clothing altering as though over the years. There are imographs taken at the entrance to a mine head. 'It's Wheal Berta.'

Josiah studies a side wall that holds a different kind of display. Squinting at newsprint, he calls to me. 'Over here.' I glance across. 'They're all cut from newspapers,' he says. 'This one's about a cave-in at the mine that happened back in 1764. That's…'

'More than thirty years ago.' I turn back to the imographs, drawn to the face of a child.

'This one's about a fire in which forty-seven miners died. There's another – a flood. They're all reports of mining disasters.'

'Josiah, look at this.' I point out the barefooted boy, who's wearing knee-length shorts and a filthy, oversized shirt that's patched and mended, his face almost as grimy as his father's. 'Recognise anyone?'

Joe stares for a moment. 'Why, isn't that Larkin?'

'It's his whole family. Check those reports for names. I've a feeling you'll find the Larkins are a recurring theme.' I move on to the third wall, the one to my left, and immediately recognise the face of Augusto Ritcott, the man whose remains were first turfed up in the Sallow Grove by a boy's dog. His likeness is on one of many cuttings taken from newspapers that plaster the wall, seven of which, including Ritcott's, have been altered: their eyes scratched through.

As I move around the wall studying picture after picture, Josiah scans the articles, reading aloud. 'Father-of-four, George Larkin. He was one of the flood victims. Here's another. Raffe Larkin, son of Myrle Larkin – buried alive in the cave-in.' Josiah makes the sacred sign.

I chastise him. 'I've told you before. Using the sacred sign will one day…' A memory flashes in my mind: Stanley Larkin in his shop, making the sacred sign at the mention of Mumford's obituary. 'Why didn't I see it before?'

'I don't understand,' says Joe. 'Larkin's a silker but that boy's clearly a threader.'

'Larkin is a threader in the guise of a silker. We both saw him make the scared sign. We've found the Seraph. He's killing for revenge. He's keeping a tally of his victims here on this wall and there are others he has in his sights.' A thought startles me. 'And I've a feeling he's not at home because he's going after Lord Draker!'

'Why?'

'You saw this morning's papers. That idiot Bretling's put himself directly in the line of fire. What's more, before I left his office this morning, I overheard Sergeant Huntly telling him Larkin wanted to meet. Bretling said he'd be at the Sallow Grove from two.'

Joe checks his pocket watch. 'But that's in five minutes!'

'Come on!' I head for the doorway.

Joe follows. 'We'll never get there in time.'

'We must try!'

An excerpt taken from the gawper file,
as written by Michael Banyard.

War is on the horizon, not only for humankind but for the gawpers, also. I fear it may not be long before all young men are conscripted and sent overseas to fight. And what state the world shall be left in when it is all over, who can say?

To whom would this accumulated knowledge of the gawpers pass if I were to not return? I should hate for it to be lost to the annals of time. It is, as yet, a well-kept secret. Because of this, I have decided to find a trustworthy recipient in whose hands I may place this knowledge for safe-keeping.

23

Blood in the Snow

In which Banyard and Mingle race to the grove

Glancing over my shoulder, I see Josiah passing the table, snatching a paper. He stuffs it into his long coat pocket. We dash down the narrow stairs and meet Jinkers in the workshop, the whites of his eyes large in the gloom.

He tags along. 'What's going on? Mrs Figgins was most put out.'

'We'll explain later,' I say. 'Stay here and guard the house. There's important evidence up there.'

Out in the street, I wave frantically for the coach.

Josiah checks his pistols. 'I'd feel better if we had our rapiers, too.'

'There's no time to fetch them.'

Fletcher arrives, drawing the coach alongside the kerb.

'To Holloway, with all haste!' I say, opening the door and climbing aboard.

Josiah follows me in. From Larkin's doorway, wearing a forlorn expression, Jinkers watches us go. As the coach gains speed, I lean out from the cabin window to shout, 'Hurry, Mr Fletcher! A man's life hangs in the balance!' I take my seat.

On the bench opposite, Josiah pulls the paper from his

pocket, flattens it out and passes it to me. 'Take a look. One of Larkin's toys.'

At first glance, the diagram appears to be a technical plan of a telescope's inner workings, but then I notice there's no lens at the wider end and there is instead an arrangement of mirrors and moving plates. 'It's a kaleidoscope. So what?'

'You didn't spot the blade, then?' Josiah looks smug.

The revelation hits me. 'That's how he's killing them.'

Joe continues, feigning an imagined conversation. '"Really, sir, you must try this. It's my latest invention, a thing of wonders! Just put this end to your eye and turn the brass ring." Then, *whack*! The movement triggers a sprung blade. The viewer drops dead. As you say, a clever man, this fellow.'

The coach wheels leave the ground as we shoot over Rook's Bridge. How Fletcher keeps control on the icy road, I can't say. We dash down Bunson Street, willing the horses to go faster while fearing a terrible crash.

Joe leans out, grimacing at the road ahead. 'Tell him to slow! Bretling's not worth it!' We thunder along dangerously, part-rolling, part-sliding, often bouncing, and it seems Fletcher is a reckless driver. Still, the horses somehow keep their footing, and he manages to steer a good line down the road.

We tear past a column of large infantry steam trucks, likely heading for the docks. Half a mile more and Fletcher's tugging the reins. The way ahead is blocked by slower traffic. Unperturbed, he shouts to alert all those we approach.

'Clear the way! Mind the way!'

Carts and mules draw aside to let us pass. A barrowman abandons his barrow to dive for the safety of the pavement. Ice and dirt fly in our wake as the wheels skid this way and that. We close on the rear end of a speeding steam truck that's spewing black smoke from its funnels, but we're moving faster. It's all Fletcher can do to heave back on the horses. They slow as he guides them aside and we pass the irate steam driver, who gestures rudely in our direction.

Soon Crowlands is behind us and the road surface softens to

a gravelled track. The gutters of Bunson Street are replaced by grass verges, overhung with twisted trees, and our path is clearer here, unobstructed by the dense city traffic. When we do meet other vehicles, there's usually enough room for us to move over and fly past without issue. Fletcher takes advantage to make good progress, the coach hurtling like cannon shot, and it's my turn to lean out of the window, clamping my hat to my head, for he doesn't know the way. *Holloway*, I said, but Holloway is a big district.

'Take the next right!' I shout over the tearing wind. 'It's Tinlock's Farm. Do you know it?'

Shaking his head, Fletcher immediately cuts to the right, leaving behind an enraged farmer we've run off the road, who stands on his tilted cart to shake a fist. I shout back to him. 'Sorry, old chap. We're in a terrible hurry!'

We hurtle along another stretch. I continue to direct. 'Left at the end. Tinlock's Farm will be the next on the right.'

We rush from the coach before the wheels have stopped turning, shaken by the journey. 'Fetch the Drakers!' I call back to Fletcher, vaulting a gate to run into the first field. We're soon breathless, hampered by last night's snowfall as we track fresh boot prints in the snow. The field is patched with icy puddles. We slip, slide and wade across the open land, racing to the ring of tall sallows before us in the second field. Long before reaching it, we come across a body lying prone in the snow; blood that's sprayed from a wound to the left eye is a vivid red on the blanket of white. I stoop to examine him.

'Dead.'

Josiah cocks his head. 'It's Sergeant Huntly.'

We continue on towards the trees, noting the marks of others who've gone before us. They show the passing of three individuals – all heading for the grove – but now they're confused by a single set of returning footprints which ends at Huntly.

'He's still here,' I say, keeping my voice low. 'Hurry!'

We run to the sallows, where the shoots spring up through

the snow in broad clumps around their trunks and the weeping branches fall like beaded screens to obscure the clearing within. Josiah makes for the entrance: a gap between the trees where the footprints converge. I grab his arm and whisper, 'Not that way.' We edge the circle, seeking another path through, one that will not immediately give us away. Halfway around, we find it and push through branches and shoots to spy, screened by a thickness of growth before us.

There at the centre of the grove, Bretling stands with Larkin, deep in conversation. Larkin is smiling and talking animatedly, though we can barely catch his words.

'... of course, it's always been a fascination of mine...' I lose part of the line as Larkin turns his head. '... since childhood, really...' A bulge to the side of his coat betrays the presence of a pistol.

Bretling nods and takes his pocket watch from his waistcoat, flips it open to read the time. We push through more branches, creeping to a point behind Larkin from where we might surprise and overpower him.

Larkin reaches into his coat pocket to take out the kaleidoscope. As he does so, Josiah draws a pistol. I miss Larkin's next few words but hear, '... latest invention... working marvel... must really have a try...' He hands the instrument to Bretling who accepts in a humouring manner, immediately raising it to his eye.

'Tell me what you see,' says Larkin.

'I see reflected faces. Patterns. There are skulls. Tell me, who are these people?'

'Drop it, Lord Draker!' I shout, fighting to scramble out through the branches. 'Drop it or die!'

Bretling turns, the kaleidoscope an inch from his face. Larkin throws back his coat to reach for his gun.

'Drop it, or you'll die!' I repeat.

'There's a dagger in the toy,' says Josiah.

Bretling drops the device. It hits the trampled snow at his feet, the dagger deploying with a sudden jolt. 'By Lychling! What on Earthoria?' He rounds on Larkin. 'You would dare attempt to kill me?' He draws his pistol and levels it. He's faster than Larkin but Larkin is there before him. They stand a matter of feet apart, each with a gun now trained on the other. With Josiah aiming his at Larkin, I see little point in adding to the arsenal.

Larkin ignores Josiah and speaks directly to Bretling. 'You asked, who were the people? I'll tell you. They were my family. My father, George Larkin, drowned in Wheal Berta. Taken from me by the greed of a silker mine owner.'

Disturbed and trembling, Larkin slowly begins to circle Bretling. Each maintains his aim, Bretling turning on the spot to match Larkin's pace. 'My brothers, Jack and Raffe, both taken by the mines. Even my Uncle Amos. Gone. All gone.' As though drifting in thought, Larkin lowers his gaze, but the next moment locks back onto Bretling like a whip. 'I had a sister, too. Did you know? Angie. A pretty, innocent child she was. She used to sing like an angel. Used to dance. I loved them, you see. I loved them all!'

Bretling begins to speak. 'I'm sure—'

Shaking his pistol erratically, Larkin cuts in. 'You will hear me out!' With apparent effort, he calms himself to continue. 'My mother was, understandably, broken afterwards. We all were. Broken and lost. She used to walk here on this very spot. Oh, how she loved this place! She would spend hours here in the summer. But then, after what happened...' Larkin seems to abandon this sentence. He starts again. 'She took a rope one day, slung it from a tree. They found her...' Incapable of finishing the thought, he rubs manically at his face and cocks his head at Bretling. 'Someone has to do something. Do you see? You silkers can't get away with all this. Your papers call me a killer, but you're the real killers. Killers for profit. You sicken me. I am sickened to the marrow of my bones.'

'What happened to Angie?' asks Bretling.

Larkin fumes, jabbing the pistol towards Bretling. 'Don't you *dare* speak her name. You're not worthy for it to pass your lips!'

'Woe is me! for I am undone,' I recite, *'because I am a man of unclean*

lips, and I dwell in the midst of a people of unclean lips …'

Bretling speaks. 'You do realise there's no escape for you, whether you kill me or not? In a few moments this place will be crawling with my officers.'

'It doesn't matter,' says Larkin, shaking his head. 'Nothing matters any more. Nothing… Don't you see?'

'Lower your gun, Mr Larkin,' I say, stepping cautiously closer. 'There's no need for anyone else to die today.'

Larkin continues to glare at Bretling. 'To the contrary, Mr Banyard. I believe I have it in me to take one more soul with me to the grave.' With an almost imperceivable twitch of his finger, his gun recoils. Bretling flinches as the bullet ploughs into his arm, wide of its intended mark. With his grip destroyed, Bretling's pistol falls to the ground. Josiah shoots a hole in Larkin's pistol hand before the man can take a second shot. Larkin's gun, too, tumbles to the snow as he cries like a wounded animal. Blood drips from Bretling's arm. He clamps a hand around his wound. I collect the guns.

Closing in, Josiah holds Larkin in the sights of his pistol. He has a second barrel still loaded and two further shots readied in the gun still on his belt. 'For a moment there, I wasn't sure who to shoot,' he growls, looking from Larkin to Bretling.

'Well, I'm much obliged it wasn't me,' says Bretling, wincing. 'I imagine you're a better shot than the toymaker here.'

With his good hand, Larkin takes a handful of old imographs from his pocket to thrust in Bretling's face. 'Look at them. Look at what you have done!'

'It wasn't me, Mr Larkin,' says Bretling in a pragmatic tone. 'Your rage is misplaced.'

A gust of wind tears some of the pictures from Larkin's outstretched hand. He peers at Joe, imploringly. 'Kill me, Mr Mingle. I beg you!' He lets the rest of the pictures go. 'I want to be with them. Send me to my family!' Dropping to the ground, he claws at the imographs as the breeze scatters them across the snow like fallen leaves, like strange blossoms of the sallows.

Drakers emerge, then, lurching through the trees opposite,

Goffings among them. I call to them. 'Take him. This man is the killer.' I restrain Larkin while the others approach. 'Plead your case, Larkin. Plead your case and change the world, or all you've done will be for nought.'

'You killed Huntly!' says Goffings, stomping towards us.

'I'm a dead man. Do you think they'll listen to me now?' Larkin laughs hysterically. 'You've already condemned me. This is your fault, Banyard. This is all on you!'

The Drakers flood the grove. I release him into their hands.

'Huntly's dead?' asks Bretling. He sounds angry and dismayed.

'Back there. Stabbed through the eye, like the others,' says Goffings. While officers take hold of Larkin, Goffings forces the prisoner's arms behind his back to close handcuffs around his wrists. Larkin resists, twisting and fighting as best he can, so constrained. In the tussle, Goffings nearly loses his footing in the snow, but rights himself to punch Larkin in the gut. They take their prisoner away under Bretling's watchful gaze as another officer fusses over the wound on his arm.

'What's that?' Josiah points to a dark rectangular shape lying across the grove in the snow.

I squint at the object. 'It looks like a pocketbook. One of the Drakers', perhaps.'

We walk closer, leaving Bretling with his nursing officer. Josiah collects the book and turns the pages. After a moment he brightens. 'Why, Mr Banyard, I do believe I've had an excellent idea!' He passes Goffings' open pocketbook. 'These phrases – here, here and here... Look familiar?'

I read Goffings' case notes. 'They match the news in the *Evening Herald*, in places word for word. What are the chances of that?'

'Pretty slim, I'd say.'

'Goffings is the leak! You mentioned an idea.'

'I thought it would be a terrible shame if the book fell into Lord Draker's hands.'

In the clearing opposite, Bretling and other Drakers examine the deadly kaleidoscope.

'It would indeed!' I say. 'Quickly. He'll not linger long.'

I watch Josiah cross the clearing to pass over the evidence, see Bretling take the book, turn its pages, the revelation dawning on his face.

Lord Draker calls a sergeant to him. 'Smeaton, take some men and arrest Sergeant Goffings this minute. And see them both into the cells.'

At the grove's entrance, Smeaton and his officers approach to quickly overpower Goffings, who, in dread, locks eyes with Bretling. As they cuff Goffings' wrists in iron, Bretling rips the stripes from his uniform. 'Take the blaggard away.'

'Poor old Sergeant Goffings,' grunts Josiah, while I stoop to collect the windblown imographs of Larkin's family. 'So Bretling was right, after all. The killer was a threader.'

'A threader posing as a silker,' I say. 'Who would believe such a thing?'

24

Matters of the Heart

In which Banyard seeks answers

It's not until later, when I visit Larkin in the threader gaol, that I get a chance to fill in some gaps in the story. I find him fettered to an iron loop set into the stone floor of a confined and stinking cell that's furnished with only a roughly hewn bench. His wounded hand is bandaged, the fabric stained with blood.

'The plan of Wheal Berta my lad passed to us – was that you? You tried to kill us in the mine, didn't you?'

Larkin gazes unseeingly at the small patch of light that gleams from the solitary small window set high into the rear wall, and is silent for a time. At last he speaks, though slowly and as if waking from a deep daydream. He nods.

'We used to live out that way, not so far from the sallows. We were poor but our home was a happy one, when we were all together. We made the most of the little we had.' He appears to drift away, lost in his thoughts again, but then returns. 'I had charts of the mine. I used to work there – was a junior engineer for a time – and a good one, years ago. I didn't need Mumford's plan to build the model. I could have done it with my eyes closed.'

'Does that mean there was another reason for Mumford's

visit?'

'He wanted me back. Wanted me to return to work there. He was always invested in that mine. I wasn't interested.'

'Not in his offer, at least…'

'It did rather present an opportunity I couldn't resist. I gave him the grand tour of my toy shop, showed him my creations, how I'd turned my skills to a different line of work.'

'Including your latest invention – a kaleidoscope that kills. I suppose your other victims were all in some way responsible for the deaths in your family.'

'Some of them directly. Others less so.'

'The coal in their mouths?'

'It seemed an appropriate gesture. You found the reference. I know you understand.'

I ask again, 'Was it you who tried to kill us at the mine?' When he doesn't answer, I move on. 'Your method only worked with individuals, didn't it? Two working together presented an altogether different problem, so you had someone deposit the chart in Ebadiah's bag; you knew we wouldn't be able to resist a clandestine investigation of the mine. Was it you who followed us, or did you have someone else do it?' I try again, this time with a different tack. 'At Lancett's funeral – were you the figure I chased into the woods? And at our first meeting you bade us return. Why? To insert yourself into our investigation, to keep abreast of developments. You went to Mumford's funeral for the same reason, though you made a good show of it, presenting the widow with the automaton.'

Neither agreeing nor denying, he glances at the pistols on my gun belt. 'You could end this torture for me, Banyard. No one would blame you.'

'Why did you not attend George Berringford's interment?'

At the sound of the name, Larkin breaks into a snarl. 'Berringford was the worst of the lot! I regret killing him the way I did. A quick death was too lenient. I should have made him suffer like he made others suffer.' For a moment, Larkin's inner monster surfaces, a deep-seated rage brimming in his eyes, and then, as quickly as it manifests, it dispels. At once he is himself again, the mild-tempered toymaker of Old Town Way. 'I have money hidden away. I can pay you, make it worth your while.'

'I can't help you. Tell me about the two in the pond. Who were they? Are there others in the woods?'

'Now, now…' He looks at me sideways, smiling sardonically. 'If you won't help me, why should I help you? It goes both ways, this game we play.'

'What did happen to your sister?'

He glares at me: that same look he gave Bretling in the grove. 'She froze to death, of course, one winter's night soon after they found Mother. We were cast out into the gutter like pieces of rubbish.' Lamenting, he adds, 'It was the 17th of Elventide. We had nowhere to go.'

'I'm sorry, Mr Larkin. I truly am.'

He narrows his eyes at me. 'Sorry? You're *sorry*?'

Taking the pictures of his family from my pocket, I leave them on his bench. 'I thought you might want these back. Farewell, Mr Larkin.'

Beyond his little window a man readies a noose upon the gallows, but that must be for some other poor soul. Such a punishment has been deemed too lenient for Larkin. He is destined instead for a more protracted execution in the poisonous sands of Mors Zonam, where he will be abandoned without food or water, tightly shackled to prevent his escape.

With a heavy heart, I leave.

In the darkness of late afternoon, Magwitch finds me alone in my bedroom. Around his towering figure, particles tear by in a haze and I hear it transmitted through his senses, a noise like a rushing wind.

His thoughts come to me, sounding like sluicing gravel in my mind. *This one has seen much sorrow.*

I stare at the miasma streaming behind him and dab blood from my brow with a handkerchief. *What is that? Where are you?*

It is sand. There is a desert storm.

Shouldn't you take shelter?

Dagomites can weather such storms. It will soon pass.

We caught the killer.

Magwitch watched what happened in the grove, heard what was said. Magwitch tried to find you before you arrived.

So, you know about the suffering of Stanley Larkin. You know about the wrongs that drove him upon his dark road. Promise me, you will not pursue the others – that you will not finish what he began. There has been too much killing already. It is not the way.

If the great violation is discovered, Dagomites will destroy.

But don't you see? If you destroy those who kill others, you become the same as them. You become the violator!

I sense a great tension in his thoughts and, as he wrestles with the challenge, feel a pressure in my head. *This one has no violation. That is why Dagomites let this one live.*

What are *you? Who are* you *and your kind, that you believe you have the right to choose who lives and who dies?*

We are Dagomites, come to save your kind from themselves. This is the Dagomite way.

The strain in my head is unbearable. I drop to my knees and, sensing my discomfort, Magwitch retreats. In a moment he is gone, as though swallowed by the storm, and then my room is quiet and still and I am alone once more.

We make the papers, and not for the first time we're the talk of the city. It's even hit the front page of the *Camdon Herald*.

BANYARD & MINGLE SAVE LORD DRAKER

I pin the headline proudly to the case room wall.

We throw a modest Elventide party at the office, fetching Lame Garrett from The Dog and employing him to play his fiddle. We dance, sing tavern songs and pass around drinks and cake, although the others are not overly impressed with the *Herald*'s headline: '*We* helped. Where are *our* names?' complains Lizzy, looking particularly fine in her best party dress: a deep-blue silk with a black lace bodice.

'You're not honestly suggesting we change the company name to Banyard, Mingle, Banyard, Joseph, Danton and Fairweather – Mysteries Solved?'

'A bit long,' says Josiah, screwing his nose up.

'And why should all the men's names come first?' says Penney, hand on hip.

'A good point,' says Lizzy.

I don't have a good answer.

Josiah to the rescue. 'It's the way of the world.'

'That doesn't mean it's right,' says Lizzy.

I wait for Jinkers to demand he be added to the theoretical name, but he's just thrilled to be at the party. It's more company than he's had in years. Zadie also attends, which puts a wide smile on Josiah's face and, arriving with Myrah, even Bretling makes a brief appearance to relay his thanks, though he declines a drink when offered and seems embarrassed when Lizzy asks him to join the dance. Laughing, she grabs my arm instead to draw me into an Eyrlandian reel and I spend most of the dance trying not to meet her eyes as Lame Garrett fires quick, fluid notes from his bow.

When Lord Draker has gone and his shadow lifted, the party returns to full swing. Penney lays a hand on mine to draw me aside, her smile melancholic. 'May we talk?' We find a corner of the case room where the music is not so loud. With merciless speed, she gets to the point. 'Michael, I'm sorry, but what we had has gone. It just feels wrong. I do love you, just not in *that* way. You're more like a brother to me.'

'And you like a sister to me,' I confess. 'I didn't want it to be like this.'

'Me neither. Whatever shall we do?'

I shrug. 'Carry on as good friends? I should still hate to lose you.'

'Yes, we will always be good friends. Michael, I will always be there for you. And if you and Miss Fairweather were to sometime wed and have... little Banyards, it would be my delight to be an honorary aunt.' Penney smiles and plants a gentle kiss on my forehead. 'By the way, you'd best talk with Elizabeth quite soon. She's thinking of leaving. I rather think the poor girl has a thing for you.' With a knowing smile, she returns to the throng.

I re-enter reception to witness a touching scene and wish I could overhear the exchange, yet the music and chatter are too loud: Myrah approaches Mardon, who has been reticent and unsmiling since her arrival. They talk briefly. He brightens and a moment later drops to one knee, delving into his waistcoat pocket. He takes out a gold ring set with a single diamond and, as others notice and pause to watch, the music stops and he proposes most brazenly before us all. A great cheer erupts. The 'I will!' is mostly lost beneath the din, though her nod and smile are clear to all.

Chiming my glass with a letter opener, I garner attention. 'Ladies and gentlemen, I see congratulations are in order. I'd like to make a toast, if I may. Let us drink to the future Mr and Mrs Mardon Banyard!'

We drink and cheer again, and a merrier party I've never known, though I'm not finished yet. I note with interest that Josiah is the first to reach out a hand to Mardon and congratulate the couple.

'There is another matter to address, however,' I say when the noise has simmered down enough for me to be heard. 'The agents of Mysteries Solved have worked well and worked hard to crack the Seraph case, but there's one individual without whom we might have failed altogether – and so it is only right that I ask you to raise a glass… to our good friend and spy, Mr Jinkers!'

Jinkers is so astonished by this sudden and unexpected turn of praise that he's rendered speechless. I rather think he deems my announcement a ploy of mockery but, as he takes in the surrounding cheers, grins and applause, his concern melts away, to be replaced by a nervous smile. He raises his glass in a gesture of thanks before sipping his wine. We drink.

'Mr Jinkers, now that it's all over, I shall see to it that Lord Draker is informed of your part in our investigation. It's only right he should know.' With a word of warning for him to open it later, alone and at home, I pass him a present wrapped in brown paper and tied with string.

'Merry Elventide, Mr Jinkers.'

'For me?' He gazes at the gift in awe.

'I think it's something that will interest you.'

Thanking me profusely, he grabs my hand and near shakes it off. I can only imagine him unwrapping the file and reading the enclosed note.

> *Dear Mr Jinkers,*
>
> *Knowing our future uncertain, with war pending, and wishing to safeguard a particular knowledge within my possession, I have seen fit to make a copy of my father's case file. It is an assemblage of accounts and studies of the gawper kind to which I have also added my own findings. I place this into your hands now, with trust that you will keep it secret, keep it safely and use it wisely.*
>
> *Wishing you and Mr Kaylock a very merry Elventide,*
> *M B*

While the girls are busy admiring Myrah's engagement ring, I steal a moment with Mardon. 'What happened, cousin? I thought you said she'd rejected you.'

'Ah, a misunderstanding on my part,' he says between sips of steaming spiced wine. 'Have you ever noticed we doctors have the most appalling handwriting?'

I smile and lift my glass to his. 'Then, may it be the only misunderstanding the two of you ever encounter!'

'I'll drink to that, Micky.'

I realise Josiah is going to protest wildly about the delay I've imposed on his own proposal, but I'll just have to deal with that when it happens.

After the party, when I've sent Josiah home with Zadie on his arm and everyone else has gone, it's down to Lizzy and me to tidy up the office. We sweep the floor, clean and straighten until the place is back in good order. Collecting the last of the cups and plates from the desks, I realise my opportunity to speak with her alone is slipping by. Yet it seems I'm not the only one feeling this, for as I speak her name, she says mine.

'Lizzy…'

'Michael…' She blushes and looks away. 'Mr Banyard, Penney and I have spoken–'

'Penney has spoken with me, also.'

'–about you, and something has to be done… Wait. She has?'

'Yes.'

'Oh. Well, then…' She seems suddenly lost. 'You see, I don't think I can go on like this.'

'Agreed.'

'I'm sorry, that's just the way it is. I really think I must leave…' She meets my eyes briefly. 'Did you say *agreed*?'

'Lizzy, if you'd let me speak, I have something to say. Listen.' Now it comes to it, the words stick in my throat like pebbles. I force more of them out, feeling foolish and nervous. 'My thing with Penney is over. I think it has been for a while now. I just didn't want to admit it.' I face up to the truth, accepting it and voicing it all at once with a quickening pulse. 'I'm beginning to think it is *you* who truly has my heart.'

Mop in hand, she looks at me for a moment that seems to stretch for eternity. Her eyes shine and I wonder, is she crying, in some way insulted or angered? I fear Penney was mistaken in her earlier comment, but then, dropping the mop, Lizzy walks to me. Our faces near, as though drawn by an unstoppable force. I'm terrified and enthralled. Her lips, full and sensuous, at last part to speak. 'Finally, Mr Banyard. It's taken you long enough…'

'Please, call me Michael.'

We kiss.

'Merry Elventide, Michael.'

Epilogue

A few days after the Feast of Elventide, I find myself alone in my bedroom one evening, dwelling on the past month and its prevailing mysteries, haunted by Larkin's pleas for me to end his life. It seems we shall never truly know the identities of the two bodies in the pond. Larkin certainly can't tell anyone now. I can only conclude that they were individuals, silker or threader, who somehow got in his way and so were silenced.

Other questions endure. What became of Hanover's corpse after Larkin's run-in with the mounted Drakers? One can only assume that, after escaping that night, Larkin found a place to dispose of the body, which has yet to be found. And without a body as proof, can we even be sure of Hanover's death?

Are there still others buried beneath the trees of Black Down Forest, down beyond the grove? Again, the matter remains unresolved. I have since walked those woods and come across several depressions in the ground that I believe could signify shallow graves. Nettles grow there, which is usually a good indication. However, Bretling refuses my repeated requests for the area to be properly searched and the potential graves investigated.

Patty Primshaw's theft of the sapphires has left us barren. Oh, yes, Lord Draker will give us his consultancy fee as promised, but I've wages to pay and expenses to settle. The paltry sum won't last long. He has denied us any reward, saying *that* was only an incentive for his official investigators and so not applicable. There will be nothing left with which to aid a single threader, and I haven't even cleared the bill for Primshaw's silker wardrobe. We are, as they say, broke.

Glancing out from my bedroom window at the foggy street below, I still, at once mesmerised, harkening to a song of peculiar clarity.

> *God rest ye merry gentlemen, let nothing you dismay,*
> *Remember Christ our Saviour, was born on Christmas Day,*
> *To save us all from Satan's pow'r, when we were gone astray,*
> *Oh tidings of comfort and joy, comfort and joy,*
> *Oh tidings of comfort and joy.*

The carol is ancient, no longer favoured by the celebrating masses. The words float to me as though voiced by ghosts of a bygone age, born of the Old People in a time and place before Elventide replaced a free celebration of other long-forgotten festivals.

I spy the singer, whose angelic voice carries so clearly upon the frosty air, though never glimpse her face. Cast in quivering shades of lamplight-blue, she walks with sadness – ragged, naked feet shuffling snow – into the unforgiving night. And soon she is gone from view. I blink into the gloom, wondering if indeed it *was* a ghost I saw, and think of Larkin's poor sister.

A sudden knock at my door startles me and I open it to see Josiah standing there, a scribbled note in his hand.

'What's this?' I ask, taking the paper.

'Goffings' address. Since he's in gaol, I had Ebadiah track it down. I figured he must have Hanover's money tucked away somewhere and, well, he won't need it where he's going, so...'

Pocketing the note, I join him in the corridor. 'Of course, if that money *were* to fall into our hands, we'd be honour-bound to pass it on to Hanover's kin, even though he made it through duplicitous cruelty to others.'

'What? Would we?' Josiah seems genuinely surprised and disappointed as he follows me down the passageway to the stairs.

'I'm joking. Hanover's relatives are stinking rich and I

couldn't find a single one of them deserving of an inheritance.'

'You mean we can keep it?'

'Get your coat, Mr Mingle. To keep it, we must first find it!'

Acknowledgements

The scripture featured in *The Seraph of the Sallow Grove* was taken from the King James Bible – Isaiah 6:5-7.

The composer of the traditional old English Christmas carol *God Rest Ye Merry, Gentlemen* (now in the public domain) is unknown, although records show that it was sung within the Christian Church from the fifteenth century. First printed in AD 1760, the hymn became more popular when William B Sandy included a version of it in *Christmas Carols Ancient and Modern* (1833). Since then, it has been used broadly and is also referenced in Charles Dickens' *A Christmas Carol*. See viscountorgans.net/god-rest-ye-merry-gentlemen (accessed 4th May 2022).

Consultation and expert guidance on the crime scene forensics featured in *The Seraph of the Sallow Grove* were provided by chemist, biologist and crime-writing specialist Brian Price.

Also by B J Mears

A Banyard & Mingle Mystery
Volume I

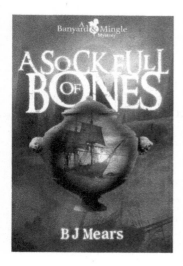

Young private detectives, Banyard and Mingle, are out of money and out of luck when a swindled widow presents a life-changing case. As clues reveal a treacherous shipwreck and a rotting corpse in a cage, they are confronted by brutal smugglers and ghoulish gawpers in a mystery that could cost them their lives!

However, in a dystopian world of slavery and greed, where silkers rule and threaders serve, it is not just the criminals they will have to fight…

Can justice prevail when the law itself is corrupt?
And how might a sock full of bones help bring it about?

'If you like your Sherlock Holmes with a heap more supernatural, a dash more social conscience and a Watson who proposes the worst ideas, this is the book for you.'
Kate Coe, Writing & Coe, Fantasy author and editor

'An intriguing mystery, set against a backdrop every bit as convincing and mysterious as Robert Harris' *Second Sleep*.'
Rev Dr Simon Woodman, Author of The Book Of Revelation

A Banyard & Mingle Mystery

Volume II

Following their success recovering King Doon's bones, Banyard and Mingle's services are in high demand.

But when a mysterious green-ink letter claims Michael's dead father was murdered, he is compelled to reopen a long-forgotten case…

Pursuing clues to a powerful, clandestine order and a missing young woman, the duo confront vengeful enemies and shocking truths – and then there's Willow, a runaway slave, who bursts back into Josiah's life with deadly effect!

With gawpers haunting and a murderer closing in, can they survive long enough to see the case through?

And if the 'green ink ghost' is revealed, will it be too late for justice to be done?

'A fascinating world, rich in detail and intriguing characters.'
*Dan Sefton, Screenwriter (*The Mallorca Files, Trust Me, The Good Karma Hospital *and Many More)*

'A real page turner. The vivid descriptions of the surroundings and people allow you to stand alongside the private investigators on every step of their earnest, funny and soul-searching, quest for the truth.'
Julian Roderick, Teacher, Author of The Felix Jones Adventures

A
Banyard & Mingle
Mystery
Volume III

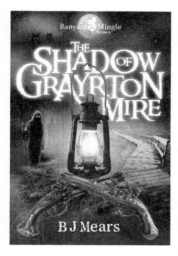

Shadowy deaths have long made Grayrton Mire a place of gruesome legend. But when a vulnerable boy is charged with the latest killing, Banyard and Mingle brave the treacherous marshes to defend him.

Confronted by suspicious locals and rumours of a terrifying beast, they stumble into a deadly conspiracy. With the clock ticking and ruthless authorities determined to protect their secrets, they will need associates Penney and Lizzy to risk their lives if they are to uncover the truth.

Can they save the boy and discover who – or what – lies behind the sinister legend?

And will they survive a final night on the mire?

'We can't get enough of these superbly adventurous mystery novels. There's never a dull moment in a Banyard and Mingle book!'
Steve Fenton, Phonotonal (Music – Words – Subculture)

'Mears' blend of compelling writing, wry style, and careful plotting makes this a highly readable mystery adventure.'
Simon Woodman, Author of The Book Of Revelation